The Second WomanSleuth Anthology

The Second WomanSleuth Anthology:

Contemporary Mystery Stories by Women

edited by
Irene Zahava

The Crossing Press
Freedom, California 95019

Dedicated to Harriet M. Welsch

Library of Congress Cataloging-in-Publication Data

The Second womansleuth anthology : contemporary mystery stories by women / edited by Irene Zahava.
    p.   cm.
  ISBN 0-89594-368-9   ISBN 0-89594-367-0 (pbk.)
   1. Detective and mystery stories, American—women authors.
  2. Women detectives—Fiction.   I. Zahava, Irene. II. Title: Second woman sleuth anthology.
PS648.D4S36   1989
813'.087208352042' 09045--dc20   89-37474
                                          CIP

Contents

Preface

Twelve years ago, when I seriously began to indulge my passion for mystery novels, I was made to feel that there was something almost shameful about it. Friends didn't bother to hide their surprise, and often their disgust, when they asked how I could waste my time on such trivial and escapist trash.

Luckily, times have changed! Now, when I get together with my friends we invariably swap mysteries and spend at least some of our time discussing our favorite authors and their fictional creations. Our tastes are certainly eclectic. Collectively we enjoy tough-talking detectives, academic environments, international settings, intellectual puzzlers, stories set in New York City, stories set anywhere *except* New York City, supernatural plots, "cozy" mysteries, etc. There is one thing we all have in common, though, and that is a genuine delight in the increasing number of mysteries being written by women, featuring women sleuths.

We are drawn so strongly to these books because, rather than searching for an escape, we are seeking to read about *reality*. More and more contemporary women mystery writers are dealing with subjects and issues that affect our lives. And the very best of the women sleuths are women we feel we know—they could be our friends or relatives or neighbors; sometimes, they could even be us. These are characters who aren't meant to be compared to Superwoman. They are fallible, hard-working, conscientous, and vulnerable. They worry about how they're going to pay the rent and buy groceries. And no matter what happens to them, they don't give up and quit; they are tenacious women who may not have all the answers but who never stop asking important questions.

Irene Zahava
May, 1989

Murder Most Musical

L.A. Taylor

The doorbell chimed in B-flat major. As Enrico braced his legs against the carpet, yapping in G, Madame Spezzacristolo let the refrigerator door slam and wiped her hands on her hip-filled red dress. The doorbell bonged again.

"Coming. I'm coming," Madame muttered, swallowing the last of her snack on the way through the dining room. She stooped to adjust the bow that kept Enrico's silky hair out of his eyes, pulled her aging bulk upright, and answered the door with a bright stage smile.

Shadowed against the dripping afternoon, the new student clutched her music to her chest. "Come in, come in," Madame Spezzacristolo intoned. "What have you brought? Schubert? Ah, a few little *canzoni, si,* a good start, good."

"What a cute dog," the student said, as Enrico snuffled at her ankles.

"*Si,* my Enrico. Out to the kitchen, *caro,* and lie on your rug, that's my good boy."

The retired soprano, despite her rotundity, strode to the grand piano in spike-heeled sandals and slid gracefully onto the bench, holding out her hands for the girl's music. Behind her, wide French doors framed a view of her lilac-bordered garden, admitting plenty of light. No need to bother with the music lamp.

"A few warm-ups first, hey?" Madame played an E-major arpeggio. "And we find out what your voice is all about."

The girl licked her lips. "Okay."

"Who have you studied with, again?" Madame asked, hands on the keys. The girl mentioned a name. Ed Block, of all people. Madame nodded. "Could be worse," she allowed, although she believed she herself did certain — many — things better than anyone else, among them vocal coaching.

"Now. Eee-ooh-aah, please on the triad." She demonstrated. The girl began.

1

Too bad. A pretty voice, but thin; a slip of a voice from a slip of a girl. Still . . . .

"Nice, okay," Madame said, her smile turned up for the second balcony. "Now again, you remember to aim the breath here, so" — yanking on her own large nose — "and from here comes the support, *capisc?*" She pulled in her abdomen with her fingers, from which a dozen rings sparkled.

The student tried again, facing an alarming spectacle: an enormous pouf of dyed red hair, a triple chin under a large-featured face accented with violet eyelids on which a false eyelash was askew, and an enormous freckled bosom rising within a red paisley tent. All her training deserted her.

A shame, a shame, Madame thought. Me, reduced to taking on whatever walks through the door, after all the *brava, brava!*

"*Brava,*" she said aloud. "Now, we really rattle the teeth, yes?" She played a chord in G, thinking of the garden behind her, where she had hoped to eat supper on the brick patio nestled in the ell of the house. Alas, it was raining, the lilacs would be rusty and scentless by morning, the bricks exhaling a dampness that at her age irritated her throat.

The student really rattled her teeth in a scream.

There followed a shot and the dissonance of breaking glass. Madame Spezzacristolo, her reflexes honed by thousands of performances, found herself crouched under the piano. She opened her eyes long enough to note the student collapsed in a heap beside her and the wound in the girl's chest, then squeezed them shut, waiting for the second shot.

No shot came. Madame held her breath, eyes shut tight, and heard first a thrashing among the lilacs, then the afternoon silence of the neighborhood punctuated by the drip-drip-drip of the rain. As a car started in the alley beyond the garden, something cold and wet touched her cheek.

Her scream, cramped as she was on her knees under the piano, shook the glass of the French doors.

Enrico Caruso yelped and backed off.

"Didum hurtum's ears?" his owner asked absently. "Momma's sorry."

She gathered up her skirt and crawled past the over-turned piano bench to bend over the student. The poor girl was clearly dead; the wound had already stopped bleeding and the blue eyes stared in soft dilation at the ceiling. "Outta here, 'Rico," Madame ordered. "We gotta leave her alone. No

2

good licking her hand now, poor kid." She picked up the wriggling Pomeranian and hustled into the kitchen.

"Nine-one-one?" she asked herself, perplexed. With the girl dead, was it an emergency? Should she call the precinct house direct, as she'd been told to do when the dirty old coot next door hadn't answered his door for four days and the assembled neighbors had decided to break into his house? As she dithered over the white pages hoping for instructions, her telephone rang.

"Madame Spezzacristolo? I'm sorry to interrupt you, but I believe Bettina Smith's having a lesson with you, isn't she?" asked a pleasant male voice — breathy, but a decent baritone if somebody took it in hand. "Could I speak to her, please?"

"Ah — no." Madame sucked in her upper lip. "She, er, left."

"Oh," said the voice. "Already? I thought she was supposed to be there until four?"

"Right," Madame confirmed. "Something more important came up."

"Oh. Sorry to bother you." The line clicked. Madame Spezzacristolo, the call she had to make becoming more urgent by the instant, dialed 911.

The police proved unexpectedly sympathetic and expectedly efficient; little more than an hour passed before the student was removed from her spot beside the piano. Photographs had been taken from every conceivable angle, including several of Madame herself, posed on her brocade couch with her hands uncharacteristically still in her lap — not as part of the investigation, but for the two cops who were opera buffs. One of them had gone all the way to New York to hear her as Cherubino! Madame felt a special warmth of heart for this man, who now prepared to question her.

"This seems ridiculous, me being such a big fan of yours, Madame Spezzacristolo," the man said, opening a notebook on his knee with an embarrassed chuckle, "but, you know rules. I got to ask you your name."

"Lena Goldfarb," Madame Spezzacristolo said crisply.

"Uh, what?"

"Goldfarb, comma, Lena. That's my name."

The cop, a big blond with the look of an aging lumberjack, stopped to consider. "I don't have to spell Spezzacristolo?" he asked.

3

"*Diretto*, sweetheart." Madame Spezzacristolo-Goldfarb flashed a humorless smile. "Just a stage name — in my day Goldfarbs didn't take to the stage. Not opera, anyway."

"But — weren't you born in Italy?"

"New York City, *caro*. Little Italy, *capisc*? Family across the hall, Graziano. Downstairs, Romano. On the stoop I played jacks with my good friends, the Lampone twins." Madame reflected for a moment, her full upper lip sucked in so that the little lines of lipstick that had run into the wrinkles above her mouth splayed out like the rays of the sun. " Course, I don't know how much Yiddish they knew."

"Goldfarb," the cop said, writing. "Address, I've got. Age?"

"Seventy."

"That's hard to believe," he remarked, pursing his lips. "I only went to New York a few years ago!"

"Not so long," Madame agreed. "Maybe twenty years."

What she knew about the afternoon's incident was quickly told: the new student, the shot, finding herself under the piano, the thrashing in the lilacs, the car in the alley.

"Must have thought he got you," the cop commented, still writing. "You tumbling under the piano so quick."

"Me?" Lena exclaimed, a thrill of fear at her throat. "I didn't think of that."

An interminable series of questions about her enemies followed. As Maria Spezzacristolo, she had upstaged most of the major singers of the past fifty years: the list was long. And, more recently, rejected students, outraged accompanists, incensed conductors, even (given that she was home all day and found much to criticize in the way the city was run) her alderman. None of them, Lena thought, likely to do murder. Not this murder. A strangling on stage, sure, the piano bench splintered over her head, an unconsidered stab to the heart with the baton — quite possible. But a shot from among her rustling lilacs? Missing so large a red paisley target, and hitting a pale slim girl smack in the heart?

No. "I can't picture that at all," she said.

"I can," the detective assured her. "And this is my profession."

"Still —"

He chuckled. "Look, do I sing high C's?" he asked. Ridiculous question for a bass.

Nevertheless, he closed his notebook and stood up. At the door, Lena twinkled her many rings at him. "*Ciao*," she said,

4

with a first-balcony smile. The other cops had already left; an earlier attack of her renowned temperament had scattered the members of the press. Alone, she leaned her head against the closed door and took a deep breath.

"Come, 'Rico," she said. "We'll shut ourselves up in the kitchen this evening. And go to bed early."

By morning, the sky had cleared to an almost painful blue. Madame Spezzacristolo sat on the brick patio next to lilacs still spangled with rainwater, sipping a cup of strong black coffee.

"Never saw anything like it," the young man repairing the French doors remarked. "Only one pane shot out, but every last one of the others is cracked."

"Two trained sopranos screamed," Madame Spezzacristolo explained. "One" — she inclined her head graciously — "with an international reputation."

"Oh, like that ad where Ella Fitzgerald breaks the wine glass?"

"Right." Madame went into the kitchen for more coffee. Poor kid, he'd never make a singer. That whiny tenor. Whooppee-whoppa-whooppee with an electric guitar, maybe, but nothing *real*. Not even little lyric *lieder*. Nothing like that baritone on the telephone yesterday, even.

She went back to the patio with her steaming mug and sat down. That morning, as a bow to propriety, she had donned her soberest dress, a well-cut tent in royal blue shot with purple and forest green. She'd even removed most of her rings, leaving only her sapphire birthstone and her father's black onyx oval. With the index finger wearing the onyx she traced the pattern of her funereal — relatively funereal — dress, puzzling over yesterday's events.

Now, wait.

S'pose you fired a shot — through the pane whose shards the police had carried away the day before — into a room where the light wasn't so good. You *thought* you'd hit Bettina Smith (no sense shooting somebody you didn't know, right?), but that fat lady in the red dropped *as if shot* and rolled under the piano! You'd leave in a hurry, and in some uncertainty, wouldn't you?

Lena Goldfarb got up and carried her mug to the trampled spot where the police had investigated most intensively. She broke off a bent but unwilted peony and turned to look into her house. Allow for this being morning and the sun shining into the room.

Even so, she couldn't see much past the piano — in fact, all she really saw clearly was the white uniform of the man cleaning the carpet. And yesterday it had been afternoon, and raining. The garden had been light, sure — Bettina Smith must have seen the man with the gun, or she wouldn't have screamed — but indoors, no. Mmmm. What could be simpler than to stop at a pay phone to make sure you'd hit the right woman? Wasn't there a pay phone in the 31 Flavors place, two blocks away? Sure.

She sipped coffee, running the remembered nuances of that voice past her mind's ear. Nervous? Something she hadn't spotted in her own agitation. Relief in that "Sorry to bother you." Mmmm.

The *nerve*! Shooting the kid before she'd had a chance to open her mouth, and using *my* telephone to check up! "He'll sing a different tune when *I* get done with him," Lena snarled, *sotto voce*.

Mmm. To shoot — or call — you'd have to know where Bettina Smith planned to be. Didn't that imply somebody who knew her well? Someone who would be expected, say, to go to her funeral?

"Hey, kid," she called to the whiny tenor.

"Yeah?"

"If you shot your girlfriend, only you thought maybe you really shot somebody else, would you call up the somebody else to see if she'd been shot?"

"What?"

Patiently, Lena repeated her question.

"I guess maybe," the tenor replied, with a sideways glance at the eight remaining cracked panes of the door.

"C'mere," Lena ordered.

The tenor looked at the glass cutter in h'' right hand and set it down carefully. "C'mon, c'mon," Lei a urged. "Yeah, right here in the bushes."

"In the bushes?" the tenor repeated, sounding alarmed.

"Yeah, right here. No, no, no, I mean turn around and look at the house. See?"

"See what?" the tenor asked nervously.

"That guy cleaning the carpet."

"Yeah, I see him."

"What else?"

"Uh, sort of the piano, and the window on the street end."

"That's it!" Madame crowed. "You couldn't see which one you'd hit if they both fell down, could you?"

"Both what?"

"Women, *balordo*, women!"

"I don't see any women."

"Of course you don't There aren't any."

"Wait'll I tell the guys about this," the tenor muttered, starting for the house with his right index finger wiggling at his temple.

How degrading! "Don't tell the guys about this," Madame Spezzacristolo implored. "Swear to me, *caro*, you'll keep this as secret as the grave."

"What grave?" whined the tenor, white showing at the tops of his eyes.

"Any damn grave you please," Madame snapped. "Just keep your mouth shut, *capisc*?"

She clacked back to the table and sat drumming her fingers on its surface for several minutes.

"I'll go to the funeral," Lena Goldfarb said aloud.

The glazier turned his head, decided the crazy old lady was talking to herself, and snapped the piece of glass he'd just scored along a neat, straight line.

The telephone rang as Madame set her cup on the kitchen counter.

"Hi, Lena?"

"Oh, hi, Ed." Madame Spezzacristolo leaned her ample behind against the counter, knocking over the empty cup without noticing.

"Hey, what happened to that student I sent you — Bettina Smith?" asked the caller. "She's dead? The newspapers don't make much sense. I guess you threw a fit?"

"Temperament, Ed, temperament," Madame said. "You're a singer, haven't you got one? What else could I do? The place was *seething* with reporters!"

"But she was murdered? I know she didn't have her gut under anything below an E-flat, but she wasn't that bad."

"I never got to hear," Madame Spezzacristolo said. "She'd sung maybe a dozen notes when somebody shot her. Through my back door."

"Honest? That's what the papers said. I figured they screwed it up, like they do reviews."

"*Did* reviews," corrected Madame Spezzacristolo, who'd had a good one not two months before. "No, they were right this time. Any idea who did it?"

"I thought they were after you."

"Me!" Madame hesitated a bit, tempted by renewed fame. "Not me, Ed," she said. "I think they were after the girl."

"Oh?" Ed sounded miffed. "I was her coach for two years, and the cops haven't talked to me."

"They will. Ed, *carissimo*, what was she like? Bettina?"

"Just a nice lyric soprano, coming along —"

"No, no. Not the voice. The girl. A brat, maybe?" Madame Spezzacristolo stretched the phone cord to look into the refrigerator. Funny, what happened to that cup of peach yogurt, she wondered.

"Brat? Would I send you a brat? No, this was a nice, nice girl. Sweet kid."

Madame hung up after a few more exchanges, unenlightened: if the girl had been threatened, if she'd had a jealous lover or had been given to injudicious upstaging, if she'd been the center of any sort of rumors at all, Ed hadn't known about it.

As she strode into her living room in her high-heeled feathered mules to see what the carpet man had done to her floor, Madame Spezzacristolo remembered belatedly that Ed was a class-A, dyed-in-the-wool gossip. *Oi*, and she'd told him all about yesterday's phone call! Well, let her suspicions spread. Maybe a guilty somebody would give himself up. Hadn't she herself been stabbed on at least a hundred occasions — as Carmen, of course — and hadn't Don Jose confessed, every single time?

Another day of intermittent thought led Lena to change her plans. Again in the more-or-less funereal blue, Madame Spezzacristolo minced up the steps of the mortuary home Thursday afternoon, right at the start of "visitation hours." She dreaded seeing that pale face again, composed and painted through it would be, but this was the best way she could think of to use her own special talent to roust out a killer, a killer with more *chutzpah* than was good for him.

Inside, a smooth middle-aged bass invited her to sign a "memory book." *Maria Spezzacristolo*, in her huge, jagged hand, barely fit into the space allotted; she switched to printing to add her address. Then, with the deep sigh of a woman about to go on stage in a brand-new role, she entered the small chapel.

Bettina Smith's parents huddled near the other end of the room, as bowed with sorrow as Lena had feared. Nearby, a dark-haired young man, obviously Bettina's brother, lounged uneasily, talking to another man who was perhaps in his middle twenties. Madame Spezzacristolo raised her chest like a spinnaker and sailed slowly across the blue carpet toward the group. The father, a trim man going grey, rose and came toward her.

Condolences came more easily than she had anticipated; the Smith family apparently held her no ill will. "This is Bettina's fiancé, Mark Crawford," the father introduced the second young man. Lena inclined her head. "Maria Spezzacristolo," she said.

"A pleasure to meet you, Madame," Mark Crawford said. "Bettina is — was — very excited at the thought of studying with you."

Him! Already! Shocked but gleeful, Lena gabbled her regret at the way things had turned out. "But I've had the pleasure of speaking with you before, haven't I?" she suggested, clutching her purse to keep her hands from trembling as she stared into the young man's blue eyes. "Tuesday — wasn't it you who called?"

"Tuesday?"

"After — I mean during Miss Smith's lesson, someone called to speak to her. Wasn't that you?" Madame Spezzacristolo found a smile to soften the words.

"Hey, did you tell the cops somebody called?" the gangly sibling inquired, in a voice that resembled his father's, even if his manners did not. "You oughta tell the cops."

"Not me, no." Bettina's fiancé shook his head. "I wouldn't have dreamed of interrupting a lesson with you," he declared.

Liar! I never forget a voice! Lena thought. "I'm so sorry," she purred. "I thought it was you. I'm not often mistaken about voices."

"Someone who sounds like me, maybe." With a small smile, Mark Crawford shrugged. "As I say, I wouldn't dream of using up time as valuable as yours would be to a singer."

Madame pulled in her chin and raised her freckled bosom to acknowledge the compliment, tottered through the rest of the social forms, and left the mortuary with relief.

9

Mark Crawford's air of certainty might have given another woman pause, but Madame had seen some marvelous acting in her time: more than one two-hundred-pound Mimi the audience would swear was a consumptive waif; more than one Rodolfo who made the ladies sigh over his stage tenderness toward a woman he privately despised. She had been known to work such wizardry herself, and with a Rodolfo who stomped on her toes during every duet.

Later that evening, the telephone rang as she devoured her third Weight Watchers' frozen dinner. "Coming, I'm coming," she grumbled, and picked up the receiver with a bright "Allo?"

"Maria Spezzacristolo," whispered the caller. "If you go to the police with your ideas about voices, you will die."

"I beg your pardon?" Lena boomed, but received only a click and a buzz in reply. "Ah," she said excitedly to 'Rico. "The chickens are flying now! Do I know acting? *Sì!*"

Over her second slice of cheesecake she began to wonder whether accosting Mark Crawford had been such a good idea. That nervous whisper . . . . She shuddered. Threats, on stage at least, had a way of being carried out . . . .

"We've talked to Mark Crawford," the blond cop assured Lena, sitting on her couch half an hour later. "True, he's got no alibi, but on the other hand he's got no reason for killing her."

Madame Spezzacristolo reared back. "Where there is love, there is reason for murder," she said. "You as an opera lover should know that."

"But as a police officer —"

"Mark my words," Lena interrupted, "that young man killed that girl. Otherwise, why call that afternoon without identifying himself? Execrable manners. Yes, that's your murderer, right there. And then, why lie to me about calling?"

"Crawford's a singer," the cop remarked. "He might think life's an opera, too."

"A singer!"

Shaken, Lena mentally played that afternoon's conversation back. Undeniable: that voice had done some singing. Maybe a lot of singing. And the voice on the telephone, so similar, hadn't seemed trained at all. "Almost like two men," she murmured. "But two men with the identical voice, one trained, one not? How is that possible?"

The cop looked up sharply and wrote something in his notebook.

Yet the girl's soprano, after years of study, had been breathy and small when faced with a new coach. Surely shooting somebody would have the same effect? Even on a mellow baritone? "Still," Madame Spezzacristolo insisted, "keep an eye on Mark Crawford. I warned him, see, that I'm on to him. Somebody threatened me because I talked about Mark Crawford's voice. Has to be him."

"You've got a point," her visitor agreed. "We'll take care of it. Don't worry."

"Thank you," Madame Spezzacristolo said with great dignity.

After the cop left, at his suggestion, she went through the downstairs rooms pulling the drapes closed for the first time in months. Sneezing heartily from the dust, she wrote herself a reminder to fire her cleaning lady.

"You'll protect me, won't you, 'Rico?" she asked the little dog, mournfully. For once, she wished she had a large dog with fearsome teeth, instead of her poppet.

The ten o'clock news reported the killer still at large. A snatch of an interview followed, not with Mark Crawford but with "Bettina Smith's fiancé's brother, Michael," a man squinting into morning sunlight as he answered a reporter's question, a man whose voice left Lena breathless. She tried to call her friend the blond detective, but found him unavailable. The nasal contralto at the other end of the line was sorry, but Madame could leave a message and wait for the cop to call back — tomorrow.

Lena looked in the Yellow Pages under "Dog Rentals" but found no such service, useful though it would be. Sighing, she carried her disappointment upstairs, exchanged her royal blue tent for another of apricot chiffon, and went to bed.

What woke her, Lena didn't know. She held her breath, listening. Nothing unusual; only the faint wheeze of 'Rico breathing at the foot of her bed. Stealthily she slipped out of the bed and tiptoed to the window.

There, in the shadow under that linden, wasn't that a man? Just standing, across from her house? Yes!

The room went cold. How dumb, to have only the one downstairs phone! With one beside the bed, next to the clock that told her it was three in the morning, she could call the police. As it was, the thought of the creaky staircase, the trek through half the living room, the dining room, and part of the kitchen, everywhere surrounded by her lovely, heavy, turn-of-the-century furniture, exposed to whoever —or was it whomever?— might be lurking behind it, was suddenly daunting. Lena sat on the edge of the bed, fumbling half-heartedly with her toes for her satin mules.

Was that a knock? A single knock, *downstairs*?

Still shoeless, she tiptoed back to the window. The man was gone.

At the moment she turned away from the glass, 'Rico yipped once and barrelled for the open bedroom door.

"'Rico, no!" Lena shouted. "Come back here!"

The man must be in the house! Lena burst into action. She slammed the door, leaned against it, and looked wildly around.

The dresser! Perfect! shove that against the door —

Lena gave the heavy chest of drawers a mighty heave. But her calf muscles, so used to her high-heeled shoes, rebelled. She felt a searing pain in her right calf and stopped pushing with a yelp and a whimper. The dresser angled a scant foot out from the wall. She'd never budge it, not like this.

The door! she told herself through her pain. Lean against the door!

No! A bullet would go right through that thin walnut panel. Lena dived for the closet. Crouched among her flowing polyester, she strained to hear the sounds from below.

'Rico yapping. Footsteps. A voice, the voice she had heard on the phone, shouting words she couldn't make out. Running steps, dog and human, on the stairs, and 'Rico, *caro* 'Rico, his heart so much bigger than his teeth, yapping, growling, yipping — then a hoarse human cry and thunder on the staircase as someone fell.

"Got him!" Lena crowed. "*Bravo*, Enrico!"

She'd cheered too soon. To Lena's horror, human steps pounded up the stairs and the bedroom door burst open. In the few seconds it took the man to cross the room she stood and filled her lungs, one fist clutching a high-heeled shoe. As she raised the shoe over her head the memory of the last act of *Lulu* flashed through her mind, the lady of the evening about to be slaughtered by Jack the Ripper, only this time it would be a Jack with his arm incredibly lengthened by a gun—

As the closet door was flung open, she let her *Lulu* scream rip loose.

"Police," squeaked the man, as the shoe descended on the arm he jerked up to protect his face.

Several minutes later, the uniformed cop who had opened Lena's closet door sat on her couch, rubbing his forearm and shaking his head to make his ears stop ringing. Paramedics had just arrived to take away the man who had fallen down her stairs. Lena shivered, telling herself it was the draft from the open French door that raised her goose bumps. The big blond cop she had begun to think of as a friend thumbed off his walkie-talkie and grinned at her.

"Feel okay?" he asked.

Lena gathered Madame about her. "Of course I do, *caro*."

"I have to apologize. After our talk this evening, I had some men watching your house, but the suspect slipped past us and we didn't know he was inside until we found a pane of glass knocked out of the French door. When Officer Anderson heard him fall down the stairs, we didn't know whether he'd already found you or not."

"Unh," said the man on the couch.

"Fortunately not." Madame Spezzacristolo flashed a fifth-curtain-call smile at the unhappy uniformed officer. The paramedics wheeled a stretcher out her front door, bearing Michael Crawford away. A broken left leg, both bones snapped at the ankle, and a concussion, but he'd recover to stand trial.

"The younger brother," Madame said, as the door closed. "Aren't families amazing? He sounded almost exactly like Mark when I heard him on television — and I suppose the telephone only emphasized the resemblance. Did you get my message?"

"Just now — a little late, but you'd already given me a good reason to check up on brother Michael, and you were absolutely right."

Madame felt rather proud of herself. "But *why?* That's what I can't understand."

"That I can't tell you," he said. "Yet."

The policeman returned the next morning. Lena saw him get out of his car and stop to watch the whiny tenor replacing the glass in her bedroom window. She hurried to the door. "Come in, come in," she said. "Have you found out some more?"

"Yes, indeed." With an oddly nervous grin, the big man followed her into the house. "The guy you saw at the funeral home yesterday was Mark Crawford. The one who broke in was his younger brother, Michael."

"That I already know, *caro*."

"Seems Bettina was dating Michael, but when she met Mark — they were both in some operetta, Gilbert and Sullivan, I think —"

"It would be," Lena muttered.

" — Bettina broke off with Michael and started dating Mark. Michael wasn't too pleased, shall we say. Then, when Bettina promised to marry Mark, all he could see ahead of him was a lifetime of hating his brother and, er, lusting after his sister-in-law."

Lena rolled her eyes upward. "Kids! They think everything lasts forever, like on stage!"

"I guess. Anyway, Michael couldn't bring himself to get rid of his own older brother — there's less than a year's difference between them and they grew up almost as close as twins — so he took the only other way out he could see. He hoped people would think he'd been aiming at you, that's why he did it here. But when Mark mentioned that you'd thought he had called you, Michael saw the danger. That's what brought him back."

"Oi!" Lena shook her head. "Talk about Gilbert and Sullivan! No, too grim for Gilbert. Some Italian librettist. Piave, maybe — the man who wrote the book for *Rigoletto* oughta drool over this!" she shook her head. "Ridiculous! That stuff went out eighty years ago."

"Ah, speaking of librettists."

A little thrill of — not quite fear, but something close – touched Madame Spezzacristolo's throat. He couldn't be thinking of lessons? Another amateur? "Yes?"

"I was thinking. You lost a student, and I used to do some singing . . . ."

"Yes?"

"I thought maybe you could help me get my voice together . . . unless you think it's too late?"

"Probably no," Madame said briskly. "What did you have in mind?"

"Uh, the *Winterreise*, for starters?"

"Absolutely no." Madame put her foot down. "No Schubert. I have just developed a terrible allergy to Schubert. How

14

about, mmm, Mozart? Yes, some nice, light Mozart. Songs, not arias."

Outside, the whiny tenor started to sing, off-key, country and western, an all-too-appropriate ditty about rejected love. I suppose he'll be wanting lessons next, Madame Spezza-cristolo groused to herself, as she wrote the big cop's name in her appointment book.

Perfect Timing

by Judi Lind

"Blast it, you're late again today, Fiske!" Lieutenant Chamberlain bellowed for emphasis.

"No, sir." Detective Carlye Fiske pointed at her watch. "I'm right on time."

Chamberlain jabbed a finger at the wall clock. "Get a new watch. You're even later than usual."

The clock over his door read 8:31. How could Old Reliable be wrong? She always kept her watch 15 minutes fast, and now it was 15 minutes slow.

Carlye began to mumble an apology.

"Save it," Chamberlain muttered, shoving a scrap of paper into her hand. "We've got a homicide over in Wood Park. Murphy's already there, and forensic's on the way."

Carlye looked up sharply. "What do we have so far?"

"Not much. Victim was female, early forties. Apparently lived alone. Found this morning by her car pool. Get on over there before Murphy screws it up."

Carlye headed out the door. She knew her partner, Ed Murphy, would have everything under control.

As she neared the Wood Park exit, Carlye checked the address: 1448 Orlando Avenue. Her eyes widened in surprise. Only last night she'd had dinner with friends on Orlando. It was a block-long cul-de-sac, so obviously the murder victim must have been one of Louise's neighbors.

Louise Goodhue was a local celebrity of sorts. She had a regular food column in the paper and was considered *the* hostess of Santa Dominga's social set. She also taught gourmet cooking, which was how Carlye had met her. At their last class, Louise had invited a few students for an impromptu swim party Sunday evening. Now, first thing on Monday, Carlye discovered number 1448 was the house next-door to Louise Goodhue.

Carlye flashed her badge and went inside. A woman in her

mid-20s was seated on a sofa in the living room. Her eyes were red, and Carlye noted her hands were shaking, but apparently she was under control. She was being questioned by two detectives.

She found Ed Murphy in the kitchen, as the medical examiner filled out forms.

The kitchen was bare of clutter except for tufts of fluffy material scattered over the terra-cotta tile floor. She scooped up a fragment that looked like kapok stuffing from a pillow.

Carlye nudged Murphy. "What have we got?"

"Margaret Canter, age forty-two. Divorced. One daughter, lives in L.A. Get this! Her ex is *the* Arthur Canter of the Fortune Five Hundred. I heard the divorce was real nasty."

"Interesting. Motive?"

Murphy shook his head. "Place has been ransacked, but it doesn't look like anything's missing."

Carlye took a closer look at the bullet wound in the victim's neck. "Any fix on the time of death?"

"Pending autopsy, Doc estimated between six and ten last night."

Carlye paled. She'd been right next-door from seven until almost eleven last night. They'd even been outdoors, lounging around Louise's pool, yet had heard nothing.

She asked, "Any way to cut that time closer?"

"The daughter in Los Angeles said she spoke with her mother at eight o'clock last night. It was a ritual: She called every Sunday night at eight."

A vague memory flashed through Carlye's mind. "Anyone interview the neighbors yet?" she asked.

Murphy shook his head.

"Check out the ex's whereabouts last night," Carlye said. "I'll talk to the woman who found the body, then take the door-to-door."

She returned to the living room and conferred with the two detectives. The girl's name was Nancy Morales. She worked with the victim at a large law firm downtown. They'd been car-pooling for about six months but didn't go out socially.

"Any reason why not?"

"Margaret's a lot older than me. Was." The girl dabbed at her eyes with a soggy tissue. "Besides, she was involved with her boyfriend."

"What's his name?"

17

"She never said."

"Then how did you know about him?"

"Margaret never mentioned his name, but she talked about him a lot."

"Didn't that seem odd?"

Nancy Morales whispered dramatically, "I think he was married."

When further questioning produced no new information, Carlye started the door-to-door.

There were only six houses on the block. After getting no answer at the first three houses, Carlye got lucky. Mrs. Swanson, an old lady who lived directly across the street, apparently spent a lot of time perched in front of her window "keeping an eye on the neighborhood." Nothing escaped her faded blue eyes.

She gave Carlye an accurate description of the cars driven by Louise's guests, including her own. Mrs. Swanson knew nothing about the victim's alleged boyfriend, nor had she seen any strangers prowling about. No, she'd heard nothing that sounded like a gunshot.

"The only person I saw over there yesterday was Louise. Reckon her husband is out of town. Didn't see him."

"What time was that?"

"Last night, it was around eight o'clock."

Carlye nodded. That fit. Louise had gone over a few minutes before eight to borrow ice. Carlye remembered glancing at the mantel clock when Louise mentioned that she'd better hurry, that her friend's daughter would be phoning at eight sharp.

She thanked Mrs. Swanson and walked quickly back to her car.

Carlye reviewed her notes. The haphazard ransacking combined with no evidence of forced entry meant the killer was probably known to the victim. They must turn their attention to Margaret Canter's family and friends. Find the mysterious boyfriend. Or maybe old Arthur had gotten tired of paying alimony.

Carlye closed her eyes. There was an elusive fragment of knowledge just out of reach... but it would come.

Suddenly, all the pieces clicked into place. A couple of interviews would nail the lid on this one.

Later that evening, she knocked on Louise's door.

"Carlye! What a surprise. Come in."

"Thank you. But I'm afraid this isn't a social call."

Louise led the way into the living room and offered Carlye a seat on the brocade sofa. Louise sat down and appraised her guest.

"Of course, I had forgotten you were a police officer. Are you investigating dear Margaret's death?"

"Yes." Carlye took a deep breath. "Louise, were you aware that your husband was having an affair with Margaret Canter?"

"What! That's the most preposterous...."

"No," Carlye cut in, "it's the truth. Was he going to leave you?"

Louise stood up and said coldly, "Ridiculous. I thought you were my friend. I think you'd better leave."

"I can't do that," Carlye said. "Louise, I have a warrant for your arrest."

Louise's face flushed a deep scarlet. "On what charge?"

"Murder, first degree."

"You can't be serious. Margaret was alive after I went over there last night. She talked to her daughter. Why, you're a witness to the fact that I was here until almost eleven. The news report said she was killed between eight and ten."

"I know," Carlye admitted. "That's the part that had me stumped. Then I remembered my watch was wrong this morning."

"I don't know what you're talking about," Louise blustered.

"Then let me explain. Knowing your husband would be out of town this weekend, you carefully set up this pool party. That was clever. Naturally, everyone here took off her wristwatch.

"Then while we were splashing merrily away, you went inside and reset all the timepieces, figuring that later no one would attach importance to a watch being fifteen minutes slow."

Louise glared, but some of the starch was weakening in her stance. "This is your little fairy tale."

"Let me go on. So after our carefully choreographed swim, you brought us all inside for drinks. Then, lo and behold, you, the perfect hostess, ran out of ice. 'No problem,' you said, 'I'll just borrow some from my dear neighbor Margaret.' Of course, you made a big production out of pointing out that the time on the mantel clock was five to eight. Perfect alibi, right?"

"You said it, my dear." Louise seemed to be regaining some of her confidence.

Carlye continued, "And that, *my dear*, was your mistake. There was no way my watch should have had the same time as your mantel clock. I'm continually late, so I keep mine set fifteen minutes fast.

"I checked with the other women, and theirs were all slow this morning too. So when we thought it was five to eight, it was actually about ten after. Margaret had already talked to her daughter. You smuggled the gun, and one of your throw pillows to muffle the sound, out in your ice bucket. Then you calmly walked next-door, shot Margaret and came back here and played the charming hostess. But you know what really ticks me off? You knew I was a cop, so you used me for your alibi."

The color drained from Louise's face as Carlye snapped on the handcuffs. "Louise Goodhue," Carlye intoned, "you have the right to remain silent. . . ."

Trouble on the Beat

by Elizabeth Pincus

I was nursing my third cup of joe and building a desktop house out of business cards when I first heard the footsteps. I quickly peaked the roof with two more cards and shoved a half-eaten pack of Licorice Whips into my trouser pocket. I turned to flash her a winsome smile, Miss Congeniality, the customer is always right. She was a she, that's for sure, all five-feet-one of her with every inch counting.

She spied me and picked up her step as she crossed the last stretch of cement floor. Her lips, pursed a bit in tension, formed a smile that may have been meant for my card house instead of me.

I cocked a brow. "Admiring my sculpture?"

"That too," she said, meeting my gaze and extending a paw accustomed to serious business. I stood to shake it, careful to withhold any comment on her diminutive stature. I was short myself — on cash, that is.

Her eyes swept up vertically. I was glad I'd worn my string tie with the rhinestone cowboy boot clasp. Really jazzed up my slapdash outfit. I'd hire me in a second.

"I seem to be lost," she said, glancing around the dank warehouse space cluttered with canvases, art supplies, and department store mannequins. She read from a slip of paper. "614 Tennessee Street. Hmm. Do you know where I can find Nell Fury?"

"You found her. In the flesh."

"Oh! I assumed you'd be, you know, in an office."

"It does the trick. I used to work out of a penthouse at the Fairmont, but I was getting all the wrong kinds of clients."

She laughed politely. I groaned inwardly. God, Fury, be cool.

"It's a friend's studio," I explained. "She paints at night, so she let me put in a phone and do business here during the day."

"The mannequins?"

I grinned. "They keep us both company."

I whipped a business card from the desk, causing a whoosh as the house scattered across an otherwise bare surface. I handed it over, realizing it was the first time I'd used one. Phoebe had made them up for me, partly in jest. Pale pink bond with embossed gold lettering: Nell Fury, Private Investigator — 'I Like to Watch.'

Now she really chuckled. "I would've thought this private eye business was real serious stuff."

"It is," I said. "Deadly." I nodded her into the easy chair, a tattered affair of magenta leather, and resumed my seat. She told me her name was Lydia Luchetti. Half an hour later, I had my first real client in over a month.

I walked her to the studio door and watched her, all pint-sized vim and earnestness, drive away in a mud-colored Datsun B210. Circa '75, I'd say, strictly utilitarian. I caught the peeling remnants of several bumper stickers pushing various harmonies — global, sisterly, whatever. The Frisco fog hung cool and silky over China Basin, a bayfront melange of industrial buildings, mangled railroad tracks and defunct hash houses. I scouted the sidewalk. No would-be clients, no rival dicks checking out the competition. No one at all for that matter. Not a neighborhood for foot traffic.

I strolled back to my desk chewing on leftover licorice. Brain food. I picked up my trimline princess and dialed Barbary Coast Taxi. I'm glad Phoebe switched over from Yellow — they would never page her.

Barbary Coast was ever solicitous. "Barbary Coast Cab."

"A message to 678, please."

"Is that Nellie?"

"Yeah, hi Ling."

"She's down 'round Burlingame."

"Well just tell her to meet me at Francine's when she gets in."

"Will do. Give that bouncer a wink for me, will ya?"

"Yeah. Right."

Sure, Ling. I swear, even straight women are suckers for leather these days.

Happy hour sounded nearly ecstatic when I rolled past the entrance of my favorite dive and Kryptonited the old

Schwinn to someone's Harley. I sauntered in. "Get a job," I mugged to the dozen or so denizens clustered noisily around Francine's pool table, eclipsed by smoke, cue sticks, and a growing collection of Corona bottles.

I thought I heard some vintage Eagles on the jukebox.

"Hey — are dykes musically illiterate, or what?" I quipped to the bartender, throwing her a nod and the hint of a grin.

"What do you want, Anne Murray?"

"I've had worse."

She guffawed and slapped a Bud and some change onto the bar, "Go on, give us some of your Patsy." With 'I Fall to Pieces' oozing its tinny elegance throughout the barroom, I slid back onto my stool.

"Mary Lou, what've you got in the way of hors d'oeuvres?"

The bartender leaned forward and tucked a rebel curl behind my ear. "It's Lou, and for a woman who sucks Bud you're getting some fancy ideas about food. Hors d'oeuvres!"

"Nah. You know me, Louie, anything in cellophane."

She pulled a jumbo bag of generic snack product from beneath the bar and cracked it open into an ersatz straw basket. I ventured a taste.

"Great. I love you, Lou."

"Ha. Here, have another beer to gag it down. Phoebe coming?"

I nodded. And settled in to wait.

Phoebe Grahame was a hack par excellence, a tireless confidant and the lender of an innocuous old Plymouth Duster when I had to do surveillance. She also knew her way around Bay Meadows, and promised to buy me a sporty Mazda if she ever cleaned up on the Pick Six. I told her I'd always wanted a Volvo. None of that dirty talk, she'd say, as she dropped a few more Andy Jacksons at the pari-mutuel window.

She dropped another on the bar when she cruised into Francine's and ordered the house red — Phoebe called it the health potion of the rank and file. She'd justify anything as a show of solidarity with The People.

"So you got a case?" Phoebe asked. "The big time?"

"A routine tail. Can I use the car?"

"Sure, love, what's in it for me?"

"'Til death do us part," I chimed, and flashed her my private smile. Phoebe and I were lovers once and I hadn't quite recovered. Nor had she, I suspect, and we still flirted around to confuse our admirers. Not that they were waiting on deck, or even warming up the bullpen. Hard to figure, I thought, fixating on the fine, hollowed cut of Phoebe's throat and the wine-stained treasure of a mouth that saved smiles for truly special occasions.

This wasn't one of 'em, though any new client was a significant coup for me in this business of detecting. Only months ago, after three years as an operative for Continent West Investigations, I had secured my solo license and a line of type in the yellow pages. The phone was still slow to ring. My cohorts at Continent West talked me up around town, but it's a funny profession — no one I could stomach could ever afford to hire me, even at my relatively discount rates. Or so I thought, until Lydia Luchetti signed a contract that very morning.

Phoebe was swinging her leg — clad in black and white chef's pants — to some new pop tune. Phoebe loved top 40. She turned to ask me about my new client. I replied, somewhat sketchily, even with Phoebe.

"Luchetti, Lydia —"

"Oh. From *Re-View*."

"Yeah." I smiled. Mary Daly fever runs rampant. Detractors were quick to dub the magazine *Rear View*. "You know her?"

"No. No, I just recognize the byline. Politics, right? The city beat?"

"Not any more. Now she does the books, sells ads, all the business stuff. 'Fiscal Facilitator,' she said. They're a collective, though, eight women, so everyone shares, well, I mean, it's all a little vague, who does what."

Phoebe laughed. I shrugged and finished off the basket of salty treats. I'd spent five years on the staff of London's *Spare Rib*, so I knew a thing or two about group decision-making. Ever respectful, that's me, but it was no accident I'd chosen this solo sleuth routine. Now I could do as I pleased, privately suffering my own long-nurtured idiosyncrasies.

In my estimation, *Re-View* was a sophisticated feminist monthly, not too polished, still rough and angry. Too much poetry, perhaps, but the essays were strong and the staff beyond intimidation. A pleasure, since the local "alternative" papers had wimped away into resource guides for consumers. Hey, another article on cappucino-makers. There's grist for revolt.

Lydia Luchetti was one determined journalist. I explained her worries to Phoebe.

"They're a tight group. All the paid staff go through rigorous interviews, but they take volunteers, too, almost any woman who walks in the door. Luchetti told me they're needy for help and scraping for funds —"

"Sounds like you, Nell."

"Yeah, well. I don't know, this is the weird part. Luchetti thinks one of the new volunteers could be a mole. She found her in the business files and — collective or not — only the paid staff handles that stuff. The woman says she wants to learn how to run a magazine, but Luchetti, well, felt something was wrong —"

"Christ," muttered Phoebe. "Feelings. Paranoia, now there's a feeling."

"I know, it seems that way. But plenty of people would like to see *Re-View* go under. Maybe someone's looking for a tax slip-up, you know, to sic the IRS on 'em. Or maybe a competitor wants to expose some questionable funding sources. God, you don't think *Re-View* has taken any grant money from Coors, do you?"

"Ugh!" Phoebe shuddered.

"Anyway, there's another thing. Luchetti says the volunteer wears 'Lesbian Power' T-shirts and all this lavender shit . . . really pushing it. Like that's the way to be a hip feminist–"

"It's not?"

"Maybe for hacks like you," I said.

"Anything for tips, sweetheart."

After a bit more banter, Phoebe and I exchanged keys and parted ways. She unlocked my crusty bike and tooled off toward the Castro Theater to see *The Hunger*, for about the fifth time. Phoebe couldn't resist that scene where Catherine Deneueve spills wine on Susan Sarandon's blouse and has to help her, ah, clean up. I found the Duster parked by a fire hydrant and headed for my apartment. I wanted to check the mail and prepare for surveillance.

Earlier in the day I had tried to make some inquiries about the volunteer in question, Suzanne Delaney. Nobody with that name was listed in the Bay Area directories, nor did the name show up when I pulled a few strings and checked the usual records — utilities, DMV, DSS, voter registration, etc.

Delaney had told the *Re-View* staff she was a nurse at San Francisco General, but that turned up a dead end, too. It was possible she was new to town, or had just fudged on revealing her employment, but it was more probable 'Suzanne Delaney' was a sham.

For some reason, I trusted Lydia Luchetti's instincts. She was a sharp cookie who was emptying her wallet to investigate Delaney, all out of concern for *Re-View*. Hmm. That *was* why she hired me, wasn't it?

I pulled onto Ramona Avenue and parked haphazardly across the sidewalk. I wouldn't be long. Ramona was a sleepy little block tucked into a narrow triangle of roads where the Mission abutted into Market Street. The best thing about my tiny apartment — besides the wild cast of characters in the neighborhood — was its close proximity to the It's Tops Coffee Shop. Heavenly.

Grabbing my scanty bundle of mail, I zipped upstairs to get a sweater, a novel and some food. I packed a grocery bag with Fig Newtons, root beer and a few tomato sandwiches. I loved tomato sandwiches because you could slather on lots of mayo, but also because Harriet always ate them in *Harriet the Spy*. Harriet stole my heart when I was a kid — maybe that's what made me a dyke. Or a private eye.

Heading back outside I loaded up the Duster, checking to make sure a blanket and empty coffee can were still stowed under the seat. I had no idea how long I'd be in the car. Luchetti had asked me to shadow Delaney when she left the *Re-View* offices that night, after putting in her scheduled evening of volunteer proofreading. Meanwhile, I was supposed to meet Luchetti at the offices during suppertime, when the place was usually cleared out. Though Luchetti had found nothing missing from the business files, she said I could look around myself, just to get a feel for things. If any other workers were there, I could pretend to be an eager new volunteer.

The *Re-View* offices were located way out in the Richmond District, on Cabrillo Street between Thirty-seventh and Thirty-eighth. It was a middle-class, residential neighborhood, an unlikely spot for a radical feminist magazine. The word was that a well-off lesbian had left her home to the *Re-View* staffers, who had gladly settled into the spacious rooms in 1985 after years of sharing cramped quarters in the Haight.

Heading for the Richmond, I cut across Market and hung

a right at Divisadero. I watched the scenery blur from lush greenery and pristine Victorian facades to barren lots and weathered clapboard as the street rose up, then down, then up another incline. Cutting left at Turk, I drove due west, cracking a window to let the salty air seep in as I neared the ocean. I was at *Re-View* within ten minutes and parked half a block away. I snuck a Fig Newton before sauntering up the walk, taking in the turquoise window trim, pale blue stucco and tasteful women's symbol knocker adorning the *Re-View* front door.

Luchetti greeted me coolly, a faint nervousness playing around her eyes. Two of her co-workers were there. I rushed through phony introductions and settled in to wait in some kind of archives room where back issues neatly lined one wall and a current events bulletin-board hung on another. Suddenly this whole venture seemed absurd. Suzanne Delaney was probably a well-meaning woman fresh out of the closet, which would explain her over-eager lavender clothing and skittish behavior. I sighed, then decided I might as well check out what *Re-View* was up to in 1978, its first year of publication. I was pulling the dusty volumes off the shelf when my client stepped in to tell me the coast was clear to explore the business office — her fellow staffers had gone out for dinner.

"How long have you worked here, Lydia?" I asked, as I reached up to reshelve the journals.

"Oh. Since the early '80s. I —"

She balked. I followed her gaze. She seemed to be focusing on the collection of magazines from 1979, just to the right of the bundle I'd disturbed. Indeed, whereas the coat of dust was uniform across most of the old *Re-Views*, the cardboard container holding the '79 issues was dotted with fingerprints. Luchetti grabbed a nearby foot ladder and hopped up to get a closer view.

"Have you been looking at these?" she asked, sharply.

"No." I frowned at Luchetti, puzzled, slightly annoyed. "What's the problem? These are here for people to use, right?"

Luchetti caught my expression and struggled to compose herself. "Yes, of course. I'm sorry, Nell. I'm worried — I mean, we only have one copy left of some of the older issues and —" She giggled. An odd sound out of her determined, no-nonsense mouth.

Before she could object, I yanked down the '79 volumes and gave them a quick scan. Unlike the '78 *Re-Views*, the '79 bunch was loose. Volume 2, Number 7 was clearly missing from the collection. Casting a narrow glance at Luchetti, I reached to give her a hand down from the ladder. She took it, fixing me with pale brown eyes gone suddenly cagey.

"Maybe a collective member borrowed it," she said.

"Humph. Got an index for these things?"

Half an hour later I was slumped in the driver's seat of Phoebe's old clunker waiting for Suzanne Delaney to emerge from the blue stucco house. I took another bite of tomato-on-sourdough. That's the nice thing about San Francisco, sourdough to anchor your mayonnaise. Something fishy was going on. Scanning the index for Re-View magazine, Volume 2, Number 7, I had noted the variety of articles — i.e. "After the White Night Riots: Where Do We Go from Here?", "Lesbians Gear up for Historic March on D.C.", "Women's Music or Wimmin's Music: Does Patti Smith Count?"

But one title had leapt out. "The Separatist Manifesto: You Don't Suck the Cock of the Oppressor," by Meg Halliway. Halliway, Halliway. That name was ringing some faint bell in the back of my brain. Was she a Londoner? I had asked Lydia Luchetti about her, but my client had just shrugged and become all business-like again, as if her moment of fluster was a figment of my imagination. Fishy indeed. Anyway, the business files had revealed not one wit of info to help me, as far as I could tell, and Luchetti had hustled me out of the offices. So I sat in the deepening gloom of a cool San Francisco night, one eye peeled to the front door, the other to my fast-diminishing sack of supper.

I cracked a root beer and rifled through my mail, which I'd left scattered unceremoniously on the dash. My heart flipped over when I saw the return address and familiar scrawl of my daughter, Pinky. Her real name was Madeline, but she'd always been called something else. As a tiny kid she became a rabid fan of the Sex Pistols and insisted on the name Sid. Now, a few names later, she was into the folk revival, the beats, Roland Gift, and the handle Pinky. I had recently sent her a black satin jacket with "Pinky Fury" lettered across the back in pink sequins. She loved it. I knew she'd be wearing it next year when she came to the States for our long-awaited trip to Graceland.

Pinky lived in London with her other mom, my ex-lover. It worked out okay, except I missed her a lot. I was hoping she'd come stay with me awhile before sprouting completely out of teenhood. Ripping open the envelope, I pulled out a short note and a poem she'd published in her local community newsrag. My daughter, the poet. Oh well, it could have been worse. She could have decided to become a lawyer.

I was still wide awake and brooding about Luchetti, Delaney, Margaret Thatcher, and the Cubs' pitching staff when I caught eye of some movement at *Re-View's* front door. I pulled out my pocket watch. I'd been huddled in the car for almost three hours. As I watched, a trickle of women left the offices. Suzanne Delaney was easy to spot from my client's precise description.

Though unremarkable in appearance, she was a bit older than the average *Re-View* volunteer, maybe pushing 45, and wore a crisp purple bandana around her neck. All her clothes looked too new, from her lavender dungarees to her shiny nylon knapsack. Delaney walked with little jerks, as if her flat shoes were somehow an obstacle to graceful movement. She nodded goodbye to the other workers and headed for the red Honda hatchback parked a few hundred feet ahead of me.

That confirmed it — Luchetti had said that's what Delaney drove. I wrote down the plate number and noticed Delaney dig something from her glove compartment before turning over the engine. I waited until a cacophony of car motors broke the night's stillness before kicking the Duster into action. Keeping my lights off, I let Delaney pull ahead to a distant stop sign and then set off on her tail.

I'd done it a million times, it seemed, but I still got a secret kick out of surveillance. When I worked for Continent West, we always worked in teams: a few cars, two people per car. It was really tricky to pull off by yourself, but I liked giving it the old macha try.

The red Honda was blazing a simple path eastward along Cabrillo Street and I followed steadily behind, though I had to move closer when Delaney turned left, then right again after a few blocks. She was heading toward Pacific Heights, seemingly oblivious to the cranky old Duster snaking behind her through the tony neighborhood. The Honda lurched to a halt before a stately home along the higher reaches of Jackson Street. I passed on by, hung a right by Alta Plaza Park, jumped from the car and hustled back on foot. Did Delaney live here? If so, I'd be holding vigil all night. As I skirted the bend to bring the Honda back into view, I saw Delaney slam the car door and walk toward a well-lit side porch. Her movements were still awkward, but there was a new urgency in her step. She held her shoulders taut, her arms crossed in front, her neck bent with unwavering purposefulness.

The night seemed suddenly eerie beyond belief. Before I could register the sickly fear in my gut, I saw a man throw open the side porch door, only to be met by a volley of bullets fired point-blank from the gun in Suzanne Delaney's outstretched arm.

Afterwards, I wondered why I didn't go after Delaney. I guess it was that polished chrome weapon still clutched in her hand as she ran off on foot down Jackson Street. A picture of moderation only moments before, she now looked maniacal. Delaney apparently didn't see me. I watched her trot away into distant shadows before I ran up to the porch. Mr. X was beyond my help. Way beyond. A few bullets had caught him in the chest and another in the throat, leaving a wide-eyed glaze of horror across his craggy face. That face. Shit. I'd seen it before.

I gingerly snapped a wallet from his back pocket, and pulled his driver's license. Pervis Culhane. It clicked. His photo and name were splashed all over town on campaign placards: Pervis Culhane for District Attorney. A wave of nausea ripped my gut as I remembered why I knew the name Meg Halliway. Culhane's chief rival in the upcoming election was one Margaret Halliway, a recently emerged player among the city's liberal politicos. Good grief. Meg Halliway, lesbian separatist, running for the highfalutin' D.A.'s seat.

The nausea came on fully. I let fly a trail of vomit into a nearby shrub, disturbing its crisp topiary. I shivered convulsively, sweat building despite the chill, and fought to regain my equilibrium. Then I quickly wiped down Culhane's wallet, tucked it back in his pocket and hightailed it for the Duster. As I sped away I heard sirens zeroing in on Jackson Street. Neighbors must have heard the shots.

There're a couple of pay phones perched high in Alta Plaza Park, like rinky-dink modern sculptures paying homage to technology. I hoped at least one of them functioned. I stopped the car and scrambled up a grassy slope — there was no one in sight. From the hilltop vantage point you could see clear across the San Francisco peninsula. Everything seemed unnaturally twinkly, from the boxy grid of downtown high-rises to the bobbing lights in the harbor to the flashing red domes atop the approaching black and whites.

Luchetti had given me both her home and work numbers. I found the piece of paper in a breast pocket, still intact, if a bit crumpled. Her home phone yielded a staticky answering machine which I cursed, involuntarily. I dialed the *Re-View* offices.

"Hello." It was Luchetti.

"I need to see you immediately," I demanded.

"What? Nell? What's going on?"

"That's what I need to ask you!" I could sense my anger mounting, focusing on my client for lack of a coherent alternative. I took a breath, counted to three. "Look. Your volunteer just killed someone. Pervis Culhane, I believe. You want to tell me what you know? *All* of what you know?"

I heard her gasp in shock. Sounded real enough, though at this point I didn't know what to believe. Here I was, a low-rent private dick only fourteen hours on a case and I had a fresh corpse, a missing assassin, an untrustworthy client, indigestion, and almost no clue about what was happening. Maybe I'd be better off playing the ponies with Phoebe.

"Nell, I'm sorry," Luchetti finally blurted out. "I had no idea Suzanne Delaney was violent. Oh god. Where is she now? What happened?"

"She ran off. After shooting Culhane in Pacific Heights."

"Are you all right?"

"Peachy."

Luchetti gulped. "Listen. I'll tell you everything, I promise. But we need to find Meg Halliway. I'll explain on the way." I agreed, grudgingly, and told her to pick me up at the park.

Now we were careening madly toward Halliway's apartment in North Beach. Traffic was slight as we ran a few lights, jumped a curb and sped across Van Ness and into the Broadway tunnel. I cast Luchetti an appreciative glance — the woman could drive. And she was sure hell-bent on seeing Halliway that night. I pumped Luchetti for more information as we cruised smack into the inevitable traffic jam at the neon-washed corner of Broadway and Columbus.

"Damn!" Luchetti craned her neck, straining to find a way to circumvent the intersection.

"How do you know where she lives?" I asked. I was still hungry for details.

"We used to be friends." Luchetti bumped her wheels into a loading zone. "It'll be quicker to walk over to Kearny Street — she's up there. Let's go."

A fuller explanation finally tumbled out as we hoofed it down Columbus. Luchetti and Meg Halliway had been acquainted since 1981 when they'd overlapped on the *Re-View* staff for about six months. Meg — now Margaret — was a mentor to Luchetti, but she'd grown more distant after entering law school. Luchetti said she didn't hear from her much, and when she read Halliway was running for D.A., she figured the former separatist's politics had, to put it mildly, mellowed. Then Luchetti met the new volunteer, Suzanne Delaney — and realized it was the same woman she'd seen at a restaurant a mere week ago on the arm of hotshot candidate Pervis Culhane.

"I figured Culhane was using her to dig up some dirt on Meg," Luchetti explained. "You know, get some proof on her lesbian past, leak it to the press. All the employee records are in the business files. And that article! Suzanne Delaney must have found it after all — I didn't think she'd had a chance to check the back issues."

"Why didn't you just confront her? Or give her Halliway's article up front? Why should you help Meg hide out in the closet?"

"Nell." Luchetti's face flushed. "There's a lot riding on the D.A.'s race. We need someone who's not hand-in-glove with the cops. Culhane's a corrupt asshole."

She caught my look of skepticism. As if other high-powered dudes were as clean as the Easter bunny.

"Besides," Luchetti continued, "Culhane sent someone to spy on us! It's so sleazy!"

I stopped in my tracks. "What do you think you hired *me* to do? Lick your boots? Or maybe I'm just your patsy, is that it? I rake the muck and you become the next Woodward-fucking-Bernstein."

Luchetti's flush turned two shades deeper. I could've fried a couple of eggs on her cheeks.

I burst out laughing. "So. You wanted to write an exposé on the juiciest secrets of the D.A.'s race. I'll be damned. I thought you'd left the city beat behind, anyway." I kept chuckling.

She sighed. "I miss it. I wanted to scoop the dailies, you know, from a feminist angle. What's wrong with that? I thought if I brought in a private eye I could unearth Culhane's sleazebag tactics and maybe find out what Meg was up to. If I tried to investigate myself, I would've tipped my hand. Maybe I should have been more straight with you, Nell. But I like to work. . .privately."

"You and me, honey. You and me."

Luchetti and I had come to a halt near the entrance to an Italian cafe. Strains of live opera wafted out across the sidewalk. La la la. I was exhausted. There were still a few questions muddling this whole hangdog affair.

"Lydia, why are we going to Halliway's? What does this have to do with Culhane's murder?"

"I . . . I'm worried about her. I thought Culhane's boys might think she was responsible for his death."

"What makes you think she wasn't? Maybe Delaney's a double-spy."

She shot me a look of anguish. "No. No way!"

Luchetti peeled off into the residential streets of North Beach. I followed, an aria reaching its breathy climax behind me. Good thing I'd worn my trusty oxfords — run faster, jump higher. I finally understood. Luchetti and Halliway must have something going on. Why else would Luchetti be so obsessed with safeguarding Meg's reputation? Why else would she be so worried?

As I rounded onto Kearny, I could see Coit Tower glistening up ahead in the moonlight, a cylindrical monument looming coyly over the City That Knows How. I also saw three people jostling in a driveway, their testy voices rising. One of them must be Halliway, the lean figure with a helmet of silver hair and in incongruous shorty nightgown with ruffle at the neck. As I neared the trio, the woman bowed her silver head and broke into a tired sob. Luchetti, herself choking a muffled cry, reached over to encircle Halliway's quivering shoulders.

The odd woman out was Suzanne Delaney. She eyed the embracing lovers with panic rising in her haunted face and turned, bolting in confusion. For the second time that night I watched Delaney dart off into the darkness, her revolver still bobbing, flashing, trailing glints of light as she faded slowly from view.

I found out later that Margaret Halliway had nothing to do with Culhane's premature demise. The way the papers called it, it was all the work of Delaney, whose real name turned out

33

to be Carla Mayes. She and Culhane were having an affair, an abusive one apparently, and he'd been double- and triple-timing her on top of that. Coercing her into snooping around *Re-View* was the last straw. She had snapped. Mayes had allegedly aced Culhane with his own revolver that she found sequestered — illegally — in the glove compartment of his little red Honda.

Luchetti didn't get the scoop. It was plastered all over the San Francisco dailies, pieced together from speculation by Culhane's relatives, friends, even some *Re-View* staffers. Carla Mayes herself was still on the lam. And I kept my own lips sealed about witnessing the murder — I didn't get on so well with the city's finest. Halliway emerged from the whole thing unscathed, maybe stronger. Her authorship of "You Don't Suck the Cock. . ." remained mysteriously under wraps.

I still didn't understand why Delaney — I mean, Mayes — went over to Halliway's apartment. Luchetti told me she thought Mayes wanted validation from Halliway. Maybe Mayes thought the candidate would be grateful to her for getting rid of Culhane, and offer up an alibi. I don't know. I may never know. But Luchetti said I could read all about it in the next issue of *Re-View*. She was publishing some theoretical piece on the psychology of women and crime. Sounded like baloney to me.

I was sitting in a booth at It's Tops the morning after the murder. Eleven o'clock had come and gone, but I hadn't slept much and the cracked linoleum counter kept swimming in and out of focus. Dirty cups and English muffin crumbs lay scattered across the table. I tried to focus on Pinky's poem. Just then, a flash of orange and blue metal rolled past the window — must be a Barbary Coast Taxi cruising for a meter.

Sure enough, Phoebe strolled in a few minutes later.

"Hey!" I beamed. She looked adorable. "How'd you know I was here?"

"You're always here. Besides, I saw your carrot-top in the window."

Phoebe had a *Chronicle* under her arm. She threw it on the counter, eyebrows raised quizzically. I didn't say anything as she slid into the booth across from me. She'd hear about it, sooner or later.

"Pinky sent me a poem," I said, handing Phoebe the mimeographed newsletter. I sipped some more coffee as she read it once, then again.

"Not bad. For a poem."

"Yeah. Not bad."

Crime Time

Helen & Lorri Carpenter

It really wouldn't be fair to complain, Emma Twiggs thought, contemplating the narrowness of her small office. After all, Jim had finally relented and granted her a cubicle, no matter how tiny, that positively established her right to claim private investigator status. *'Amateur sleuth until further notice'*, she amended, remembering her nephew's warning. Nonetheless. . . .

The septuagenarian's thoughts were interrupted by the appearance of Nancy Barnes, her good friend and peerless secretary to James Galveston, Private Investigator.

"Jim wants to see you in his office, Em," the dark haired young woman said, stepping through the doorway.

Emma's brows peaked with interest. "My nephew has a case for me?"

"He's meeting with a client," Nancy said. "He wants you to bring a pad and pencil."

Emma pushed back her chair with a resigned sigh. She would have given her bridgework for a chance at a real case, but her closest brush with anything remotely related to detecting was transcribing her nephew's indecipherable scribbles onto a floppy disk. Lately, in order to avoid further eye strain, she'd volunteered to be present whenever he felt the need to write down the pertinent facts conveyed by a client, but she hated the task.

"I suppose he wants me to take more notes," she said to Nancy as she picked up the required items, exited her drab office, and followed the fashionably trim secretary down the hallway to Jim's opulently appointed inner sanctum.

"Ah, Aunty, I'm glad you're here." James Galveston, tall, flawlessly groomed, and clearly in a good mood, rose to his feet as Emma entered. He gestured gallantly to a velvet couch situated to the left of his client, "Have a seat."

The man lounging indolently in the chair in front of Jim's walnut desk turned to look at Emma. He was lean and slightly balding, with a long, unhappy face and eyes that reminded Emma of iced flounder at the fish market.

"This is Marvin Simonson. Mr. Simonson works as a clerk at Willaby's Art Gallery. He wants to hire us." Jim sat down. "Please continue with what you were saying, Mr. Simonson. Emma is my . . . . special assistant, and the firm's chronicler. You can speak freely in front of her."

Marvin Simonson's flat eyes blinked at Emma, and he shrugged, his shoulders scarcely moving the fabric of his baggy suit jacket. "I'll start again," he said through tight lips, as if having to deal with a woman was a major inconvenience. "Some years before Mother passed away, she bought a floral pastel from a relatively obscure artist. When my father discovered how much money she'd wasted, he was furious and refused to allow her to hang the still-life in the house. Mother had it wrapped in linen and stored in the attic. I forgot all about the painting. Last week I decided to do a thorough cleaning of the house and found it.

Marvin Simonson paused, and Emma, who had been staring out the window behind Jim's head, became aware that he was waiting for her to start taking notes. "Please go on, Mr. Simonson," she said, positioning pencil over notepad.

"Knowing some American art has appreciated immensely, I took the pastel to my employer for his appraisal. Mr. Willaby became very excited and told me the work was of top quality, worth in the neighborhood of $300,000. Since sales at the gallery have been slow, he offered to act as my agent, for a slight commission."

A flurry of emotion crossed his face. "I couldn't decide whether to part with the painting or not. I kept remembering how much Mother loved it." Marvin Simonson stopped speaking and pulled a crumpled handkerchief from his back pocket. He proceeded to dab at his eyes, then wadded the square of fabric into a ball.

"What a fool I was for procrastinating a week . . . ." He wiped his hands on the wrinkled hanky. "With the money from the Gemstone Flowers —that's the name of the painting—," he directed this to Emma, "I would have been set for life. Now it's all gone. My valuable pastel has been stolen!"

Emma, finally letting her interest show, remarked, "Surely, since you worked for an art dealer, you knew such an expensive item should be properly insured?"

"I did. But I'm not a wealthy man," Marvin Simonson

pointed out. "When I spoke to my insurance agent he quoted a very high premium. I couldn't afford it. That's when I knew Gemstone Flowers would have to be sold. The insurance company agreed to issue a temporary rider to cover the painting until the sale was consummated. Unfortunately, it was for only a fraction of the pastel's worth."

Jim leaned forward, his face showed mild impatience. "Can we please get back to the theft?"

Marvin Simonson pushed the mutilated hanky he'd been twisting into the recesses of his pocket and went on with his recollection of the crime. "Last evening, at two-forty-two a.m., I was awakened by a loud noise. When I went to investigate, I discovered the electricity was off. I found my flashlight and made my way to the living room. There was a rustling noise behind me, and as I turned, someone hit me over the head."

He paused again in his narration. Emma, writing as fast as she could, looked up and saw him pointing to a black and blue mark on his forehead. "It was four-seventeen before I regained consciousness," he continued. "The entire house had been ransacked. The painting was missing. I telephoned the police immediately. A detective came out, took my statement, and suggested I file an insurance claim."

Jim leaned back in his leather chair and laced his fingers across his tailored suit. "I'm not sure I understand why you need a private investigator," he said, his smooth brow puckering. "The police can pursue a simple burglary as adequately, and certainly much more cheaply, than I can."

"As I told you earlier, Gemstone Flowers was insured for approximately a quarter of its true value. Recovery of my pastel would bring me a greater monetary gain."

Jim brought his steepled fingers to his lips and frowned in concentration. Emma re-read her notes and tapped the end of her pencil against the pad in sudden comprehension. "What sort of clock do you have at home, Mr. Simonson?"

She could see her question annoyed both men. Jim dropped his hands to his desk, and shot her an irate glance. Marvin Simonson twisted in his seat. His mouth was stretched in a thin, hard line. "Excuse me?" he asked.

"Your clock at home," Emma repeated. "Would you describe it for me, please."

The pale man stared at his scuffed shoes. "It's just an ordinary digital alarm, the plug-in kind they sell at any discount store." He raised cold eyes to hers. "Why do you ask?"

"Just trying to get at the truth, Mr. Simonson. I think you stole your own painting."

"Aunt Emma!" Jim's reproving tone changed to surprise as Marvin Simonson leaped to his feet.

"You're crazy!" he shouted at Emma.

Jim dashed around his desk and caught Simonson's hands as they savagely tore at the pages of Emma's notepad. He easily subdued the surly art clerk with a hanmerlock, then forced him to return to his seat.

A badly shaken Emma retrieved her pencil and straightened her skirt. "Please call the police," she said to Nancy as the secretary rushed through the doorway. "It seems we've captured a thief."

When the room was crowded with uniformed officers, Jim flashed Emma a cynical smile. "All right, Aunty," her nephew said. "Would you like to explain to all of us what convinced you of Mr. Simonson's guilt?"

"It was the time," Emma replied, keeping an eye on Marvin Simonson, whose pale lips hung open in apparent disbelief. "He knew it was precisely 2:42 a.m. when he heard the first noise, and he knew to the minute when he regained consciousness. People who own digital clocks usually express time that way."

"Tell us more," Jim invited.

"Marvin said the power was out, and of course his digital clock couldn't work without electricity. He wouldn't have know the exact time unless the power was really on — which it was — proving his story is a fabrication."

"I see," Jim said. He leaned back in his chair and waited.

"Mr. Simonson said the insurance policy covered only a fraction of the painting's real worth," Emma went on. "If I had to guess, I would say Gemstone Flowers was probably an inexpensive print that Marvin Simonson destroyed. When these officers question him and Mr. Willaby, I think they'll find the two of them cooked up this scheme to defraud the insurance company. Mr. Simonson has admitted he isn't a wealthy man, and," she paused to consult her mangled notes, "he mentioned sales at the gallery have been slow, which means his employer also needed money. One-fourth of $300,000 isn't exactly a paltry sum."

"But why would a thief hire a private investigator?"

"To throw suspicion on someone else."

"There you have it, gentlemen!" Jim exclaimed with pleasure. "Another case well solved by Galveston Investigations. If there is anything more you need, my secretary is at your disposal."

When everyone had filed out, Jim grinned at his elderly relative. "Very good, Aunty. You've passed the Galveston Agency's private investigator exam with flying colors."

Emma stared at him in open-mouthed astonishment.

"I'm sorry I let Marvin frighten you," he said hurriedly. "I wanted to make you aware of what a dangerous business detecting can be."

Jimbo, you're an insufferable fraud, Emma thought, before she said, "Are you telling me this was a set-up?"

The younger man nodded and with quicksilver speed added, "However, you handled yourself admirably."

Still not quite believing him, Emma rose from her seat, moved across the room, and dropped the notepad into the wastebasket. Then with thoughtful concentration, she turned in her nephew's direction.

"Would you concur with my conclusion that I can scrap "amateur status" from my title?" She pretended to study her manicure while she waited for his answer.

Jim contemplated her with familial affection. "Let's just say you're on your way to becoming a valuable asset to this agency, Aunty."

"In that case, I have a request," Emma announced, smiling to herself.

"A raise?" her nephew enquired with complacent aplomb.

"No," Emma said. Making sure her voice conveyed exactly the right touch of benign determination, she told him, "I want an office just like yours."

A Nose for Crime

Helen and Lorri Carpenter

Emma Twiggs stood indecisively in front of the large display of waterbed sheets. The flowered cotton print was practical, but the pale peach satin set, which had jumped into her hand of its own volition, was the one she really wanted. As the septuagenarian sleuth considered which package to take, her contemplation was interrupted by the sound of high heels briskly approaching from the main aisle.

She turned and saw her friend, Nancy Barnes, walking toward her. Jim Galveston, her tall, sublimely handsome private investigator nephew, trailed his pretty secretary by a few steps.

"Buy the cotton, Aunt Emma," Jim advised, when he reached his relative's side. "It suits you better."

As always, his remark had the effect of committing Emma to a course of action she might otherwise not have taken. "For your lifestyle, maybe, Jimbo. My night life demands satin," she informed him, hefting the package, and feeling the same small thrill she'd felt as a child whenever she defied authority.

Nancy giggled. "I wish I could say the same." She wistfully touched the silky material through an opening in the wrap. "Unfortunately, I'm the cotton floral type."

Jim cocked a dark eyebrow at his secretary, then glanced at the slender Rolex adorning his wide wrist. "This detour to QueBee's was supposed to be a quick stop," he reminded his aunt. "It's already been half an hour. Couldn't you have bought your sheets after we took Nancy to lunch?"

"I didn't mean to ruin your birthday celebration, Nance," Emma said contritely, putting a hand on her friend's arm. "Actually, the sheets aren't the real reason. . . ."

Emma's explanation was cut off by the shrill blast of a police whistle. Startled, she pivoted around.

Near the store's entrance, a security guard scuffled with a brawny man wearing baggy camouflage pants. Before Emma

40

could speak, Nancy exclaimed, "A shoplifter!"

As QueBee's finest raised his radio to call for help, the nearly-apprehended suspect swung his fist in a jaw-breaking right uppercut. The blow sent the grey-suited guard sprawling across the floor. Free at last, the robber raced for the exit.

At that moment Jim leaped into action. In less than a heartbeat, his long legs covered the distance between the homeware department and the fleeing thug. He executed a forceful tackle and the two men fell to the floor.

Emma, riveted to the scene, heard the thief's breath escape in a loud wheeze. Before he could recover, Jim straddled him. Pressing his knee into the small of the thief's back, he immobilized his captive until the remaining security force could dash across the store.

While the bewildered crook was being led away, Jim strode back to Emma and Nancy. Brushing dirt from his hands, he paused to acknowledge the smattering of applause from the gathered crowd.

"Another perp apprehended," he said to his secretary and his aunt. He smoothed his well groomed Clark Gable mustache and grinned. "That's what detecting is all about, Aunty, being in the right place at the right time. Now can we get on with our luncheon?"

"Not yet," Emma said. She refused to let her nephew get the best of her. "As I was going to say before we were interrupted, the sheets weren't the real reason for my coming here today."

Jim frowned, "What do you mean, Aunt Emma?"

"There has been a series of petty thefts at this store lately. Today's incident is the third in less than a month. I think the crimes are a cover for something else."

Jim was skeptical, "Shoplifting is an ongoing occurrence, more so during certain seasons."

"There aren't any holidays in August," Nancy interjected.

Emma felt obliged to interrupt. "Whenever the security force intercepts a shoplifter, an expensive shipment of electronic equipment is stolen from the truck bringing in the week's warehouse order."

Jim didn't doubt her now. "Let's walk to the back of the building, after you pay for the sheets."

Emma tossed the package onto the shelf. "These can wait. Solving a case is far more important."

"If there is a case," Jim replied. "And if you're right, I don't want you to intervene. Six months of observing me doesn't give you enough experience."

"Can't he sing any other tune?" Emma muttered to Nancy, as the two women followed Jim's purposeful stride to the rear of the store. "How am I ever going to become an associate? He won't allow me to work with him until I'm experienced, and I can't gain experience unless I work with him."

"You're learning more every day," her friend consoled her. "Even though Jim won't admit it, you practically solved his last case on your own."

Big deal, Emma thought to herself. Still, she supposed Nancy was right. Despite her nephew's insistence on a hands-off approach, she had managed to make the most of her unofficial position.

One of these days, Emma told herself, as she followed Nancy and Jim from the store into the hot sun, Jim's going to have to start taking me seriously.

Shielding her eyes with her hand, Emma squinted into the bright sun and saw a large tractor-trailer parked beside the loading dock. The driver, obviously dazed, lay on the ground next to his rig. Jim and Nancy broke into a run. By the time Emma caught up, the man had recovered enough to sit up and rub the bruise on the back of his head.

"Cleaned out again! I gotta call the police."

As the trucker stood, Emma mentally made notes. Height: tall; hair color: red; distinguishing marks: the name Sam embroidered over his shirt pocket.

Jim extended a steadying hand and asked, "Can you tell me what happened?"

"They cleaned me out again," Sam repeated, his face taking on the same ruddy hue as his hair, "the third time on this run. My company's beginning to wonder if I'm involved." He made a gesture of disgust and started toward the store to find a phone.

"I might as well investigate before the police arrive," Jim said. He instructed Nancy to keep a look-out, advised Emma to stay in the shade, then stepped to the rear of the rig and hoisted himself inside.

When her nephew was safely out of sight in the cavernous interior of the truck, Emma began her own inspection of the surrounding premises. In addition to understudying Jim, she subscribed to *Mystery Monthly Magazine*. According to an article on police procedures in the latest issue, the scene of any criminal act should always be observed carefully for useful clues.

She glanced around. The concrete area at the back of the department store served as an unloading zone, as well as a parking lot for incoming trucks. The only vehicle in sight was the one Jim was investigating. Emma felt sure he wouldn't find any clues inside the trailer.

Check the ground, she reminded herself, and bent to scrutinize the pavement. The absence of rubber tire marks indicated the thieves hadn't left in a hurry, but otherwise the area yielded little insight into the events preceding or following the robbery.

She straightened and saw her nephew stroll to the edge of the loading platform to talk to Sam. Hoping to reach the truck without Jim seeing her, the stealthy sleuth cut across the parking lot. In her haste, she stepped in a puddle. A momentary observation convinced her that the irregular splotch was one of the mysterious fluids necessary for the survival and maintenance of a large vehicle. No time to investigate, she thought, hurriedly completing her dash.

Nancy was taking notes when Emma emerged from the shady side of the trailer. "What exactly was stolen?" Jim asked the driver.

"An entire load of stereos." Emma heard Sam's sigh of resignation as Nancy jotted down his answer.

"The same m.o. as the other robberies?" her nephew questioned.

The red-haired trucker shot Jim a suspicious glance, and answered with a query of his own. "Are you a cop or something?"

Jim plucked a leather folio from his shirt pocket, extracted a business card and said, "James Galveston, Private Investigator."

Sam examined the card dubiously. After a long moment he came to a decision. "Okay, I'll hire you. If you can solve this mystery I might get to keep my job."

"No need, friend," Jim said. "According to the flyer in the front window, QueBee's management is offering $10,000 to anyone with information leading to the arrest and conviction of the robbers. I plan to collect the reward."

Emma eyed her nephew with something akin to astonishment. So he'd seen the flyer, too. She should have guessed.

"You forgot to mention the reward, didn't you, Aunty?"

Jim acknowledged Emma's presence with good-natured affection, then turned to Sam. "Will you answer a few more questions?"

"Sure," Sam replied promptly. "The police haven't come up with anything. If you can figure out what happens to those shipments, maybe my boss will get off my back."

"Were the previous thefts committed in the same manner?" Jim returned the business card holder to his pocket.

"I've never been clobbered before," the red-haired driver said. He touched the back of his head and winced. "I usually go inside and get the floor manager to sign for the merchandise. The last two times, I come out, and bingo — the truck is cleaned out.

"The first load my boss writes off as an insurance loss. The second, he starts thinking something's fishy. So today I had a rider with me. Joe gets the paper work taken care of, while I stay out here with the shipment. Except someone snuck up and nailed me when I wasn't looking."

"Where is this Joe?"

"Inside with the manager."

"I'll talk to him next," Jim said.

"I'd like to know why the security people weren't keeping an eye on my rig," Sam mused. "My boss called the store especially to make sure someone would be here."

"They were subduing a shoplifter," Emma answered.

"That's right," Jim interrupted. "And I'm sure when I check, I'll find out the guards have been busy each time your rig has been hit. If the disturbances inside the store coincide with the deliveries, then my guess is the shoplifting is a smokescreen designed to keep security busy while another bunch of crooks steals the contents of your truck."

Sam eyed Jim with admiration, while Emma glared at her nephew. He'd managed to do it again. Her idea, reworded, had suddenly become his inspiration.

"What puzzles me," Emma said, "is how the thieves manage to escape so fast."

"Yeah, Mr. Galveston," Sam chimed in. "The police and my boss would like to know, too. The whole job takes less than ten minutes. The crooks seem to vanish into thin air. How do you suppose they do that?"

Sam looked at Jim expectantly. Nancy, pencil poised above her notepad, stood ready to record his reply. Even Emma leaned forward in anticipation.

"You'll be the first to know when I find out," Jim said dryly. "Right now I'm going inside to talk to Joe and the manager. Aunt Emma, you stay here with Sam and wait for the police. Nancy, come with me."

As soon as Jim and Nancy disappeared into the store, Emma walked to the puddle of liquid. Dipping her finger into the diminishing circle of wetness, she raised it to her nose and sniffed.

"Odorless," she said, disappointment clear in her voice.

"Looks like water from an air conditioner," Sam commented.

Emma's eyes swept the concrete lot. On the other side of the sun-filled expanse she saw a mini-warehouse and an overflowing dumpster.

Sam heaved another huge sigh. "It's hot out here. I'll be in my truck if you want me."

Emma wended her way slowly across the hot pavement without finding another wet spot. She was ready to start back when the heat seemed to well up around her. Pausing, she sucked in an unsteady breath. Her eyes fell on the nearby dumpster. She stepped into the cool rectangle of shade with relief. The last thing I need is sunstroke, she thought, leaning weakly against the metal container. Jim will never make me an associate if I pass out in the middle of a case.

To get her mind off her discomfort, she practiced investigative techniques by peering over the top of the dumpster and studying the long, high-roofed warehouse. The building was divided into seven connected units, each fronted by an over-sized roll-up garage door. The owner's name and phone number were printed in what appeared to be blurry square letters on the cement block side.

Emma lowered her lids, and inhaled deeply, imagining herself on the top of a mountain. But instead of piney fresh air to clear her head, her nose caught the unmentionable odors arising from the overflowing dumpster. Mixed with the unpleasant smell was the acrid scent of cigarette smoke. The sleuth's eyes flew open, and her dizziness faded quickly.

A moment later, she ran across the parking lot to the tractor trailer rig. Jim emerged from the store and crossed the loading platform to her side. "Something wrong, Aunty?"

"Yes," the breathless sleuth said succinctly. She waited for her racing heart to calm before she added, "I know how the thieves have been escaping so quickly."

45

As disbelief spread across Jim's face, a police car, siren engaged, arrived on the scene. A uniformed officer stepped from the vehicle. He peered at the sun, removed his hat to wipe his brow, and grimaced in commiseration as Sam climbed down from his rig. "Another theft, huh?"

Sam nodded and gestured at Emma. "This lady says she has the answer."

The officer looked expectantly at Emma, but Jim moved forward. "James Galveston. I'm a private investigator. My aunt . . . uh, associate, and I have been working on this case."

"If you've come up with anything, we wouldn't mind listening," the officer said mildly. "We've turned this town upside down and haven't found a clue."

Jim glanced at his aunt. Emma, enjoying her role of newly appointed associate, smiled gently at her nephew, then spoke directly to the policeman. "I believe you'll find the thieves, as well as the last shipment, behind door number one," she said, waving a hand grandly at the mini-storage buildings.

"What I'd like to know, Emma," Nancy said later, over a superb, though somewhat delayed, birthday luncheon of Beef Ragout, "is how you figured it all out."

Emma set her wine goblet on the table. "I wish I could say logical investigative techniques, but that would be an insult to both Jim and the police." She grinned at Nancy. "Actually, the credit has to go to my nose. The cigarette smoke made me realize someone was in the warehouse."

Jim shook his head in mock amazement. "One of these days you're going to be as good as I am, Aunty." Ignoring her startled sputter, he studied his neatly trimmed nails. "Of course, your methods need refining, but I can't complain about today's results. The $10,000 fee Galveston Investigations earned for an hour's work isn't bad at all."

Emma dabbed the corners of her mouth with the linen napkin and eyed her nephew innocently. "As soon as you make me an official partner, I'll be more than happy to share my reward money with you." She paused to let her words sink in. Then, winking at Nancy, she added, "After I purchase QueBee's most expensive satin sheets, of course."

Drowned in Affection

Helen and Lorri Carpenter

"Your theory puts Todd Cahan in the middle of the whole mess. That spells murder!" Emma Twiggs drew a breath after her emphatic statement. As a junior associate of Galveston Investigations, Emma spent many hours in front of a mirror practicing the art of impassivity. This was an opportunity to put her skills into action.

Flattening her tone, she added, "Tell me more."

"The coroner's report states death was accidental," her new friend, Arnie Bracken, said. His voice rose sharply. "Tell me how anyone as healthy as Jo Fernley could have died by 'accidentally' drowning in a bathtub."

Emma remained silent, willing Arnie to present her with a clue. In preparation for this, her first undercover case, the septuagenarian sleuth had become a certified water aerobics instructor and secured a position at Happy Haven Retirement Community.

Now, after a week of listening to bits and pieces of misinformation and gossip, she sensed she was being offered a solid tip. She waited with impatience for the retired accountant to continue.

Arnie glanced furtively at the other Happy Haven Retirement Community residents congregated around the pool deck. When he was sure his outburst had gone unnoticed, he said in a calmer tone, "By his own admission, Cahan was in Jo Fernley's apartment. That gives him the opportunity for murder."

Arnie had already mentioned his desire to be a private detective. Emma, hoping his hobby had led him to some bit of tangible evidence, leaned closer. "And the motive?" she prompted.

"Money," he said. "Jo Fernley was a wealthy woman."

Emma averted her eyes. Arnie mustn't notice my interest, she thought, knowing all her practice hadn't prepared her for actually being in the forefront of a murder investigation. To cover her enthusiasm, she asked her friend to repeat himself.

His note of irritation told her Arnie mistook her diversion for disbelief. "Money," he stated again more emphatically. "Jo had a meeting with a representative from her life insurance company the week before she died. From what I heard, she changed the beneficiary on her policy."

Emma leaned into the thick cushions of her lounge chair. Arnie's theory of murder for money coincided with that of Galveston Investigation's client, the insurance company. But so far, he hadn't given Emma the lead she was seeking.

Before she could question him further, Arnie's prime suspect, Todd Cahan, strode into view. The sight of the alleged murderer had the same effect on Emma's heart rate as an aerobics workout. In an effort to maintain her nonchalance, she lowered her gaze and pretended to watch the swimmers while she surreptitiously studied him.

Happy Haven's tall, middle-aged physical therapist still had the enviable ability to turn women's heads. He moved around the pool with the easy stride of a jungle cat. His animated smile acknowledged each of the grey-haired ladies who greeted him, but his blue eyes sparkled only when he approached a slim woman clinging to the edge of the pool.

"Evie Donner," Emma whispered to Arnie. She watched the scene unfolding before her with a jaundiced eye.

Evie, Happy Haven's newest retiree and an enthusiastic member of Emma's afternoon workout class, was suited in a mauve bikini that barely covered her dimples. When she extended a hand so the therapist could help her from the water, the scraps of cloth slipped downward, and for a moment her slim body hovered on the brink of exposure. Laughing prettily, Evie stepped from the pool and wrapped a towel around herself. She and Todd moved across the deck toward his office.

Disgruntled, Arnie said, "I see Evie's headed in the same direction as Jo Fernley," and his gaze locked on the retreating couple. "I'm going to practice some surveillance, Em."

Only Emma's quick action stopped Arnie's chair from tipping over as he leaped to his feet and rushed after Evie and Todd. Annoyed by the abrupt end to their conversation, Emma rose from the chaise lounge and walked across the unsplashed pool deck to the clubhouse. As she entered the arched portals, she was still thinking about Arnie and bumped into her nephew.

James Galveston, tall, broad-shouldered and impeccably handsome, caught her arm. "I've been looking for you, Aunty."

"Jimbo!" Emma hastily performed her own version of Arnie's furtive glance. Satisfied that no one was watching, she asked, "Are you trying to ruin my cover?"

"It's not your cover I'm worried about," Jim said grimly. Still holding her elbow, he guided her toward The Happy Haven Grill. "Let's have lunch."

"Your treat?"

When he nodded, Emma allowed him to sweep her along. She kept silent until they were seated in the restaurant. Then, unable to restrain herself any longer, she asked, "What *are* you worried about, Jim?"

"Aunty, you've been a mother to me for thirty-five years," he began gently, in his best protective-nephew-worried-about-elderly-aunt tone.

"Are you thinking of taking over my case?" Emma interrupted. Even before he opened his mouth, she knew the answer. The anxious hand, brushed over his neatly trimmed mustache, gave him away. Nonetheless, she waited with exaggerated patience for him to speak.

"I wish I didn't have to say yes, Aunty." Jim looked truly distressed. "I received some information today that makes me think you're in too much danger to continue this job."

Emma leaned forward to ask what he'd learned, when a disheveled Arnie burst into the restaurant. His gaze swung across the diners, then settled on Emma. He wove through the tables and stopped at her side.

"I want to apologize for running out on your earlier," the big man said, barely acknowledging Jim's presence in his rush to account for his actions. "I hope you'll understand once I explain that Evie Donner is almost family. Her husband was my best friend. Before he died, I promised to watch out for her."

Prompted by an impulse she didn't care to examine, Emma said warmly, "My nephew, James Galveston, and I were about to have lunch. Would you like to join us?"

Arnie grinned. "Did you say James Galveston? I've always wanted to meet a famous private eye like Big Jim Galveston in person." He pumped Jim's hand enthusiastically.

Emma watched a wide smile spread across her nephew's face. Pulling his ensnared hand free, he ran a finger over his trim mustache. "And rightly so," he remarked.

Emma mentally rolled her eyes. Of the ten Galveston children, Jim was her favorite, but occasional glimpses of his inflated ego made her doubt the wisdom of her partiality. Before Arnie could issue another compliment, Emma brought the conversation to earth. "We're both detectives," she said sweetly. "I'm working undercover for Galveston Investigations."

The retired accountant's mouth dropped open, and he eyed Emma with new respect.

"My aunt is a junior associate," Jim clarified. "She and I occasionally collaborate."

Arnie pulled out a chair and sat down as the waitress arrived with the menus. After she scribbled their orders and left them, Arnie said, "I'd like to finish telling you my theory about Cahan."

At a nod from Emma, the older man continued. "I'm sure he seduces lonely women, gets himself set up as their beneficiary, and then kills them. Jo Fernley wasn't the first, you know. I heard our man was arrested in Miami for the murder of an elderly neighbor who just happened to be very wealthy."

"He's right, Aunt Emma," Jim interjected. "That's why I should handle this case myself." He turned to face Arnie. "Because of information I received this morning, I've been trying to convince my aunt this case is too dangerous for her. She should let a more experienced investigator take over."

Emma's silence was eloquent. Jim took her hand and softened his tone. "I'm doing this for your own good, Aunty," he said. "Before I drove over here, the Miami police report on Todd Cahan came into the office. Several witnesses testified they heard the victim tell Todd she had revised her life-insurance policy to benefit him."

"I knew it," Arnie said.

"However," Jim continued, ignoring the interruption, "because the policy was never actually changed, the money went to Shady Lawn Retirement Center, where the woman had been living. Since the police couldn't come up with a motive and the coroner ruled that the death was accidental, all charges against Todd Cahan were dropped."

"He was lucky," Arnie said.

Jim agreed. While he eyed his aunt, apparently debating his next words, a short, red-headed man strode briskly into the restaurant. Glancing neither left nor right, he crossed the parquet floor and headed toward the kitchen.

"Marty is up in arms about something," Arnie remarked, as Martin Grumbach, the retirement community's commander-in-chief, disappeared through the swinging doors. The sound of his lusty voice filled the dining area. Apparently the chef was being informed of a complaint made by a patron. Emma strained to overhear.

"Please, Aunt Emma," Jim said. "This is no time for eavesdropping."

"I'm listening, not eavesdropping. Finish telling me why you're going to steal my case." Arnie covered what sounded suspiciously like a chuckle with a loud slurp of iced tea from the glass the waitress had just set before him. Jim looked at his aunt in mild reproof and was silent until their lunch was placed on the table and the three of them were alone again.

"There wasn't enough evidence to bring Todd to trial, Aunt Emma, but you must admit this information makes the case too risky to pursue on your own. A more experienced investigator should step in."

Emma made an impatient gesture. "Does Marty know about Todd's arrest?"

Jim lifted his eyebrows and shrugged. "He must. He was working at Shady Lawn Retirement Center at the time."

"Then why did he hire Todd to work at Happy Haven?" Emma wondered aloud.

Before Jim could comment, the kitchen doors burst open, and Marty Grumbach once again appeared in the dining room. Wending his way through the clustered tables, he came to halt before Jim, Emma, and Arnie.

"Bracken," he said jovially, clapping Arnie across the back, "and Mrs. Twiggs." He smiled at Emma, then turned to Jim. "I don't believe we've met. But I must say I recognize you from the newspapers. You're the famous detective, James Galveston." Jim accepted the accolade with his usual sangfroid, rose halfway from his chair, and shook Marty's proffered hand.

"What brings you to Happy Haven?" the red-headed director questioned, his eyes narrowing. "Business?"

"Not at all," Jim assured him. "Emma is my aunt."

Marty's gaze returned to his water aerobics instructor. "Mrs. Twiggs never mentioned any relatives — at least, none so famous."

"Say, Marty," Arnie interjected, "I've learned something interesting about another member of your staff." He paused as Marty's cool eyes swung in his direction. "Cahan has a police record." The words hung baldly in an extended silence.

After a moment Marty said, "If you're trying to make something of Jo Fernley's death, idle speculation causes nothing but trouble. Todd and I discussed his past problems. He's made a clean start and a new life here at Happy Haven. As far as I'm concerned, that's the end of the matter.

"The truth is, I believe in people. Whether Todd was guilty or not — and since the police cleared him of all charges, he evidently was *not* guilty — he has been open and honest with me, and I see no reason to continue to punish him for being in the wrong place at the wrong time."

The director's glance shot across the table's three occupants and settled on Jim. "I hope you are only here to visit your aunt. We don't need more trouble at Happy Haven." Without waiting for a reply, he hurried from the restaurant.

"He certainly was emphatic," Emma remarked, once he was out of earshot.

"That spirit makes him an excellent fundraiser," Arnie replied. "The Center was in the red until he took over last year."

Jim picked up the ham on rye the waitress had placed before him and sank his teeth into it. Conversation was temporarily shelved as they all ate hungrily. After the coffee was served, Jim leaned forward. Elbows set on the table in disregard for the rules of etiquette Emma had tried to hammer home during his formative years, Jim rested his chin on interlaced fingers and returned to the subject uppermost on his mind. "I know I promised you this case, Aunty. But surely you can see it's not safe working with an alleged murderer."

"That very fact makes me even safer," Emma countered. "At least I know my enemy. Now I can concentrate on proving his guilt." Her nephew looked unconvinced.

"Face it, Jim. We suspected murder from the beginning. What difference does being sure make? You were willing to let me investigate before. I think I should finish the job. Besides, how would you fit in at Happy Haven?" Emma gestured around the dining room. The youngest occupant was sixty-nine. Jim's youthful thirty-something demeanor was an obvious contrast.

"You've got a point," Jim admitted. Settling back in his chair, he picked up his coffee cup and looked at his aunt sternly, "But I expect to be kept fully informed on all developments."

"I'll keep an eye on her," Arnie piped up.

Emma, hardly believing she'd managed to retain command of the case, could only grin.

"This is the best place to be in hot weather," Evie Donner said, lazily executing a scissor kick.

Over the past week she and Emma had begun to cement a friendship. Today, by mutual consent, the two of them remained in the pool after the rest of the class disbanded.

Evie giggled and added, "Unless it's with a certain handsome guy we both know."

The off-hand remark presented Emma with an unexpected opportunity. Pressing her advantage, she asked, "You mean Todd?"

"*He* sure gives a lady an ego boost." Evie sighed. "That young man has had a rough life. I've been thinking of making things a little easier for him."

Emma frowned in puzzlement. "How?"

"Probably with a trust fund," Evie lazed in the water a moment longer. "Of course I'm not sure yet. It might be better to give him the money now, so he wouldn't have to wait until I die — which I hope won't be any time soon."

Emma steeled herself for the next question, hoping her probing wouldn't strain their developing friendship. "Are you and Todd . . . ."

"Oh, no!" Evie hastened to assure her. "Todd's too young for me. He's just someone I'd like to do something for. I think of him as the younger brother I never had . . . ." She broke off as the man they were discussing strode to the pool's edge.

"Hi, Evie," Todd said. "Sorry to interrupt your session."

Evie smiled up at him with something in her eyes that Emma's years of experience refused to classify as sisterly. "You can interrupt any time, Todd."

The physical therapist returned her grin before directing his attention to Emma. His expression hardened, "I'd like to talk to you, Mrs. Twiggs. Please come to my office when you're finished." Todd smiled at Evie once more, then strode away.

"I wonder what that's all about," Evie mused.

Emma shrugged and lifted herself from the pool. "I don't know, but I guess I'll find out." The sleuth was aware of Evie's gaze on her back as she wrapped a thick terry-cloth towel around her shoulders and followed Todd's retreating form.

The tiny cubicle the therapist called his office was sparsely furnished with a desk, two chairs, and a telephone. As Todd gestured toward a chair, Emma found herself wishing Arnie were here, instead of at a banquet for retired accountants. It was surprising how comforting the big man's presence had become.

"I saw you in the restaurant with James Galveston last week," Todd said without preamble after she sank into the molded plastic chair. "I want to know why you were having lunch with a private detective. Has it got something to do with Jo Fernley's death?" His abruptness surprised Emma into silence. She had expected a session of verbal dancing.

"Come on, Mrs. Twiggs," the younger man prodded. "I'm sure you're familiar with my arrest record. I'm not going to sit by and be framed for another murder I didn't commit."

Finding her tongue, Emma asked. "How do you know Jo's drowning was murder? Her death was listed as accidental."

Todd drew a breath, and countered with, "We were talking about your luncheon meeting with James Galveston."

"He happens to be my nephew," Emma replied, rising to her feet. "If you're through interrogating me, I have things to do."

"Please, Mrs. Twiggs." Todd's pleading tone stopped her. "I need your help. It's taken me this long to find the courage to talk to you."

Emma stood in indecision. "What can I do?"

"Convince your nephew I'm innocent. I swear I'm not a murderer. Marty Grumbach gave me a second chance here at Happy Haven. Another false arrest could ruin the rest of my life."

His disarming frankness struck a chord in Emma. She returned to her chair. "If my nephew was investigating Jo's death, what proof could you offer of your innocence? Face it, Todd, the facts are damning. The woman you were questioned about in Miami was found dead exactly the way Jo Fernley was, and both victims intended to leave you money."

"I watch television crime shows, too," Todd said, "and I can tell you I had no motive in either case. When they were alive, both ladies were extremely generous to me. After their deaths, I didn't get a penny. Wouldn't it make more sense for me to want them to live?"

He was right, Emma conceded silently. Todd gained nothing from either death. So who did? Or could it be that both women were simply the victims of unfortunate accidents? The evidence certainly seemed to be pointing to that conclusion. Yet Emma was sure something was eluding her.

"What was the depth of your relationship with the two women?" she asked, almost hesitantly. Nosy delving into what she considered private territory was the only part of detecting she disliked.

Todd grinned crookedly. "We weren't lovers, if that's what you're asking, Mrs. Twiggs. Actually, both ladies . . . ."

A scream interrupted his answer.

Todd leaped from his chair, rushed across the small office, and flung open the door. He entered the lobby, paused, then dashed toward the room housing the whirlpool baths. Emma trotted briskly behind him. As they entered the steamy room, the scene that greeted them resembled a freeze-frame from a movie.

Evie Donner was pressed against the wall of a hot tub. Her eyes, wide and frightened, were glued to Marty Grumbach's face. Happy Haven's director knelt beside the tub, one hand extended toward the frightened woman. Evie's gaze flew to Emma and Todd. "Thank goodness someone heard me," she gasped. "He just tried to drown me!"

"Now, Evie," Marty said soothingly, "you're hysterical."

Emma stared at him. The pieces of the puzzle clicked into place, forming a complete picture. Turning to Todd, the enlightened sleuth said, "Please restrain Marty while I call the police."

"Well, Aunt Emma," Jim said contentedly, fifteen minutes later, as he watched the police handcuff Marty Grumbach. "Looks like Galveston Investigations solved another impossible case."

An unladylike comment formed on Emma's lips, but concern for Evie made her swallow it. Now that the fright was over, shock seemed to have set in. Todd moved closer, and began rubbing Evie's slender shoulders. She leaned gratefully against him.

"I don't understand a few things," Todd commented.

"I'd like to know what's going on, too," Arnie's deep voice boomed. The big man strode up behind Emma. "The minute I heard the sirens, I knew something was wrong at Happy Haven."

"I'll try to explain," Emma said, turning to Evie. "Let me start by getting a few answers. Do you have any relatives, Evie?"

The slim woman's eyes flicked to Emma's face. "No," she said, apparently puzzled by the question.

"Who would benefit by your death?"

Comprehension dawned on Evie's face. "Of course," she said slowly. "How could I have been so stupid? He said he loved me. And all the while, he was only after my money."

"I think I missed something," Arnie interjected, running a hand through his hair. "Who are we talking about?"

"Marty, of course," Emma replied.

"But you told me your money goes to Happy Haven Retirement Community," Todd said to Evie. "Marty wouldn't benefit."

"Something Arnie said the other day made me put two and two together," Emma spoke up. Turning to the retired accountant, she said, "Do you remember? You mentioned that Marty put Happy Haven in the black because he was an excellent fundraiser. I think a check of his books will show how he managed to be so good at his job."

"So when I began talking about setting up a trust fund for Todd, he must have gotten nervous," Evie said.

"You mean he committed murder simply to build his reputation?" Todd's repugnance was evident, as comprehension dawned on his handsome face. "And he was using me all along to take the heat."

Jim, silently listening to the exchange, steepled his fingers in front of his face and mused, "There's only one problem left, and it's the one we started with. How did Marty make the murders appear accidental?"

"I worked out a scenario when I believed Todd was the killer," Emma answered quietly, with an apologetic smile to the physical therapist.

Arnie looked flummoxed. "Tell us, Em. This whole thing has me puzzled."

"By starting with the theory that each victim thought of the killer as her friend, as well as her lover," Emma replied, "it follows he would be allowed in the bathroom during a bubble-bath to engage in some . . . um, well, love play. Don't you see how easy it would have been? A quick yank on the woman's ankles, and a murder could be made to look accidental."

Jim's face clearly showed his skepticism. "Your conclusion falls a little short, Aunty. Aren't you forgetting there was no noise, no water splashed anywhere, and no contusions on the bodies?"

"During my training as a water aerobics instructor, I learned that when water rushes through the nasal passages with sufficient force, loss of consciousness is immediate and complete. The women died without a struggle."

Evie shuddered. "I was almost his next victim," she murmured.

"I think you've just cleared up several unsolved murders, Em," Arnie replied. "The police will have to ask the coroner to do another autopsy, but . . . ."

"*Our* theory will stand up in court," Jim finished the other man's sentence.

Emma grinned at Arnie's amused expression. Crossing the steamy room, she linked her arm through his and led him from the damp building into the sunlight. "You and I should talk about forming a detective agency. We make quite a team."

She heard Jim's in-drawn breath at the same moment Arnie caught her meaning, and closed one eye in an elaborate wink. "Let's toast our new partnership," he said, matching his stride to Emma's. "Who knows? Maybe one day we'll be as famous as Galveston Investigations."

The Rainy Night Murder

Rose Million Healey

I trudged up the five flights of stairs (the elevator was out of whack again) and peered down the murky hall. The lights were on the blink again.

Slumped against my office door was a shadowy figure. For one optimistic minute I thought *Ade's Detective Agency* might have a client. However, considering the early hour and the dearth of business lately, I decided it was probably a zealous bill collector or a tired burglar.

Reluctant to encounter either species, I began quietly backing down the stairs.

"Yo! Thelma! That you?" The shadow straightened and stepped forward. Lt. Francis X. Foyle, friend, foe and former boss from the days when I was a winsome rookie with the N.Y.P.D.

The Lieutenant can be a thorn in my rosy flesh, but at least he wouldn't mug me or dun me for debts, so I greeted him graciously. "You look like death warmed over, Francis. Been out carousing with the jet set again?"

He fixed me with a baleful glare. (His glares have been known to wither grass.) "*I've* been working. Which is more than some people can say. Open up this playpen of yours and gimme some of that mud you pass off as coffee."

"I'm not your Precinct Peon anymore," I said, moving past him to unlock the door. "Don't start pushing me around because you've flubbed another case." I gathered up the mail from the floor.

"Flubbed?" Foyle threw himself down on the couch. "I just wrapped up a big one."

"Wrapped it up, huh?" I know Francis X. If he'd been satisfied with the night's work, he wouldn't be lying here crumpled and unshaven. He'd be natty and barbered and spouting off about the efficiency of the police force in comparison to "puny private eyes."

Something was bothering him, and he wanted to hash it over with me. There was no use trying to rush the stubborn flatfoot. In his own good time he'd get around to it.

I plugged in the hot plate and started some water boiling. A shuffle through my mail revealed, surprise,surprise, more bills. Ordinarily, I'd have checked the answering machine. But why let Foyle hear messages like "Ms. Ade, this is our fourth and final notice."

Instead, I meandered over to the window. "Nice morning. Did you get caught in that storm last night?"

The Lieutenant growled. "Why can't anyone get murdered on a sunny afternoon? It's always gotta be midnight in the middle of a tornado."

"Murder?" I handed him a mug of instant.

Sitting up, he hunched over it. "Beautiful girl. God, what a waste." There was a pause while Foyle stared bleakly into his cup. I helped myself to coffee and sat at my desk. Give him time. He'd get to it.

After a moment, he shrugged. "What the hell. Nobody lives forever." Without further philosophizing, Foyle launched into the facts of the case. At eleven-forty p.m. there'd been a 911 call. A man identifying himself as Winthrope Gale said one Thea Corbett had been killed and he was detaining the guilty party at the scene of the crime. Sounds of a female voice had erupted in the background and hurriedly giving the address, the caller had rung off.

A nearby cruiser was dispatched to investigate. When the information proved correct, Lt. Foyle and his men took over.

"We go into this brownstone in the East Sixties at twelve-thirty a.m.," Foyle said. "Small building. Four floors. Four apartments. Respectable but not ritzy. You know: super in the basement but no doorman."

Foyle and his team entered the second floor apartment. It's his job to be observant, and Foyle's good at his job. He observed the small, sparsely furnished vestibule: red door-mat, bare floor, a wrought-iron halltree upon which two coats were hung. A man's cashmere; a woman's wool. Puddle of water beneath the halltree. Near the archway leading to the living room, a glass-topped table holding a red vase filled with white flowers, artificial.

The living room was spacious and brightly lit. Foyle hasn't an eye for the finer nuances of interior decoration. Neat and orderly. No signs of partying. Lots of little red scatter rugs.

The chairs and sofas looked like trampolines. Over in one corner there was a bunch of real exercise equipment.

"Sprawled in the middle of the room is the body." Foyle groaned. "It had been *some* body believe me. She's wearing a a white satin robe, and her long, black hair's covering her face. Blood's spattered on the robe and seeping into the red rug under her head. At her feet, there's this steel barbell. Eight inches. Weight, about ten pounds. Seemed to have blood on one end.

"I don't have time to see much more before these two characters come at me. They're both talking ninety to the minute, but I manage to get their names. Winthrope Gale and Jill Vermont. The guy's a Social Register type. Fiftyish. Thin on top, thick in the middle. Veddy proper. You know, the kind that, even when he's yelling, doesn't move his lower jaw?"

I nodded.

Foyle continued. "Trying to shout the guy down, and doing a pretty fair job of it, is this girl. Woman. Twenty-seven, I'd guess. No beauty, but no beast either. Nice shape to her. There's a red smear on her blouse. I don't ask why. Not then.

"I let the pair of them yammer until it dawns on me they're accusing each other of the murder. Then I shut them up and sit them down at opposite ends of the room. Mr. Park Avenue makes noises about what a bigwig he is, but I squelch him and get on with the preliminaries.

"While the M.E.'s pawing the cadaver, and the photo and print boys are busy, I glance over the premises."

Foyle had made a quick but thorough inventory of the four-room apartment. In the kitchen he found the refrigerator stocked with health food and white wine. One bottle, recorked, was almost empty. The cabinets held an ordinary assortment of glasses and chinaware. The sink was damp as was a cloth draped on a rack above it. An empty garbage pail was lined with a clean, plastic bag.

Both bedrooms had doors opening to the living room. The larger of the two belonged to the dead woman. Her initials were on some of the expensive-looking garments in the closet. Interestingly, several flamboyant dresses of a much bigger size were pushed toward the back.

Overall, the two bedrooms were tidy. The beds were made and unrumpled. In the bathroom neither the sink nor the shower showed signs of recent use. The medicine chest contained no drug more potent than aspirin. There were no ashtrays in any of the rooms.

"Okay, now I've got an idea of the layout," Foyle told me. "So I'm ready to listen to the various versions of what happened. The M.E. confirms the obvious. Thea Corbett's been done in by a blow from a blunt instrument. More than likely, the barbell. No other apparent marks of violence on the corpse. Approximate time of death: an hour to an hour-and-a-half before the examination began. Say, eleven, eleven-thirty p.m. Of course, the doc doesn't like to be pinned down until he can make further tests. The fingerprint guys reported one set of prints, probably female, on the barbell."

Foyle's men canvassed the occupants of the house. The super had been asleep in his basement apartment and had noticed nothing unusual. The first floor apartment was untenanted. On the third and fourth floors, the inhabitants were uncooperative.

"Saw no evil. Heard no evil," Foyle said. "New Yorkers. They didn't want to get involved." He held out the mug for more coffee.

Obliging him with a dollop, I asked, "Meanwhile, what were your star witnesses doing?"

"Giving each other dirty looks and chomping at the bit. I'd thought putting them on hold would calm them down. No such luck. The minute I say I'm prepared to take their statements, they begin babbling like tobacco auctioneers again. You can't make out a word either one is saying except that 'lie' and 'liar' come out loud and clear and often.

"The only thing to do is separate them. I start steering the girl into the kitchen so I can question her in peace. But Winthrope Gale blows his ever-loving top. He's too important to be kept waiting, he says. He has friends in high places, he says. Then he names a few. God, Thelma, you go much higher than that, you get nosebleed. So — I took him into the kitchen first."

"Francis!" I said, shocked.

Foyle grimaced. "Yeah, well, at my age I don't relish pounding a beat in the Bronx again."

I wondered if that was why he'd paid me this call. Kowtowing to some V.I.P. troubled his conscience? "I'd have done the same," I assured him.

"No, you wouldn't have, Thelma," Foyle said quietly. He sighed. "Well, that's what I did, and I'm stuck with it."

Leaning back, he closed his eyes and, in a flat, droning voice, recited the results of the two interviews.

Winthrope Gale began by demanding the arrest of Jill Vermont. He said he caught her *gloating* over the body of his — acquaintance — moments after the tragedy occurred.

During further questioning, Gale acknowledged a "liaison" with the dead woman. They had met at the health club where she was an instructor. That an attractive young female and an older, married man should become involved was regrettable, perhaps, but not unprecedented, he maintained.

For six months Gale had been subsidizing Thea Corbett's needs. In return, she was available when his busy schedule allowed him to visit her. Usually, every Monday evening. When pressed, the man admitted that his wife belonged to a literary society which met on Monday evenings.

Had Mrs. Gale known about Thea Corbett? the Lieutenant inquired.

"Not in tedious detail," Gale replied. "However, my wife and I have an understanding concerning — discreet diversions."

A few weeks ago, his latest "discreet diversion" proposed inviting a friend to share her apartment. A friend who would be unaware of Gale's identity *and* would make herself scarce on Mondays from eight to midnight. Jill Vermont, also an employee of the health club, was that friend.

"From the beginning things went badly between them," Gale said. "Thea complained that Jill was envious of her, and they quarrelled constantly. When she told me how frightened she was of Jill's violent temper, I advised giving the woman her walking papers, but Thea kept procrastinating. She was *afraid.* Yesterday, when I telephoned, she said she had definitely decided to evict Jill and begged me to be with her for moral support. In a sense I'm to blame for this dreadful event. I should have been here."

"Weren't you, sir? You're here now. Last night was a Monday."

"I arrived after eleven o'clock, Lieutenant. The reason I telephoned Thea yesterday was to cancel our standing appointment."

"Oh? Why?"

"My wife was ill. There *are* priorities, you know."

"You came here later, though?"

"I'd promised Thea I would slip away if I could. She'd been

terribly upset at the prospect of facing Jill Vermont alone."

"Anybody see you leave your place? Garage attendant? Taxi driver?"

"As a matter of fact, I walked. My home is only eight blocks away."

Although tempted to comment on the convenience of that arrangement, Foyle contented himself with asking Gale to go on with his account.

He let himself in with his key, as was his habit. The lights were on, but the apartment was strangely silent. While hanging up his coat, he called out to Thea. There was no answer. Upon entering the living-room, he saw why.

"Thea lay prone on the floor. A woman stood *gloating* over the body. I realized at once that Thea was beyond help and that the woman must be Jill Vermont. Her violent temper had done its worst. I ran forward and seized her wrists. We struggled. When she couldn't free herself, the wretched creature attempted blackmail. Either I allow her to escape, or she would claim I'd murdered Thea myself. Of course, I knew she couldn't possibly substantiate such a ridiculous lie. I dragged her to the telephone and dialed 911. That, I think, covers the salient points. I presume I'm free to leave now?"

In Foyle's opinion, Winthrope Gale was a hoity-toity, cold fish. But that didn't alter the fact that his story was plausible. Moreover, he had delivered it with just the proper emphasis. Neither too controlled nor too emotional. Gale hadn't pretended to have loved Thea Corbett but he seemed genuinely shaken by her death.

Jill Vermont, on the other hand, flaunted her dislike of the deceased. "Thea was a witch with a capital 'B.' I know that sounds bad, but what've I got to lose? Nobody's gonna believe I didn't kill her. Not after listening to that creep Gale's phoney baloney. I might as well tell it like it really was."

She said she hadn't been well acquainted with Thea Corbett before moving in with her. It hadn't taken long to find out that her new roommate was bossy, critical, and, in general, a pain in the neck. After the first week, Jill would have moved out, but she'd paid two months' rent in advance which Thea refused to refund.

Seeing eye-to-eye on nothing, the two of them lived together, squabbling like alley cats. Once in a while, there would be an uneasy truce. During those times Thea boasted of the rich lover whom she intended to marry or "at least take for a bundle." She told Jill she had kinky snapshots of Winthrope Gale that would ruin him. If he couldn't be persuaded to divorce his wife, she planned to confront him with the pictures and extort a fortune for them.

"I felt sorry for the guy," Jill Vermont said to Foyle. "Especially since she cheated on Gale like crazy. Thea was forever bringing strange men to the apartment and insisting I go to the movies or somewhere. I'm no prude, but . . . . Besides, it got so I was sleeping more in the Loew's Tower than in my own bed. I never got enough rest."

"Skip to yesterday," Foyle instructed her.

"Okay. Okay. Yesterday, I came in from work too tired to breathe, and Thea says, 'It's Monday,' in that nasty way of hers. I offered to stay in my room and not make a sound while Gale was here, but she had a fit. She said she was giving him her ultimatum tonight and didn't want anything gumming up the deal. We had a doozy of a shouting match. It went on for a couple of hours. Finally, she wore me down. She always did. I grabbed my coat and got the hell out."

"What time was that?"

"Must have been close to eight. Just before Gale was due."

"He didn't call earlier and cancel his appointment?"

"No! If that's what he told you, he lied. Whatever he told you is a lie. He's railroading me!"

"No one's railroading you. Just tell the truth."

"Yeah, and the truth will set me free? You'll believe me instead of the high and mighty Winthrope Gale?" Jill Vermont stared at Foyle cynically. "In a — excuse the expression — *pig's* eye."

Nevertheless, the young woman completed her statement. The movie she went to was *Rain Man*. Since she hadn't noticed the box office attendant nor the usher, probably they hadn't noticed her. No witnesses.

When the movie ended, she left the theater, intending to dawdle in a coffee shop until midnight, but discovered she had less than a dollar in her wallet. A movie ticket went for seven bucks these days. Damn it, she'd thought, Thea's love life was costing her a mint. Then it started to rain. And rain. Without an umbrella, she sloshed aimlessly up and down Third Avenue for the better part of an hour.

As she grew wetter and wetter, she became angrier and angrier. Stopping under a streetlight, she looked at her watch. It was eleven-twenty. She could be home in ten minutes. If Thea hadn't finished cooking Gale's goose by then, that would be just too damned bad! She raced back to the apartment.

"I listened outside the door and couldn't hear any noise, so I turned my key as quietly as possible. The place was pitch black. I figured Gale had gone, or the two of them were in Thea's bedroom. I didn't turn on the lights, because I didn't want Thea to know I'd come in. I felt my way to the halltree. A coat was hanging there, so I knew Gale hadn't left. After I hung mine up, I started tiptoeing toward the living room. Then I stumbled against something and stooped down to get it out of the way. It was the barbell.

"As I lifted it up, suddenly the lights went on. There was Winthrope Gale, standing at the lightswitch. And there was Thea. I thought she'd fallen or fainted. I didn't know what had happened. When I went toward her . . . I knew she was dead."

Feeling faint herself, Jill clutched the barbell to her chest. Winthrope Gale said something odd. He said it was very obliging of Jill to have put her fingerprints on the barbell. He had placed it in her path for just that purpose.

Dazed, Jill let the barbell slip from her fingers. It landed near Thea's feet. All the while, Winthrope Gale was talking. Gradually, Jill said, she began to understand what he was saying. He was explaining how and why he killed Thea.

"He smiled. The bastard actually smiled when he told me he killed her."

Gale told Jill of spending a pleasant evening with Thea: dancing, drinking, playing their "private games." Toward the end of the evening, however, she infuriated him by making certain unreasonable demands. In a momentary rage, he flung the barbell at her. Unfortunately, his aim was accurate. A less resourceful man might have panicked, he informed Jill smugly, but not he.

"No, he didn't panic," Jill said to Foyle through clenched teeth. "Gale was real proud of how fast he got the idea of framing me."

"He framed you? How?"

"By fixing it so my prints would be on the barbell. By getting rid of the evidence that he'd been with Thea all evening."

"How do you know he did that?"

"He *told* me, for Pete's sake. He bragged about it. Said he'd burned the snapshots over the kitchen sink and washed the ashes down the drain. Washed and dried some wine glasses, put the wine bottle away, stashed his *costumes* in her closet — God, I don't remember what all. He ticked them off one by one, *daring* me to find a mistake. When I said his fingerprints would be everywhere, he laughed because no one could prove when they'd gotten there. The one place fingerprints mattered, he said, was on the barbell, and his weren't there."

"Why not?"

"Gale said he'd wiped the dry end with some tissues before placing it where I'd pick it up. Then he flushed the tissues down the toilet. And I guess that's what he'd done to me. Flushed me right down the toilet. Boy, he set me up good."

"Maybe you're doing the setting-up," Foyle had said, pouncing on the hole in the girl's story. "If Gale was so careful to make it look as if he hadn't been here tonight, how come he hung around until the patrolmen arrived?"

Jill Vermont had an explanation. "I walked in on him thirty minutes early. The scumbag was getting his coat when he heard my key in the lock. He told me that had 'disconcerted' him, but he decided to say he'd caught me in the act. It might work out even better that way, he said. Who would doubt *his* word?"

For the first time, the young woman's hard facade cracked. Her lips trembled. "Jeez, Lieutenant, that's what it boils down to, doesn't it? His word against mine. He's a somebody. I'm nobody. What chance have I got?"

"End of statement," Foyle said to me, opening his eyes at last. "What do you think, Thelma? Has she got a chance?"

So that was it. That was why Foyle had come to me. Not to confess that he'd handled Winthrope Gale with kid gloves. Foyle wanted the underdog to have a chance, and he hoped I could give it to her. He'd laid out a forest of facts, thinking I might spot a trail he'd missed. Something he'd overlooked.

I have this trick, gimmick, whatever-you-call-it. By putting myself in the shoes of the suspects, sometimes I can figure out who is or isn't guilty. Of course, sometimes I draw a blank. Foyle says the latter is frequent, and the former is a fluke. Just the same, he has a grudging respect for what he calls my "empathy-schempathy approach." I knew he wanted me to use it now.

Stalling for time, I asked, "Gale's alibi checks?"

"The wife swears she had a 'frightful migraine' and hubby sat by her side till she fell asleep around eleven."

"A society wife *might* provide a false alibi," I said, "to avoid the embarrassment of a jailbird husband."

Foyle looked glum. "Yeah, but it *is* an alibi, and Jill Vermont hasn't got one."

"So you book her?"

"Looks like it. Hell, fingerprints, fights with the victim, no alibi. Plus a prominent citizen's word. What *can* I do but book her?"

"How much time have you got?"

"I ought to be at the station now. I just dropped by for. . . ." Foyle's voice trailed off.

"A cup of mud," I said, letting him off the hook. Obviously, he needed me to go into my little routine, and he needed it fast.

I planted my elbows on the desk and my chins in my hands. "What if I were Jill Vermont —" I mused.

"Awe, come on, Thelma. You know I don't go in for that stuff."

"Indulge me," I said, pretty sure that he would. "Let's say I'm this Jill Vermont. Hmmm. I'm no dewy-eyed ingenue. I've been around. But I'm not as tough as I talk. Right?"

Foyle nodded, "My impression."

"Thea Corbett's prettier than I am. Perhaps I'm jealous of her. Nobody's buying *me* expensive clothes. I'm twenty-seven years old . . . ."

"Don't you wish."

I ignored that, "And I work hard for a living. I come home, exhausted, and my roommate tries to boot me out. We have a rip-roaring battle. I slam out of the apartment at eight o'clock —"

"Maybe you didn't go out," Foyle interrupted again. "Maybe you stayed in and sulked and then bopped your chum with a barbell."

I thought that over. "No. My coat was wet. There was a pool of water under the halltree, remember? I must have been out in the rain at some time. And the storm didn't begin until ten-thirty."

"All right," Foyle conceded. "You did go out. What does that prove?"

"It proves I was probably telling the truth about being at the movies and being caught in the rain on the way home."

"It proves no such thing. You could have gone out after it started to rain."

"Why would I do that without a raincoat or umbrella?" Did a faint bell ring?

Foyle was scowling. "This is getting us nowhere. What difference does it make when you went out? You were back by eleven or so. Wet and mad, you could have stomped into the apartment and started tossing gym equipment at your roommate."

He had a point. "Let's see: wet and mad, I stomped into the vestibule —" Now *my* voice did the trailing off. That bell was clanging. The vestibule. I visualized it as Foyle had described it.

He was jabbering away, but I paid no attention. The vestibule. Doormat, table, halltree, two coats. Two. One wool, one cashmere. Something missing. What? Bong! I thought I had it. I hoped I had it.

". . . the matter with you, Thelma? Lose your concentration?" Foyle waved his hands like a hypnotist. "You're Jill Vermont, see? You're . . . ."

"No. No, I'm not," I said. "I'm *you*, Francis. I'm *you*."

"Great," he said disgustedly. "Am I having fun?"

"You're looking around that vestibule. What don't you see?"

"I don't see a lot of things. Mainly, I don't see what you're getting at."

"There was no wet umbrella, Francis. No umbrella at all."

"So?"

"Gale said he walked eight blocks to Thea's apartment and arrived after eleven. That means the storm had already begun when he left his house. Yet he . . ."

". . . didn't take an umbrella," Foyle finished for me."

"And he didn't wear a raincoat. He wore cashmere." I crossed my fingers. "How wet was the cashmere, Francis?"

Foyle slapped his forehead. "Dry! Gayle's coat was bone dry!"

"I thought it might have been. I wasn't sure."

"I'm sure. I'm damned sure. I held it for him when he was leaving. I bowed and scraped to that liar." Foyle jumped up. "I never met a liar I couldn't break. Gale was there all evening. He killed Thea Corbett, and I'll make him admit it."

Lieutenant Never-Show-Emotion Foyle grabbed my shoulders. "Kiddo, you've done your good deed for the day!" Lobbing a kiss toward my cheek, he ran out the door.

I went to the window and looked down at Lexington Avenue. Foyle was almost skipping when he emerged into the sunlight. I felt very pleased with myself until I remembered that good deeds don't pay the rent.

No use postponing the inevitable. I might as well find out what else I owed. Plodding to the answering machine, I flipped it on.

"Ms. Ade, my name is Martha Van Clyde. Yesterday, my husband disappeared, and the police say they can't help me. A Lieutenant Foyle recommended I hire you. *Money is no object —*"

Forget what I said about good deeds. Mine, it seems, paid off retroactively.

Bite Your Tongue, Clio Browne

Dolores Komo

"I guess I just find it hard to understand, Mama," Clio Browne said with a cluck of her tongue as she studied her mother's latest purchase. "The cabinet has doors so you can hide what's inside, only somebody paints the outside to look like what's on the inside is a mess — books stacked up on the shelves, a cracked plate, mismatched cups, and what's that? A mouse?" One of Thalia's Siamese cats leaped up to sniff at the picture of the mouse.

"It's called trompe l'oeil. Isn't it just the damndest thing you ever saw?"

"You can say that again." Clio ran her mahogany fingers through her short natural, then patted down her hair where she'd ruffed it. "No wonder they call it tramp-louie."

Thalia didn't answer at first, standing back to admire her antique find. At last she spoke. "It's trompe, Clio, not tramp, and it means trick of the eye in French. It'll be perfect against the foyer wall. Give that space a little color."

"Perfect? It'll remind me every time I come through the front door of what I forgot to put away or pick up."

"Don't be so hard on yourself, honey. You may have a little clutter problem but you're not really a slob."

"Well thank you very much." Clio pulled her hands to her hips, pooched out her lip and pretended to be offended. "Maybe you can refinish it, paint out the picture so it'll look like a cabinet is supposed to look."

"Bite your tongue, Clio Browne. This is a masterpiece, a genuine antique, and furthermore, it was a bargain. Why I could turn around and sell it for twice what I paid."

Clio nodded her head. "I'd dearly love to see you make a profit like that, Mama."

Thalia narrowed her eyes, casting her you've-said-enough

70

look and Clio knew better than to pursue the matter further. Of course she'd learn to live with the piece just as she had done with the overstuffed horsehair loveseat in the living room and the carved, stiff-backed Spanish chairs that surrounded the Duncan Phyfe dining room table.

With no further conversation possible, Clio helped her mother maneuver the new antique into its place against the foyer wall before leaving for work.

When Clio arrived at the office of the Browne Bureau of Investigation, she was met outside the door by a highly agitated man. "Clio Browne? I'm Dennis Murdock," he said before Clio could turn the key in the lock.

"Well, Dennis, if you'll give me a minute to slip out of my jacket, I'll give you a minute to calm down."

"Ms. Browne, I . . ."

"First names only, please."

"I found your agency's name in the Yellow Pages listed under private detectives. To be honest with you, I picked you out because the name impressed me. Browne Bureau of Investigation has a ring of authority." Dennis followed Clio into her office.

Clio reached over and pressed the button on the HOT SHOT that sat on the credenza. In a moment the reservoir was steaming with hot water. She released it into a mug and let a homemade teabag steep for a moment. "Here," she said soothingly. "Sit and drink this. It'll settle you down."

Dennis obeyed like a zombie. He sipped and winced because the tea was hot. "This is very good, what is it?"

"I haven't the slightest idea. My mother grows her own herbal cures for everything from bunions to brains. Some of her potions came over with our ancestors on slave ships."

"She's tracked her roots that far back?"

"She's a bloodhound."

Dennis took another hefty swig of the tea and set the mug on the desk. "Then you come by your profession naturally."

"Mm, that along with two degrees in criminal studies and my father's sleuthing genes with which he so generously endowed me."

"Whew!" Dennis's gasp was not because he was awed by Clio's credentials. His face reddened and perspiration beaded on his upper lip because the tea was hot and highly spiced.

"Tea getting to you, hon?" Clio handed him a tissue to pat his face.

He pulled up his glasses and blotted beneath his eyes. "I came straight here from Lambert Field. My plane from Kansas City landed just about an hour ago. It's my sister."

"What about your sister, Dennis?"

"She's a brilliant young business woman but I don't trust her judgment when it comes to other aspects of life."

"That's no crime."

"I'm fifteen years older than Joanna. I've raised her since she was ten when our parents died in an accident." He stared off into space for a moment.

"Go on, Dennis."

"I feel responsible for her." He took another swig of the tea. "Maybe you've heard of J. Kramer Griswold."

"Of Pine & Griswold? Last I heard he committed suicide in the home of his . . . ." Clio bit her lip as she realized who Dennis's sister must be.

"They're now calling it murder and Joanna has been accused."

Clio raised her brows, "I was out of the city for a few days. I didn't know the police had changed their minds."

"The story changed when Griswold's wife was going through his papers. She found a letter Joanna wrote. It was postmarked weeks ago."

"What was in the letter that led the police to think Griswold hadn't put the bullet hole through his own head?" Clio stuck her pencil into the electric sharpener on her desk, then blew the sawdust away from the point.

"It was typewritten on Joanna's own Olivetti and signed with her initial *J* the way she always signs personal letters to friends. In the letter, she says she'd see him dead before she'd see him back with his wife."

"That doesn't prove anything, Dennis. Surely, the police have more than that."

"One of her thumb prints is on the letter and several finger prints are on the gun that killed Griswold. Joanna claims she came home and found him sprawled on the living room couch with a hole through his temple. The gun had fallen from his hand and lay on the floor. Without thinking, she picked it up."

"Apparently the police believed it was suicide until now."

"That's all I know. I came as soon as I could get a flight out this morning. Joanna's a genius when it comes to her work, but she's very unsophisticated about other matters. Griswold was a glib, charming man-of-the-world. At least that's how Joanna described him to me. He moved in with her while he was waiting for his divorce to become final."

"How was she able to get out of jail?"

"She took care of her own bond."

That didn't quite fit with Dennis's image of his unsophisticated sister. Clio leaned back and studied him. He was wearing a dark business suit, a crisp white shirt and an expensive looking burgundy tie. The suit was well tailored but for all she knew it might be the one reserved for weddings and funerals. "I get two hundred fifty dollars a day plus my expenses. Think you can handle it?"

Dennis chuckled. "Murdock Engineering made the Fortune 500 last year."

Clio smiled back, happy with the thought that there'd be no trouble getting paid for this one. "I think the first thing I should do is check with the police — see what they've got on your sister." Clio picked up her pencil. "Where can I reach you?"

"I'll be staying at Joanna's. She's been restoring one of those old townhouses near Lafayette Square." He wrote the address and phone number on a sheet of blue paper from Clio's notepad.

Captain Felix Frayne, Clio's good friend in the homicide department, had gone on a fishing trip down the Current River for a few days. Lieutenant Rosemary Budd, the rotund veteran of the St. Louis Police Department, brought out the folder containing information on Joanna Murdock. Clio liked Rosey, if for no other reason than she made Clio feel positively petite standing close to her.

"Little girl's prints are all over the gun," Rosey said in a voice that rumbled like spring thunder. "She and Griswold were lovers and made no effort to hide that fact. He spent many nights at Joanna's townhouse before he finally moved in with her. Soon after, there was a break-in at her place." The Lieutenant raised her half-moon glasses to the tip of her nose and let the rims settle onto her plump brown cheeks. "A neighbor saw her come home around the time of the murder and apparently she was very nervous. He says she jumped a foot and dropped her keys when he said hello. She seemed to have a lot of trouble finding the keyhole and she ignored him when he yelled a second greeting. In addition," Rosey paused to suck in a deep breath, "Joanna Murdock wrote a threatening note to Griswold a few weeks ago. We have the note and the typewriter in custody."

"Hm!" Clio felt a sudden tightening around the mandarin collar of her shirt. "Anybody hear the shot?"

"Richard McCharles, the neighbor, heard a snapping sound fifteen minutes before he saw Joanna on the front porch. He can't swear it wasn't backfire. He'd been welding in the backyard. He's some kind of artist, does those preposterous things with rusty iron."

"He works at home?"

"Has a studio in the carriage house out back. There's a high juniper hedge that separates the McCharles and Murdock properties. McCharles says he saw Joanna slam out of the terrace doors. She was in a big hurry to get to her car in the alley and got away before he could turn off his torch. He heard the car zip away."

"He saw all this fifteen minutes *before* he saw her on the front porch?"

"You got it!"

"He welds things together, you said, Rosey. I suppose he wears protective glasses or a welder's helmet with one of those little windows. And then too, a welding torch makes a bit of noise if I'm not mistaken, a kind of blowing sound."

Rosey frowned and consulted her notes. "Nothing here about that," she said, raising her head again.

"It could be important. After all, he claims he saw her *slam* out of the terrace doors after hearing a — what did you call it? A snapping sound? He may not only have been looking through some kind of eye gear but a very small break in the hedge. And I wonder if acetylene torches don't sometimes snap or pop to say nothing of crackling."

"Whatever you're fishing for, Clio forget it. It doesn't matter anyway. With the letter and the gun, we've got her dead to rights.'

"Where did the gun come from?"

"It's registered to Griswold. Joanna says he brought it to her house because of the burglary."

"Were Griswold's prints on the gun?"

"Mm, yes. A left thumb and index."

"Then . . . ."

Rosey sucked in her cheeks until her lips resembled a complacent flounder's. "Joanna claims she rushed home after getting a call from Griswold. Said he was very upset because he couldn't see any way out of their dilemma. He said he intended to kill himself."

"Well, maybe he did?"

"A man like that? Civic leader? Human dynamo? I have to admit we bought that for a little while. But then Mrs. Griswold found that letter in the desk drawer in his den, where he kept his important papers. Here it is, Clio. See for yourself. It's addressed to him at his home and postmarked a short time before Griswold moved into Joanna Murdock's house. The mailperson," Rosey smiled mischievously, "remembers delivering it because it was highly perfumed and her pouch smelled great for days. And Clio, it's a scent that is specially blended for Joanna Murdock because she has some sort of allergy to commercial perfumes."

Clio took the note from Rosey's hand and sniffed it. Her forehead wrinkled and her brows raised as she read it through. It was poignant at the beginning, expressing undying love. But it turned hostile in the last paragraph which read: If I can't have you, then nobody will. *J.* "What kind of signature is that?" Clio knew what Rosey was going to say.

"Unique. She signs all her personal notes like that. And please take notice of the nicely engraved letterhead with her name in fancy Old English script, gold yet."

"Anybody could have typed that note, even Griswold, although I admit I can't think of a reason why he would. Couldn't whoever broke into the house do this?"

"Clio, that break-in was a sham, an effort to try and explain away the note. Don't you think I had the same idea? What happened was this. Joanna Murdock knew where Griswold kept his gun. When he changed his mind about leaving his wife, she fetched the weapon, knowing his prints were on it. She put a bullet in his head while he was napping on the couch and then had the gall to cry suicide."

"You believed it at first."

"Oh, we were a little skeptical without a suicide note. But that skepticism evaporated with this letter."

"Still, there's a doubt. Griswold himself might have written . . . ."

"Not a shadow." Rosey explained. "According to Elizabeth Griswold, her husband *had* decided to come back home. She'd ordered the locks on the house changed in order to keep Joanna Murdock from getting in with a set of duplicate keys she'd had made. It's all sewn up nice and tidy. Joanna asked Griswold to meet with her one last time. She became angry when he made it clear that their affair was over. She got the gun and ventilated his head. She had motive, opportunity, means, and pre-meditation."

Clio stood up and headed for the door. "Any ideas about why the neighbor might have seen her leave fifteen minutes before he saw her arrive at the front door?"

"We think she shot her lover then slipped out through the terrace doors without realizing McCharles was there. She then made a deliberate effort to be seen at the front door."

"But why?"

"McCharles has a case on her himself. He likes to think he's looking out for Joanna. He may have thought he was giving her an alibi of some sort. Besides it don't make a bit of difference."

"Maybe McCharles was jealous and . . . ."

Rosey Budd shook her head and smirked. "The man's an artist, a laid-back kind of guy. Joanna didn't take him seriously. You're barking up a dead tree, Clio. I'm all but stamping this file closed."

Clio stopped for lunch at a little diner on Chestnut Street. She ordered a chili dog even though she knew it meant an afternoon of heartburn. It was just that the air was crisp with autumn and her tastebuds refused to consider anything else. As she savored each bite, she thought about Joanna's dilemma. It wouldn't be the first time a woman reacted with hostility when she was told an affair was over.

After lunch, she drove south on Twelfth Street and turned right at Lafayette. Joanna Murdock's house was easy to find. It was freshly painted a sedate blue-gray and trimmed, Victorian style, in purple, lavender, and puce. She pulled the car up in front and turned off the engine.

She was on her way up the steps when she spotted a bushy-haired man sanding a piece of rough metal that resembled a twisted length of railroad track. He was standing in the front yard pretending he wasn't curious about her.

"Hello," Clio sang out, walking in his general direction. If this was the neighbor who'd provided the police with so much information, he didn't fit the image Clio had formed of an artist who worked with iron. His hair added at least three inches to his rather short stature. He didn't look as if he could hoist a sack of groceries. She handed him one of her cards. "Interesting piece of work. What do you call it, Mr. McCharles?"

He ignored her question. "Private detective?" His eyes lowered and his brows raised as he took her in slowly from the tips of her I. Miller business pumps to the padded shoulders of her newly acquired Harris tweed suit.

Clio wondered if he was assessing her for a later abstract rendering in rust. "The BBI's been in business for over forty years."

"You on the Griswold case?"

Clio nodded. "I've been talking with the officer in charge of the investigation."

"I told Lieutenant Budd everything. If you've seen her then you know as much as I do."

Richard repeated his story for Clio anyway.

"Thank you, Mr. McCharles. I would appreciate your calling me if you should think of anything else."

Clio started away.

"She never should have taken up with that scum."

"What's that?" Clio pivoted around

"Griswold. He got what he deserved if you ask me." McCharles's tone was cold and sour. With a shudder Clio headed for the house next door wondering if Richard McCharles could type. As an artist, he might easily have imitated Joanna's signature initial.

Dennis Murdock admitted Clio to Joanna's house and ushered her into the parlor to the right of the elegant entry hall. Clio felt as if she'd fallen back through time to the 1870's. Joanna Murdock stood up and extended her hand when Dennis introduced Clio. Joanna's handshake was firm. Her clothes were as elegant as her surroundings. Tall and slim, her gabardine slacks clung to her hips as if they'd been custom cut for her. Her hair was long and fine, hanging past her shoulders in silky threads and her scent was subtle and distinctive. Clio knew why the mailperson had enjoyed the smell in her pouch after delivering the incriminating letter to the Griswold house.

"Please leave us, Dennis," Joanna said before asking Clio to sit down. Joanna was obviously accustomed to giving commands. Dennis almost tiptoed out of the room. After Dennis had gone, Clio eased onto the edge of an Empire couch that was covered with a dark blanket.

77

"Is this the room where you discovered the . . . ."

"Yes it is, and I'm sick about the couch."

"Finding him there?"

"The upholstery. The fabric had to be imported from England. I bought the last of it. The cleaner isn't at all sure he can get the bloodstains out."

Clio tried her best not to allow her face to reflect the astonishment she felt at Joanna's callousness.

"I don't mean to sound so cold, Ms. Browne, but if you only knew how much research went into reproducing this room to reflect the period, you'd understand."

Clio wasn't sure she would.

"At any rate, I found him there on the couch. He must have been sitting there while he talked to me on the phone. I heard a click just before he hung up. Now I know that's when he cocked the pistol."

Clio looked at the cordless phone, the only non-Victorian object in the room. "You heard that?"

"Yes. I must have broken a record getting here, but it was too late." For the first time, Joanna looked a little troubled.

"I know how painful this must be, Joanna, but tell me about your relationship with Griswold."

Joanna slouched against the tufted velvet back of the Queen Anne chair, one of her slender legs slung over the other. "Kramer had gone to see his attorney that morning to discuss his divorce. He called me at my office and said he was heading straight to the townhouse and that we'd talk when I got there."

"Did Mrs. Griswold know that he'd been to see a lawyer about the divorce?"

Joanna thought a moment. "I really don't know. But she must have known it was going to happen sooner or later."

Clio nodded for Joanna to continue.

"Of course, Elizabeth Griswold was furious at the thought that Kramer would leave her. But the two of them had been at each other's throats practically since the day they got married. Kramer said they hadn't slept together for months."

"According to Mrs. Griswold, her husband had moved back in with her a few weeks ago and was trying to figure out a way to break it off with you. She says you were harassing her and that she had to have the locks changed on her house to keep you out." Clio waited.

"Lies, nothing but lies!" For the first time, Clio noticed a spark of fire in Joanna's cool eyes. "Why would I want to get inside her house in the first place? And that business about Kramer . . . it's total hogwash. He had no intention of moving back with her."

"Elizabeth Griswold claims she found a letter you mailed to her husband during the time he had returned to their home."

Clio could tell that Joanna was genuinely confused. Her relaxed posture stiffened and she inched to the edge of her chair. "I don't know what's going on here, Clio. None of this makes any sense to me. All I know is that when Kramer called me that last time he sounded very strange, not at all like himself. And then by the time I got here . . . ."

"Tell me about the burglary you had here. When was that?"

"A few weeks back."

"Did you report it to the police?"

"There wasn't anything taken and I decided I didn't want the hassle."

"Nothing was taken? Then how did you know someone had been here?"

"When I came home, I found the electric typewriter in my upstairs office was on. I don't use it often and I heard the hum as soon as I entered the room. It wasn't the cleaning woman's day so I knew she hadn't turned it on. The door to my storage closet was open and a lid on a box of stationery had been left off. But the most obvious evidence that someone had been here was in the bedroom. The armoire had obviously been gone through. A cashmere sweater I'd just bought for Kramer was wadded up and tossed on the floor on top of my favorite robe, which was ripped to shreds. I was livid."

Dennis stuck his head in the doorway. "Would either of you care for something to drink?"

Clio shook her head. "No, thank you."

Dennis looked at Joanna. "Are you all right, honey?"

Joanna sucked in a deep breath. "I do wish you'd stop fussing over me, Den."

Joanna apparently found her brother's presence annoying. It was clear to Clio that she needed him like a frog needs a pogo stick. She watched as Dennis skulked out of the room.

"Joanna," Clio said, "who besides you and Kramer had keys to this house?"

"Why, no one." Her eyebrows raised. "Unless Richard still

has his."

"Your neighbor?"

Joanna nodded.

Clio had to wonder if Richard McCharles, who obviously had a serious crush on Joanna, could have killed Griswold. "How do you explain the fact that McCharles saw you leave through the terrace doors?"

"Richard is a quaint old fool, a throwback to a prehistoric era. He still fogs his brain with marijuana. I'd be surprised if he didn't hallucinate."

"You think he was stoned the day Griswold died?"

"He often is." Joanna rolled her eyes with a look of disgust. "I've already told the police. As soon as Kramer called me at the office and told me he intended to kill himself, I came rushing over here."

"He actually said that?"

"I told you he didn't sound much like himself, which is why I took it seriously. And yes, that's exactly what he said. I can guarantee you I would not have left work under any other circumstances."

"Mm, mm!" Clio stood up and stretched a little. "I would like to see that closet you mentioned and the armoire."

Joanna led the way back into the foyer and up the stairs. At the top landing, Clio couldn't resist a peek into a large bathroom. "You sure do have a feel for late Victorian." There was a freestanding tub on clawed feet, a marble basin beneath an oval mirror and a mosaic floor of octagonal tiles.

"Kramer accused me of having a suppressed desire to live in the past until I explained to him that this was an investment. I bought the house for a song and it has been restored to museum quality. I've been offered ten times what I paid for it." She smoothed her hair. "I'm accepting that offer as soon as this is all over. I've learned I'm really more suited to apartment living."

In the small study at the end of the hall, Joanna said, "There's the table where the typewriter used to sit. The police have it, you know." She went to the storage closet that was built into one of the walls. "There's a trick to keeping this door closed. It was ajar when I came in and heard the typewriter humming. The lid of my stationery box was off."

In the bedroom she opened the armoire doors and Clio could see Griswold's clothes, neatly hanging at precise intervals. Clio walked her fingers over the new suits while Joanna selected the cashmere sweater in question. Clio scrutinized it. Entwined around a button were two long blonde hairs, as long as Joanna's but curly as a corkscrew.

"Ever have a perm?" Clio asked.

Joanna ran her fingers through her silky hair. "Good grief, no." She watched as Clio eyed the suits. "Those things are all brand new," Joanna said, pointing to Griswold's clothes. "Kramer bought them all within the past couple of weeks so that he'd have something to wear to work since his loving wife refused to allow him in the house to get his things."

Clio carefully unwound the hairs from the button and tucked them inside her jacket pocket. "What did you do with that robe?"

"It was totally destroyed so I threw it away."

"Too bad." She wondered if Griswold could have staged the whole thing himself for some perverse reason.

Instead of sharing that thought with Joanna, she turned and started back toward the top of the stairs and led the way down. "I'd appreciate it if you'd show me out through the terrace doors, Joanna."

"Certainly," Joanna said. In the dining room Clio admired the French doors that opened onto a wide brick terrace. The high hedge through which Richard McCharles swore he'd seen Joanna leave was quite thick. He would have to have pretty keen eyesight, Clio thought, to be able to see anything very clearly through the small breaks in that juniper wall. And he may have had the added filter of protective eye gear, as well.

Back in her office, Clio flopped down in the old swivel chair behind her desk. She slipped off her shoes, wheeled around and propped her feet up on the window sill, wiggling her toes as her left heel searched for the familiar dip in the marble.

If Griswold hadn't killed himself, then who killed him? All the evidence pointed to Joanna as the likely suspect. But what if . . . . The game had begun and Clio's first musings turned to Richard McCharles. Joanna's neighbor claimed he saw her leave through the terrace doors after he heard a snapping noise. Had he made that up to conceal his own guilt? Were his feelings for Joanna deeper than she knew? Might he have used his key to get in, type the note on Joanna's stationary, and mail it to Griswold? And an artist would have no difficulty imitating Joanna's trademark signature.

On the other hand, somebody else had a pretty good motive to murder Griswold. What kind of woman was the grieving widow? Clio turned around and stretched her arms along the desk top. After a moment she took the hairs she had found on Griswold's sweater out of her pocket, slipped them into a plastic sandwich bag and labeled the bag. There was only one way to find out about Mrs. Griswold. Clio's brain revved up as she mentally ran through possible introductions to the lady. She finally asked herself a question. "Can I squeeze my size sixteen hips into my old size fourteen jeans?"

Reaching for the telephone book, Clio ran her pencil down the G's in the white pages. Griswold, J. Kramer, was listed. Dialing the number, she crossed her fingers.

"Mrs. Griswold, this is your cable television company. We've had reports of snowy pictures in your area and generally bad reception. Have you been having trouble with your cable channels?"

"I don't watch much television," came the terse reply.

"Well, ma'am, I'm going to be in your area checking out the problem first thing in the morning. I'm wondering if you'd mind if I took a look at your sets. The problem might be on the pole or it could be with some faulty lead-ins. It won't take but a few minutes and it'll sure help us give our customers the service they're entitled to."

"If it won't require my time, I suppose it'll be all right."

"You'll hear my knock at eight-thirty, ma'am."

After she hung up, Clio remembered where her mother put the yellow hardhat she'd bought at a recent garage sale. Of course, she'd have to find another planter for the philodendron. And there was her old pair of hiking boots with waffled soles that would pass for steel-toed Red Wings in a pinch. She could borrow a tool belt from the building maintenance man.

When Clio came into the kitchen for breakfast, her tools clinking together around her hips, Thalia's lower jaw dropped to her chest. "It's not dark enough for trick or treating, Clio, and anyway, Halloween won't be here for another three weeks."

Clio twirled around and winced as the suspended tools clapped against her thighs.

"Let me guess, you're invited to a masquerade and you're

going as a Chinese windchime, is that it, girl?"

"Do I look like I could climb a telephone pole, Mama?"

"You look like one of them California raisins gone berserk."

Clio sat down and sipped her juice.

Thalia popped some sausages into the microwave, cracked several eggs into a bowl and beat the daylight out of them. "If you plan to climb telephone poles, you'll need a decent breakfast."

Clio didn't object when her mother added hash browns and a toasted English muffin to her plate.

At eight-thirty Clio's cantankerous Honda pulled up the circle drive and stopped in front of the posh entry to the Griswold house. A maid admitted her and asked if she'd wait while she checked with Mrs. Griswold. A few minutes later the tall slender lady herself, wearing a chic black suit, clattered across the parquet floor in her high-heeled suede pumps. Her short blonde hair folded around her perfect oval face, except for a flip of bang that shadowed her steely blue eyes.

"I called you about the cable television, ma'am. I won't take but a few minutes to check your reception."

"I'll have Minna show you where to find the sets."

The maid reappeared and led Clio upstairs. "There're three of 'em up here and the big screen's in the den. I don't got cable TV in my room up over the garage. I sneak up here when I want to see something."

She'd hoped to get into the house and have the freedom to roam around. Now it appeared Minna would cling to her like a leech.

"If you don't mind, honey," Minna said, "Mrs. Griswold's fixing to go away and I tell you, I got more to do than a gaggle of bees. TV's are in each one of the bedrooms along the hall here. The den is that room to the right of where you came in."

Clio let out a sigh of relief. She looked into the first room that Minna had pointed to. A man's suit was neatly hanging on the wooden valet. Griswold's? Clio didn't have to wonder long. Inside the coat were his initials, where his tailor had embroidered them. She pulled open the closet door and found an extensive male wardrobe. The dresser drawers were neatly stacked with underwear, socks and monogrammed handkerchiefs. It looked as if Griswold had a room of his own, which seemed to bear out what Joanna had said about the Griswold s not sleeping together.

The next room was empty, sandwiched between Griswold's and the master bedroom. A demilitarized zone, Clio thought.

The master bedroom was elaborately decorated in mauve and lavender, satins and velvet. Clio slid the closet doors along the track that ran the full length of the room. Mrs. Griswold had an enviable wardrobe. Clio couldn't resist peeking at the labels sewn inside — a sequined gown by Bob Mackey, two Givenchy suits, a cocktail taffeta by Galanos. Being in the neighborhood with such elegance sent a thrill stirring in her stomach — or was it that power breakfast she'd put away earlier? On a shelf above the hanging rods were several hat boxes. She had to have a look. The first one contained a broad-brimmed Laura Ashley felt number. For those times when Elizabeth wanted to shed her sophistication in favor of a more innocent country look? Clio couldn't resist popping it onto her head and ogling herself in the mirror. With time being of the essence, she knew she was using hers poorly. She put the hat back and pulled out some drawers of Elizabeth Griswold's dressing table and found nothing of interest. But then, in the drawer of the nightstand, she found a snapshot of the Griswold's in a happier time. Elizabeth had long, very curly blonde hair. When, she wondered, did the lady get her haircut? In the adjoining bathroom, Clio found Elizabeth's hairbrush and noted several long curly hairs. She hadn't been wearing her current style very long or else she doesn't clean her brush very often, Clio thought. She pulled several hairs from the bristles and put them into her breast pocket.

Downstairs, she went to work in the den with a sense of urgency. She had no idea what she was seeking as she opened the desk drawers one by one. There was nothing in any of them, not even a stray rubber band. The papers Mrs. Griswold had been going over when she found her husband's note from Joanna had apparently been removed.

Clio slumped onto the chair and lifted the corner of the desk blotter. There was a sheet of paper with the letter *J* written several times in a row. There was also a receipt from the OPEN UP KEY SERVICE, for replacing all the locks. It was dated four days ago. An older receipt from the same key service, for a single key, was dated a month before, the very same day Joanna Murdock's house was burglarized. At that moment Clio heard the door knob turn. Letting the blotter drop, she leaped up and made a dash for the television set.

"Are you about finished?' Elizabeth Griswold asked.

"Yes, ma'am," Clio said. "I do believe I've solved the problem."

Clio's waffle rubber soles made squeaking noises along the marble hall leading to Lieutenant Budd's office. The door was open and she walked in. Rosey was on the phone but she took time out from her conversation to let out a large guffaw when she spotted Clio's outfit. Hanging up in a fit of laughter, she said, "Just what is it you're moonlighting as, Clio?"

"Did you ever hear of trompe l'oeil?" Clio asked.

"That the guy who designed those tight jeans you're wearing?"

"It simply means a trick of the eye, Rosey," Clio said with authority.

"What kind of trick do you have up your checkered sleeve, Clio Browne?"

"Do me a favor — a small one," Clio said, easing onto a pull-up chair, careful not to sit on the hammer claw.

Rosey nodded cautiously. "Make it simple."

Clio pulled out the plastic bag with the hair she'd found on the button of Kramer Griswold's sweater, then retrieved the strands she'd pulled from the brush in Elizabeth Griswold's bathroom. "Have these checked out for me. It shouldn't take but a quick look under a microscope. I need to know if they came from the same head."

Rosey scratched her chin and eyed Clio suspiciously. "Trick of the eye, you said. Is this what you were talking about?"

Clio smiled. "Just do it, hon."

Against her "better judgment," Rosey called for a lab tech and when he came, she let Clio tell him what she wanted. They both sat back and indulged in small talk while they waited. Not too many minutes later the telephone rang.

"This is Budd." Rosey riveted her eyes on Clio. "Yeah! Yeah!" Rosey said into the phone. She listened for another minute before hanging up. "Well, Clio, you weren't kidding about tricks were you?"

"What do you mean?"

"What are you trying to pull, girl? Those hair samples came from the same head."

Clio let out a pleased sigh. "Now, let me explain it all to

you. Sample A was wrapped around the button of a sweater that had never been in Griswold's house. Sample B came from Elizabeth Griswold's hair brush. I think if we check her hairdresser, we'll find that the lady had a haircut very recently." Clio had Rosey's undivided attention. "And that's not all. There's a sheet of paper tucked under the blotter on the desk in Griswold's den. This paper shows that somebody has been practicing making the letter *J* just the same way Joanna Murdock does it to sign her personal letters. And it may not mean much, but there are also two receipts from a key shop with very interesting dates on them. With a little effort, I'll bet you'll find Mrs. Griswold somehow got a duplicate key made to Joanna's house, typed the incriminating note, doused the envelope with Joanna's perfume, and then mailed it. It was just bad luck that Joanna Murdock's fingerprint was on the paper." Clio had run out of breath.

After taking a deep one she continued. "Griswold himself never saw the letter. It was all part of Elizabeth's plan to frame Joanna. She wanted to get rid of her husband—permanently—when she found out the two of them were seeing each other. What a neat little package Elizabeth created. She even had Joanna Murdock gift-wrapped for the police."

Rosey was listening intently, her eyes as wide as silver dollars.

Clio went on. "The click Joanna heard when Kramer called her on the telephone was Elizabeth cocking the gun after she'd forced him to make that call."

"I won't even ask how you found all this out, Clio," Rosey said.

Lieutenant Budd ordered up a car to take her to Elizabeth Griswold's home. "Mind you, Clio, I'm merely going to ask the lady about her hairstyle. What you just told me is still conjecture."

Clio smiled, confident that Lieutenant Rosemary Budd would have the full story before the day was over.

Clio drove over to Lafayette Square to update the Murdocks.

"That bitch!" Joanna exclaimed. "She ruined what might have been the most powerful team in the bond business. With Pine retiring from the firm it was going to be Murdock and Griswold. What's going to happen now?" Joanna shrugged and slapped her hands against her thighs. A moment later a smile spread across her face, and it was obvious to Clio that an idea was taking shape behind those clear, cold eyes. "There's really nothing to stand in the way of Murdock and Associates, is there?"

Clio could not suppress a shudder. Joanna Murdock was every bit as calculating as Elizabeth Griswold had been. J. Kramer Griswold had fallen out of the frying pan right into the fire. Either way, his goose would have been cooked.

Joanna rubbed her hands together. "Dennis," she said to her brother, "you'll be able to leave on the evening flight." Turning to Clio, she said, "Ms. Browne, send me the bill for your services."

Clio felt sorry for Dennis Murdock. This was not the innocent child he'd rushed to St.Louis to save. She was a business machine operated by microchips instead of living cells.

"Just help me get this thing off," Clio said to Thalia when she arrived home. The buckle of the tool belt had somehow gotten stuck. "I don't want to have to wear this damned thing for the rest of my days."

Thalia fiddled with the buckle as Clio explained her theory about what must have happened on the day Griswold died.

"The click Joanna heard on the phone was Elizabeth cocking the gun, not Griswold.She probably shot him just after he hung up. By the way, Mama, thanks for teaching me about that trick-of-the-eye business. I couldn't get it out of my head. When Richard McCharles insisted he saw Joanna leave her house just after he heard a noise like a gunshot, I thought he was mistaken. But with your trompe l'oeil in mind, I began to think about tricks. It was actually Elizabeth Griswold he saw."

"Will you stand still, girl. I can't get this thing to budge. Hold that pose while I get my can of Liquid Wrench."

"Liquid Wrench?"

"Trust me!" Thalia pleaded.

When she returned from the basement with an oil can, Thalia squeezed a few drops onto the belt buckle. In a moment the lock was released and the tools and belt clattered to the floor scattering the two cats that had been affectionately rubbing up against Clio's boots.

"Whew!" Clio exclaimed. "I was beginning to think I'd be clanking through life like Morley's ghost."

"It seems to me I should get an apology for the fun you made of my little find."

"You are absolutely right, Mama. If it hadn't been for that ridic . . . that 'find' I might not have started to think about tricks the eye can play."

"Then how about lunch?"

"Sure, what've you got in the fridge?"

"You know that's not what I meant, Clio." Thalia undid her apron. "There's a new place I've been wanting to try — over on Euclid Avenue. Louisiana-Oriental named Yu All's. They fill their egg rolls with red beans and rice and feature cajun won tons."

Clio's eyes squeezed together and her hand flattened against her chest, imagining the heartburn to come. There'd be no getting out of this. Thalia wouldn't be satisfied until she'd sampled everything on the menu. "What do they do for fortune cookies, Mama?"

"Why, they put them in the hush puppies," Thalia said.

Clio shook her head, "I had to ask."

My Lover's Deadly Diary

Bonnie Morris

My name is Adar Bennett. I will be honest. I am a snoop. I am excessively curious about other peoples' lives — well, other women's lives, anyway. I'd be bored stiff otherwise. Like Harriet the Spy, my favorite fictional heroine when I was a kid, I want to KNOW, to know EVERYTHING.

Like Harriet, I began keeping a diary at age eleven, and after several years of recording my inner ethical and romantic anguish in great detail, I considered the possibility that other girls might also be keeping diaries in which they confided hot stuff. I became friends with a classmate named Mary Camille Smith, and we exchanged journals. Hers was filled with flattering remarks about me. Mine was filled with flattering remarks about her. To this day, I am wildly interested in other women's journals. Not so much to see what is said or not said about *me* — but because as writers we tend to delve deeply; conversation rarely reflects the whole imagination of the speakers. But with pen in hand, a woman will dredge up wilderness. And I love the wilderness in a woman.

Which brings me to the present. My lover, Alison, had been preoccupied and moody of late. It was a pretty lousy time for those of us in the lesbian community anyway; two young men had been harassing and even molesting women as they left Ernestine's, the local women's bar. The men had yet to be apprehended by the authorities, although most of us had been hassled by them at one time or another. It was admittedly difficult to identify them, as they always wore ski masks. Anyway, all of us were on our guard, angry, irritated at having to be on our guard, disgusted with the city's lack of protection for us. Alison had been verbally abused by these two guys; they kicked her bike out from under her and took off. I thought this might be why she had been so silent and brooding lately. Though she occasionally spoke tersely of revenge, she was otherwise noncommunicative about the incident, and I was beginning to run out of patience with her ongoing moodiness. I guess that's when I decided to read her journal and see just what she was *feeling*. Love leads you to weird actions and weird ways of caring.

One afternoon while Alison was out coaching her soccer team, I walked boldly into our study and removed Alison's leatherbound diary from the bookshelf, where it sat among volumes of Adrienne Rich's poetry. I flipped quickly to the most recent entry. Ah! Here it was:

> None of us like what's going on in our town — the violence against women makes us all feel so helpless and depressed. Only I seem willing to do something about it — something daring, but CONSTRUCTIVE.

Then, to my horror, the next page began:

> Begin by severing the vein at the base of the neck. Hold him with your left hand firmly over his head. Be sure to protect your hand with a towel. Draw the knife from the head down through the base of the abdomen . . .

I slammed the diary shut and jammed it back on the shelf next to *A Wild Patience Has Taken Me This Far*. Alison's wild patience had taken her *around the bend!* How could my sweet, gentle, *Quaker* lover be plotting to *carve up* her assailants so methodically? Was this the reason for her moody silences? She didn't want to involve me in the crime? Well, I wanted those dudes stopped too. But *severing* . How could I make love with a woman who was about to commit murder? And how could I confront her without admitting I'd riffled her diary?

Needless to say, I was not myself at supper. I nervously served Alison poached bluefish, secretly searching her face for signs of an emerging Jekyll and Hyde persona. She ate docilely. Then the phone rang. It was Alison's best friend and ex-lover Tasya, who now ran a wind-up toy store. They usually had hour-long conversations. Alison finished her meal in two giant bites and vanished into the study with the phone.

I paced. Was Tasya in on this? Alison almost always took

her calls in front of me — why the discreet exit to the study? Perhaps Alison felt more able to confide her murderous urges to Tasya: they had lived together for four years, whereas Alison and I had only been together for two. The flush of curiosity was turning my face tomato red, and before I knew it I had my careful fingers under the receiver of the kitchen phone and put my ear to the receiver.

A roar of laughter assailed my eardrum. Then I heard Alison say, "Look, it's not funny. I've *never done anything like this before.* I feel totally uncomfortable and out of my league. I just know I'll do something wrong and wreck everything. Then everyone in the lesbian community will suffer for my mistake. It's a tremendous responsibility."

"You'll get the hang of it," Tasya's rich voice soothed. "Where's your confidence? True, it's a serious undertaking — and since you volunteered to do the job, you'll have to take the rap if anything goes wrong. I know you, hon — you're not the first person I'd nominate to wield a butcher knife. But there comes a time when these skills can benefit the entire community. And I think you're damned brave to try. After all the trouble those men have caused us, your solution is ingenious!"

"Let's just go over it again," Alison begged.

"Okay." Tasya chuckled hideously. "Here are the instructions:

> Make sure first that your victim is dead — by striking a conclusive blow on the head. Remove the anal portion and the eyes — these operations may be performed with a pair of scissors "

That was all I heard. With cold, moist hands I cradled the phone back onto its hook and bellowed, "Alison — I'm going out for some air!"

I walked for an hour and seventeen minutes. I longed to stop in at a friend's house to pour out all I'd overheard. But who would believe me? Who was more credible: Adar Bennett, a reader of other women's journals, an eavesdropper on other women's conversations, an alarmist, an imaginative fruitcake — or Alison Leroy, hale, hearty, feminist soccer coach? Besides, nothing had happened — yet. Those two macho jerks were still at large in the community, rubbing excrement on lesbians' cars and spray-painting the sidewalks in front of Ernestine's. Sure, I wanted them stopped. I even wanted them to suffer as we had suffered. But was I prepared to find severed limbs and eyeballs around town — with lab reports tracing the fingerprints on the butcher knife back to my honey? And what about Alison's job? She'd had a hard enough time keeping it when the high school found out their best gym teacher lived with a woman. As a murderess, Alison would be out of work permanently — and both of us depended on her slim salary while I completed my Ph.D. dissertation on the childhood journals of a radical Welsh feminist.

I arrived home pale.

Alison looked alarmingly cheerful. "Where'd you run off to?" she demanded squeezing my arm. "I didn't get to thank you for that nice fish dinner."

I sensed deception. "Did you and Tasya have a nice talk?" I managed to snarl. "You haven't confided that much in *me* lately."

"Oh. Yeah. Sorry. Uh, — we're working on a — well, a — a project. Kind of a weird surprise. I can't tell you about it yet, and anyway, you wouldn't believe me," Alison said rolling her eyes. "But you'll find out soon; probably at the same time as the rest of the women's community. And, um . . . I hope you'll be proud of my initiative..."

"I can't wait," I said, feeling sick.

Well, things went on like this for another week and a half. Alison was preoccupied and mysterious, and tired at odd times, but told me little of what was going on. In desperation, I'd wait for her to go out jogging or to leave for an appointment with her therapist, and then I'd race to read her journal entries. They had become even more grisly. The list of "instructions," which I assumed Alison was receiving from Tasya, were unlimited in their lust for blood.

> Make an incision just back of the eyes and cut out the face.
>
> Overcome the worst of the opposition by instantly chopping off the head.
>
> Kill with a sharp blow to the head or by slipping a noose around. . . .

Tasya phoned three more times, but I could only bear to eavesdrop once. When I heard her tell Alison, "You're ready to cut up the carcass — but to cut the body apart you need to place the carcass flat on its back." I hung up in horror, convinced the crime had already taken place. Where were they keeping the bodies? They must be hacked into little pieces by now. The only place I could think of was our basement freezer. Alison had been bringing home oddly shaped parcels for days, whisking them into the cellar. I had naively assumed they were surprise gifts for my birthday. But if the crime had already been committed. . . . And weren't several of our sharpest kitchen knives missing?

My hand was on the freezer door when I heard Alison behind me.

"*Don't open that door.*" It was a gravel-voiced command.

I felt sweat break out between my toes and in the crook of my elbows. Slowly, I turned around. Alison's tall, athletic frame filled the doorway at the top of the cellar stairs. She descended fiercely, one Reebok at a time. "Don't look in the freezer," she hissed.

"Damn it, Alison, what is going on?" I was almost crying. "You can't keep them here. I don't care how much damage they've done to the women's community, this is my house too. You've got to get rid of the bodies!"

"Bodies? What the hell are you talking about?" Suddenly I noticed the long knife in her hand. The missing butcher knife. I backed away from the freezer and whispered "Alison . . . no . . . ."

"Wait a minute." Alison drawled, still gesturing with the knife. "What do you think I have in the freezer?"

The jig was up. Never had I been so sorry for my perverse curiosity about women's lives, my absurd interest in their diaries. But for that curiosity, I might have escaped the status of accessory to a murderess — or the fate of being her next victim. "I know what you did," I breathed. "I heard you planning it. You and Tasya . . . ."

"Me and Tasya? For Goddess' sake. Have you been listening in on the kitchen phone again? I *told* you, just because Tasya and I are ex-lovers doesn't mean we're going to rekindle the romance. She's my best friend. Hey, I thought you were over this jealousy trip. But I *know* you've been reading my journal. I saw your typewriter-ribbon-stained *thumbprint* on one of the pages, you dumb graduate student." But her voice was tender.

"This has nothing to do with jealousy!' I shrieked. "I *heard* you two planning the — the executions. I *saw* it in your diary. You killed those guys and cut up their carcasses! And they're right here in our *freezer*, alongside the old Girl Scout cookies and my mother's frozen kreplach!"

Alison began to laugh. I stood with head bowed, aghast at her macabre sense of humor. I thought I'd been living with Lucretia Mott all these months. Here she revealed her true identity: Lucretia Borgia.

With an abrupt swing of her well-muscled arm, Alison pulled the freezer door open. I gasped involuntarily in apprehension. But I was never so surprised as I was then. For, instead of the grisly limbs and eyeballs I'd expected, our freezer revealed layer after layer of shellfish. Not just lobsters and crabs, but even stranger delicacies: eel, octopus, and something I guessed to be terrapin. It was all packed neatly with straw and ice. I turned to Alison, who was still laughing uncontrollably, the first real laughter I'd heard from her in weeks. Swallowing hard, I managed to whisper a request: "Will you please explain all this to me before I flip out for real?"

Twenty minutes later, Alison and I were in the hot tub, her arms around me. "Those weren't instructions for murder that you read in my diary and heard Tasya explaining," she said. "Those were *recipes* — for preparing crab, lobster, even chicken. This was supposed to be a surprise for your birthday, but I guess I could have explained it all days ago to assuage your pathological curiosity."

"I wouldn't use the term 'pathology' so lightly," I responded, but I was beginning to relax in the hot, bubbling water. "I was almost ready to turn you over to the authorities, you know."

Alison grinned. "Well, you were right about one thing. Tasya and I did make a pact to catch those two guys who have been hassling the lesbian community. Our plan is to have a gourmet dinner party at Ernestine's — we'll sell tickets, and the money will go to provide better street lighting, escort services, things like that. It's also a good way to get all the women together at once. We plan to advertise the event all over town, so those two guys will know there's going to be a party. Then we figure they'll be sure to show up, maybe even with a few of their friends."

"But isn't that kind of dangerous?" I asked, rubbing my foot against Alison's shin. "I mean, those guys are bad news . . . ."

Alison's grin elongated. "That's the best part. We've got two undercover policewomen who will come to the dinner and later act as set-ups for the punks. They'll bust those jerks in three seconds. Both women know karate, and they're really on our side. One is a lesbian who just came out to her chief, and the other one has a lesbian sister who was just assaulted last month. We're all set to nab those suckers."

I shook my head in amazement. "I can't believe it. Those were *recipes?*"

"Straight out of *The Joy of Cooking,*" Alison assured me. "I wanted to make all the fancy gourmet stuff myself. I've always let you do the cooking — guess it was kind of a point of butchy pride with me, but the time's come for me to learn my way around the kitchen. And I wanted to surprise you, to take your breath away. I know I've been moody and tired lately, and I wanted to make it up to you with the best birthday party you'll ever have. So Tasya was calling me up and reading me the recipes over the phone, and I was putting them into my journal. I knew you'd get suspicious if you saw me walking around with your *Joy of Cooking* in my hand. What have I ever made for you except Fruit Loops?"

Alison was right. I do get suspicious. So, after we had had a good soak in the hot tub, and had toweled each other dry and then made love on the sofa and gone to bed, I sneaked down to the kitchen with a flashlight and took out *The Joy of Cooking.* There it all was — every line I'd seen in Alison's diary or heard Tasya read over the phone. Pages 386, 409, 384, 393, 406, and 419: recipes for crab, lobster, other difficult creatures from the briny deep. I had no idea a cookbook could be filled with such graphic detail!

Well, to sum up, the dinner party at Ernestine's was a rousing success. Alison did a fine job preparing the marine buffet and we raised about $500 for services and repairs to assure the safety of women in our neighborhood. The plain-clothes policewomen were downright adorable: I discovered that I'd gone to junior high school with the one who was insisting she was straight. Right. She certainly had a good time that night, no less than her openly lesbian partner. Best of all their set-up worked, and two young men with prior records of "malicious mischief" found themselves grabbing the arms of two highly talented karate artists. The boys went to jail — and word quickly went around town that you better not mess with amazons coming out of Ernestine's, or any woman at all, for that matter.

As for me, I've learned to relax and let Alison do some of the cooking. It's true that my excessively curious nature can get me into trouble sometimes. I still have to fight the temptation to read other women's journals. But Alison is helping to cure me of this syndrome. She's bought herself a new diary with a lock and key.

I wonder what she's up to.

No Woman is an Island

Linda Wagner

1.

"Look, Ma, we've had this same argument eight times a week for the last two years."

"But Livia, this isn't why your father and I sent you to law school. Who would want to marry a girl detective?"

"Girl detective? What am I, Ma, Nancy Drew? Not many guys want to marry a 'girl lawyer' either. I know. I took a poll. They find the idea castrating."

"Don't talk dirty to your mother, Livia. Some profession you chose. You learn to talk like that. And to your mother . . . ."

I held the phone away from my ear. I thought about putting it in the desk drawer. Had I said eight times a week? It had to be more like eighty times a week. The lines were all familiar, cliché-ridden and truly wearing thin. It was like a long running, badly written play. I wished fervently that my contract would expire and they would get another actress.

"I gotta go, Ma. I got a call on the other line." Strangely enough, this was true. I was so surprised to see the blinking light on the phone that I didn't hear my mother's parting shot. I had probably heard it before, though, so it really didn't matter.

"Spotlight Investigations. Livia Day Lewis speaking."

"Livia? Tom Jennings, here."

"Oh." I didn't want to sound disappointed, but I really couldn't help it. I hadn't had a business call in weeks. People not only did not marry what my mother termed "Girl Detectives," they apparently did not hire them either. It had been a lean two years and things were taking a turn for the worse. Business was no longer thin. It was non-existent.

It wasn't Tom's fault, but his controlled British demeanor made me even more aggravated. "Look," I snapped, "I don't have time to chat today." Liar. All I had was time.

"Hold up, Livia. I've got a lead on a couple of weird murders. You just might be able to provide some assistance to the police. Can we meet?"

The only real crisis I was anticipating was an upsurge in the cockroach population in my office. Maybe something would turn up with Tom and I could afford to buy a new Roach Motel. Tom was a freelance reporter and he sometimes got a jump on interesting things. My mother had always hoped that he would get the jump on me, but we continued to be friends and nothing more.

"How about the Choo-Choo Lounge in the Terminal Tower? About an hour?" He agreed to meet me there. I tidied my already tidy desk, locked up the old penthouse and drove into the thriving metropolis of downtown Cleveland. Driving from the West side to downtown is always a fun gig. Which bridge might be open today? How crazy are the people on the shoreway at this particular time of day? Which lanes of traffic will be closed? It is a game of skill. I came out victorious for a change.

I found a cheap place to park, only about forty miles away from where I needed to be and hiked back to the Terminal Tower. I hit the Choo-Choo about fifteen minutes early, so I warmed my behind on a barstool and my insides with a vodka gimlet. I've never been sure if it's the drink I like or the way the words sound.

The Choo-Choo is one of my favorite joints, mainly due to the decor. It's done up like an old railway car with lots of gold bric-a-brack and red velvet. It's cool and dim. It's also one of the few places where a lady can sit at the bar unmolested. Tom arrived precisely on time. Everything about Tom is precise. Tall, lanky, with hair the color of straw. So Anglo, with blue eyes and the sort of looks that you turn to follow on the street. I've known him for years, yet I'm always somewhat startled by how handsome he is. I keep forgetting. He's awfully smart, too. The only truly dumb thing he's ever done, to my knowledge, is to hang around me. He's had the evil luck to be around when I've wanted to take it out on someone. Several times. Why, I wondered, does he keep coming back for more?

"Hi, Livia." What a smile! Another forgotten virtue. Maybe my mother's not as ignorant as I think. "How are you?"

"About ready to call the prestigious law firm of Sanders Squire and Dempsey. I'm gonna get on my knees and ask them if they'll give me a job sweeping up. They're the biggest pack of attorneys in town. They can afford to be magnanimous."

"Been talking to your mother again, huh?"

"What was your first clue? Yes, I've been talking to my mother. Or rather she has been talking to me. Endlessly, interminably, nauseatingly. But then, who else do I have to talk to? I haven't had a case in months. I'm about to starve and she knows it. Say, I have an idea. Why don't you marry me and take me away from all this?"

"I tried asking once. You turned me down as I recall."

"Maybe you shouldn't have given up so easily. Maybe twice would have done it."

"I'm allergic to rejection. Besides, I rather like being pals."

I laughed. I didn't know if he really meant it, but I knew we were better off that way. "So, what's on your mind, pal?" The smile, which had momentarily deserted him, was back.

"Pirates."

"That's not funny, Tom. Just because I happened to pen a term paper on the subject is no reason for you to trot it out when you need a chuckle on a dull morning." That paper was still a sore spot with me. Three months I spent on the research. The history professor for whom I had written it felt that it was an insignificant topic and forced me to write another paper on a topic chosen by him — the correlation of shoe styles to political climates in the modern world. After all this time, it still smarted that the tyrant had won.

"There are," I said firmly, "no pirates drifting about on Lake Erie."

"I wouldn't be so sure. The coppers are beginning to wonder. They've just turned up a third body that appears to be the handiwork of some buccaneer."

"In your own vernacular — are you having me on?"

"Not a bit of it, me hearty. The first unfortunate was shot with what seems to have been a musket of great age, complete with very old ammunition. The second and third victims had their throats cut, hacked actually, with an old cutlass, which has been recovered from the scene of the last murder and identified as the murder weapon."

"Tom, I saw that movie, 'The Island,' too. I didn't believe pirates in Bermuda, why am I gonna believe pirates in Ohio?"

"'Cause just maybe this guy saw the same film — or one like it. The police think they're dealing with a guy who thinks he's a pirate. But, what's bound to interest you is that on the blade of that very cutlass, beautifully etched, in flowing letters is the name 'Rackham.'"

"Calico Jack?" He had been the chief subject of my unacceptable term paper.

"Righto. Now, soon as I hear this famous name, I tell the coppers that I know someone who is very intimate with the very same old blackguard."

"Me?"

"Two in a row! She's on a roll, folks! The prize in this case is an appointment with Chief Beardsley a.s.a.p. I have here in this manila envelope all of the info on the murders and victims which I, generous soul, am turning over to you, pirate expert, for your perusal and edification."

"And you get —?"

"You embarrass me, ma'am." He paused. "I get whatever you give the law, right after you give it to them. They don't want anything in print yet, but when this breaks, I want to be ahead of the pack. I will also want the benefit of your piratical expertise for feature background."

"You'll spell my name right, I trust?" He nodded. "OK. I'll take the envelope back to my hole and read it over, then go see Beardsley. I'll call you afterward."

"Fine. And Livia?"

"Yup?"

"You want to marry me?"

I hesitated. "Well, you surely do have a certain amount of charm that's extremely difficult to resist, sir. And your flowery speeches are attractive, but I think not."

"OK, lady. Just don't say I didn't ask a second time."

"Righto." I left the bar alone.

2.

I took the envelope back to my office to study its contents. I'm fairly sturdy, but I have to admit to feeling chilled when I saw the grisly photographs that accompanied the report. The victims were all male and seemed to have nothing else in common. The first was a businessman in his forties, graying hair, wearing what I would consider a very bad suit, a bad suit made even worse by the large hole in it. The other two were even harder to look at. One, a young college student, another,

100

middle-aged and well-dressed. Their throats had been savaged. There was blood over everything in the vicinity.

The cutlass was indeed a beautiful piece. It looked old enough to have been Jack Rackham's, but it could have been a reproduction. I couldn't tell from the photograph. I might be able to find someone who could tell me where it came from. It was the one concrete point from which I could start.

Each victim had been found with a piece of red striped calico cloth tied around his left wrist. Old Jack had earned his nickname by always wearing pants cut of this cloth. It had become his trademark.

A newsman named Tom Jennings (his note was in the file) had suggested the connection between this case and a pirate who had been dead for two hundred years. The police, up until that point, had not known that Jack Rackham was a famous dead man. They had probably tried to look up the name in the local phone book until Tom set them straight.

I returned to the awful photographs again, trying to become more objective. Whoever was responsible for this had to be totally psychotic. This is the sort of case where you can't look for motive. You can look for patterns and connections.

The phone rang. Startled, I grabbed it and yelled, "Hello?"

"What, no more detective agency?"

"Mother, you just scared the hell out of me."

"If you lived in a better neighborhood, you wouldn't need to be so jumpy . . . or maybe if you were in a legitimate occupation."

I really didn't need this twice in a single day. "Please, lets not discuss this now. I'm working on a case."

"Case? You've got work?" Snide . . . so snide. "All I called for, Livia, was to ask you to come for supper this evening. Unless, of course, you have something else planned?"

"Yeah. OK. Any special reason?"

"No . . . ."

Was that a pregnant pause I heard? Suspect my mother's motives? Uh huh. There always was a motive. But I really didn't want to argue just then so I agreed to be there about six.

Chief Beardsley was expecting me, but apparently he was not expecting me to be me. When I identified myself as the P.I. Tom Jennings had mentioned, he looked me up and down.

"You're a woman."

"No kidding," I shot back. "Well that explains a lot of things I've been wondering about. Thanks for the info."

"Sorry," he said. He wasn't, but at least he was aware that he had been insulting. "Jennings never told me your name so I didn't realize."

"It's Livia. But you can call me Ralph if it makes you more comfortable. I'll even try to lower my voice an octave or so."

He tried to smile, making a bad job of it. "How do you think you can help us?"

"I don't know yet. Can I see the weapon?"

"No," he said glumly.

"Why not?"

"Because it's . . . lost."

"Look, if there's some reason you don't want me to see it, tell me."

"Lady, watch my lips. The thing is missing. Plain and simple. It got lost when it was transferred from one department to another."

"You're kidding." I knew from his face that he wasn't. "How could it happen?"

"If I knew, it wouldn't have happened." He was trying to think of something to say. I wasn't in the mood to wait around.

"I'll be in touch," I growled, halfway to the door.

I went for a drive, hoping it would clear my head. Before I knew it, I was cruising through the wealthy Chestnut Hills section of Cleveland Heights. I had grown up here on the East side and knew this section well. This is where everybody would like to be able to live. I wondered momentarily if people would jog out of their houses and tell me to get my crummy car off their nice, neat street. My mother will not ride in my ten year old, semi-rusted MG. She seems to think it is beneath her dignity. "What do I do now?" I drove in large, graceful circles. I thought simply in circles.

I glanced at my watch and threw on the brakes. I was due at my parents' house ten minutes ago. I was about ten minutes away if I put the car in "fly." That would make me twenty minutes late, which meant a good half hour of recrimination. I threw the car into reverse, making one heck of a noise as I abused the gears. I got myself successfully headed in the right direction — the White Rabbit, late again for the

Red Queen's tea party.

Thus I arrived, panting, twenty-two minutes late, in front of my parents' house. English Tudor, tasteful landscaping, and a strange car parked in the circular driveway. I should have known. Obviously my mother had run into one of her endless parade of friends who just happened to have a son my age. Another frog waiting to become a prince at a wave of my rusty wand. Maybe I was being too suspicious. I rang the bell.

The door was thrown open by my chiffon-clad mother and, as she began her I-thought-you-were-killed-in-that-awful-car speech, I looked past her into the living room and there he was. No breaks for Livia tonight. I suddenly realized that a portion of my mother's tirade had to do with my jeans and sweater. I had an answer for that one. "You didn't tell me it was black tie, Ma. You never mentioned company."

She was caught there and had to back down. No matter, she would make it up in points later.

At least this one was easy on the eyes. Broad shoulders, dark hair, dark eyes. A type I've always liked. Intelligent looking. He was George Armitage, I learned, home from Harvard for a break, (grad work, of course). An Ivy League frog of the highest quality and darned attractive, as well. I shook hands with him while my mother suggested that we go into the dining room, although she wasn't sure that supper would still be edible. My father now joined us. He had been working in the library on a research project. He has never pressured me. I think that, although he would never say so, he is secretly pleased to have produced a maverick like me.

Froggie spoke. His voice was pleasant enough. "Your mother tells me that you're an investigator. Do you work for an insurance company?" What else, I wondered, had she told him?

"No, private sleuth. You know, like Sherlock Holmes."

"You mean a private detective?" One of his eyebrows was slightly raised.

"Does Philip Marlowe mean anything to you? How about 'drop the gun, Louie?'"

"Oh."

My mother flicked me one of her fabled why-are-you-doing-this-to-me looks. Temptation overwhelmed me. "I'd show you my rod," I camped in my best Bogart, "but I don't generally pack it on social occasions. Of course, there was this one time." I lowered my voice and leaned toward him. "I was on this divorce case, tailing a very promiscuous lady from shack-up to shack-up and — "

My mother tried to stop me. "George is a philosophy student. I'll bet that's really interesting." She was desperate. I chortled into my veal cutlet. Glancing down the table, I could have sworn my father was chortling into his.

George gallantly took up the challenge to fascinate us with some safe table talk. "Last semester, I took an elective course that was really exciting. Your mother mentioned that you like old movies. This course was devoted to silent stuff — D. W. Griffith and Mack Sennett. The social commentary inherent in Sennett's treatment of authority figures is one of the earliest media expressions of . . ."

I couldn't stand it. "That's a crock. It's unadulterated bullshit. Mack Sennett made funny movies. He made people laugh. That's all he was trying to do and that's all he did. No social commentary, no psychology. He made a buck throwing custard pies. Period." When I finally shut up, it was really quiet in the room.

"Get out of my house," said my mother, her voice shaking. "You are rude and I want you to leave." She was, in effect, sending me to my room, which was now across town.

Simultaneously, my father said, "Now, Helen —" and George said, "Please, Mrs. Lewis . . . ."

I interrupted them. "I just hate pompous bullshit." It wasn't an apology so it made matters worse.

Ma's expression was edged in purple. "You and your gutter mouth, get out now!"

I left without saying anything further. I hadn't intended to make a disaster of the evening. Or had I? If only she wouldn't push. Why didn't my father stop her? He didn't like her meddling any more than I did. She had dominated him for so long, even when he disapproved of her tactics, he did nothing.

I sat in the car, my forehead on the steering wheel, my eyes closed, trying to stop shaking long enough to get the key in the ignition. A hand touched my shoulder. I looked up. It was George Armitage. "You were absolutely correct," he said quietly. "It was pompous bullshit. I apologize for thinking you would be impressed by that stuff. Can I call you? I'd like to see you again. Under different circumstances."

I was grateful to him. I gave him one of my business cards. He read it and nodded. "Will you promise me you'll tell me the rest of the story about the promiscuous wife later?"

"Yes, though she's an ex-wife now. Would you answer one question for me?"

"Shoot. No . . . wrong terminology. What?"

"What's a nice frog like you doing in a pond like this?" I roared out of the driveway, leaving him looking truly puzzled.

I was so muddled that I nearly hit a police car parked almost at the foot of the drive. The female cop in the car didn't even look up, so I counted myself lucky and drove a little more carefully.

3.

Returning to the office seemed like a better idea than going home. A more or less commercially zoned neighborhood, it was pretty quiet at night. My locks are sturdy enough to at least let me know if someone is breaking in, and I do have a rod in my desk drawer. I've never actually carried it, much less used it, because most of my cases are about as exciting as an income tax form. But I keep the gun in case of emergencies and clean it faithfully once a week to ensure that it is in good working order.

I walked to the desk and fiddled with my answering machine. It always recorded perfectly. Playback, however, was a little iffy. Sometimes I would give up, figuring that if it was important, the caller would try again. Suddenly the gizmos snapped into place and the magic box began to spew faithfully-reproduced voices.

An electronic beep. Tom's voice came on. "Get in touch, luv. It's important." He sounded worried.

Another beep. A breathy, deep female voice said, "Calico Jack is ours. Keep your distance. One more throat is easily cut."

I spun around from the window and stared at the machine which was now silent. Cautiously rewinding the tape, I heard Tom's message, beep and . . . "Calico Jack is ours. Keep your distance. One more throat —"

The hair on my neck stood at attention. In two years of following unfaithful spouses and searching for runaway children, I had been threatened by more than one hysterical person. This was different. Quiet, sincere threats are the ones that get carried out. This threat was direct, to the point, no rhetoric.

After a few moments, my brain began to function again. I had thought that the killings were the work of a psychopath with the delusion that he was Jack Rackham. But who was this woman? What did she mean by "ours"? Whose?

Rewinding the tape one more time, I tried to listen to the voice without hearing the words. It was an educated voice with near perfect diction. No detectable accent. The words were spaced evenly, deliberately, with no hesitation. I guessed she was young, maybe in her twenties.

I turned the thing off, thought for a while and came up with a handful of nothing. Enough for one night. I would call Tom in the morning when everything was a little calmer. I'd take the phone off the hook at home and get a little peace.

4.

The morning was warm and sunny, a rare thing in the Land of Cleve. I drove with the top down thinking that while life was fragile, it could at times be pleasant. The woman on the tape was probably a crank who had somehow heard about the murders. I still had the photo of the cutlass. Maybe George Armitage would call. Yes, sometimes in the bowl of pits, there were one or two small cherries.

The five flights of stairs up to my penthouse office dimmed my enthusiasm just a bit. I dialed Tom's number, humming. There was a knock at the door. I sang, "Come in," and voila! — there was Tom Jennings, standing in front of my desk.

"Boy, that was fast service," I chirped. "I just dialed and here you are already." He was definitely not looking amused.

"Why didn't you call?" he asked quietly.

"I was just calling you. You didn't answer. You're not there. You're here."

"I mean last night, as I requested."

"Lighten up, Tom. I was at one of my mother's match-maker events. What's the matter?"

"I was just worried when I didn't hear from you. I phoned here and the phone just rang. I called you at home and the phone just rang. I went to the house and you weren't there. Look, three people are dead. I should never have involved you. I'm beginning to regret it." His worry worried me. For him, this

106

was out of character.

"Wait a minute. I thought this was my break and your scoop."

He was silent for a beat, then made a decision. "OK . . .I got a weird phone call last night. It was a woman. She said, 'Calico Jack is ours. Tell the woman to keep her distance. One more . . .'"

"'throat is easily cut,'" I finished for him.

"How did you —? Christ! She called you too?"

"It was on the answering machine. I came back here after dinner. When I ran the tape, there were two messages on it, yours and hers. I was replaying it when the machine jammed, so I never hooked it back up."

There was a knock at the door that made us both jump. It was a delivery boy with a box. "I didn't order anything."

"Name Lewis?" He spoke in shorthand.

"Yes, but . . . ."

"For you then. Fella said Lewis. This office." I took the box gingerly. The delivery boy vanished. That bothered me. He hadn't waited for a tip. I looked at Tom and weighed the box in my hands. He raised his eyebrows a trifle. We were thinking the same thing. The warning referred to a knife, but that didn't make a bomb out of the question.

"We're being silly," I said. "Bull by the horns, what?" I plunked the box down on the desk and lifted the top. "What the —?" A custard pie nestled on top of a paper doily. I picked up the card that lay next to it. "To throw at the next pompous asshole you run into," it read. "With apologies, George."

I fell into the desk chair, laughing hysterically. Tom was watching me, waiting for an explanation. I was just getting a grip on myself when the phone rang. I picked it up.

"You received it then?"

"Yes, George. A splendid peace offering. Come over right now and I'll share."

"I can't right now, but if you're free this evening, I have a movie projector and a closet full of old films. Shall we say eight o'clock?"

"If I'm not free, I'm at least inexpensive. It sounds lovely." I gave him my address and said good-bye. I opened my mouth to explain the joke, but Tom spoke before I could say anything.

"I really don't care to hear about it," he snapped irritably. "I'm late for an appointment. Call you later."

I fiddled with the answering machine until I was totally frustrated. I decided to drop it off on the way to the Museum of Art, where I hoped to find someone who could help classify the missing cutlass. I thought about taking my gun. I decided that it was a better traveling companion than none at all. I slipped it into the large shoulder bag in which I carry nearly half of everything I own. Indeed, the bag's contents are so varied that I often spend an entire evening amusing myself and others by rearranging them. Well, possibly the others are less amused.

I couldn't get an appointment to see anyone really important at the museum. However, some deft lateral movement through throngs of underlings led me to one of the guards who was an expert on old weapons. Photo in hand, I wandered through the galleries until I located Willie Hubbard in a room filled with French Impressionist paintings. The man looked an awful lot like Lon Chaney, Jr., playing Lawrence Talbot in "The Wolfman." I do a passable imitation of Maria Ouspenskaya, but the seriousness of his demeanor made me feel it would be churlish to display my talent at this particular time. "Mr. Hubbard?"

His shoes squeaked across the parquet floor. "Ma'am?"

"I was told by several people that you might be able to answer some questions about the authenticity of an artifact." His shoes squeaked a few steps closer.

"It's a private weapon — or supposed to be," I went on. "All I have is a photograph. I thought you might be able to help me decide if it's real or a copy." He nodded as I held out the picture. He studied the photo, frowning. When he finally looked up, he smiled. At least, I think it was a smile.

"A copy. Good . . . but surely a copy. And there's the lettering, of course. If this thing existed, I would know of it. It is a copy," he repeated firmly.

"Do you know of anyone who can do such work?"

"There are several people who are capable. There is one here in this city who is probably the best. He did it too well, too often, and went to jail." He paused. It was an effort for him to speak more than two sentences. "His name is Israel Chance. He runs a small jewelry store. Old Arcade. Downtown." I would have thanked him, but he was already squeaking away into the distance.

After leaving the museum, feeling fairly confident, I bought popcorn from a street vendor to feed the carp in the nearby lagoon. The day was soft and sweet. The sun shone down warm still, and I reveled in the park-like surroundings. If I had spent less time mooning around, I might have had the opportunity to speak with Israel Chance. As it was, by the time I arrived the crowd outside the jewelry store stood watching the police remove the corpse. And there was my old friend Chief Beardsley. He looked as if his lunch had disagreed with him. When I approached he turned on me, snarling like an insulted Doberman. "Another one! That's four. Are you supposed to be helping here? 'Cause you sure aren't, near as I can tell. Now we got four. Jeez!"

"Hey, c'mon, I didn't kill the guy. I was on my way to talk to him. He might have made the cutlass which, by the way, you guys lost." The best defense, I reasoned was a good offense.

"You were —? Oh, great. Why didn't you call us? He hasn't been dead half an hour. We could have been here earlier. Maybe even caught the killer."

"Look, I just found out. You could have had this information yesterday if you'd made a decent effort."

Beardsley sputtered somewhat more quietly. "This isn't the only case we've got, lady." How could someone make the word 'lady' sound like a poor career choice? He walked off grumbling in the direction of the receding stretcher which bore the remains of the late Israel Chance, my only lead.

From one of the other cops, I got some details. It seemed that Calico Jack had a brand new cutlass and had tried it out on the old gent.

Somehow he had gotten in and out of the shop without being noticed by anyone. It's like that most of the time. People look, but they don't see anything. It isn't that they don't want to get involved. They look at the ground, at store windows, wrapped up in their own problems, seeing nothing that goes on around them. It gives the police a migraine. It gives the victims an opportunity to fulfill their roles.

It was pretty clear that Israel Chance was the artisan from whom the original cutlass had been obtained. He certainly had provided the instrument of his own death. I tried to talk the officer guarding the shop into letting me look around inside, but he said I would need the chief's permission. I didn't think it would be the ideal time to ask.

I turned to leave. Through the thinning crowd, I made eye contact with a young woman. Not otherwise unusual looking, she was about six feet tall. Her large, intelligent gray eyes were definitely observing me. Although she looked away quickly, the contact had been obvious. She moved towards the exit. I followed.

She moved quickly through the crowd, but her height allowed me to keep her in view. She left the arcade and moved up Euclid Avenue, turning up Sixth Street. That was where I lost her.

Lunch at Moriarity's left me feeling that maybe my mother was right — I wasn't much of a detective. My only consolation in all of this was that the police seemed to be doing no better than I was. I headed back to the office, feeling a touch desolate.

I didn't see her standing in the shadows of what the building management loosely refers to as the lobby. If I had, it probably wouldn't have done me much good. I could, therefore, do very little about the arm she wrapped around my throat from behind. Except, of course, to gag and struggle.

Finally, I stopped wriggling. I pride myself on my ability to recognize a hopeless situation when it occurs. The pressure on my throat lessened slightly. "That's a good girl. Now stay still," she growled softly. The voice was familiar. She spoke again. "Now listen, you were warned off once. It looks like you don't take a hint very well. We'd really prefer it if you didn't screw things up."

I wanted to see her face. I knew if I attempted to turn I would be flirting with a crushed windpipe followed by reconstructive surgery. "Who's 'we'?" I ventured.

"That's real cute. I'm not stupid. You'll find out when everyone else does. In a while. After there are a few more. But you stay out of it. Understand?"

Just as she finished, several things happened in rapid succession. The lobby door squawked open, someone yelled, and my assailant let go of me and ran like hell out the door and past Tom, who was standing there. "Follow that woman!" I hollered. Tom is well trained. He took off after her, while I nursed my abused throat.

Now you may think that I'd be scared. Wrong. All I could feel was delight. This was the break I so badly needed. I was so completely elated that I dismissed the fact that my life had been threatened. Now, at least I knew I was not after a nut committing random and motiveless murders. There was a plan. Any plan forged by a human mind in relatively normal gear can be figured out by another human mind in roughly the same condition.

Tom came back, breathing heavily. He spoke. I noticed he suddenly sounded very British.

"Followed her to a building about three blocks up. She went in, grabbed the lift. Figured best not to tangle with her. Too many people about. Tall bird, strong-looking, too."

"Your accent gets thicker when you're excited. Did you know that?" I thought it was an interesting observation.

"My —? What's the matter with you? Do you get what just happened?"

"I sure do, oh indeed I do. I just got my first break in this miserable case. Now show me which building."

For some reason I couldn't quite fathom he seemed irritated. He said nothing as we walked up the street to the building where she had taken refuge. Grabbing at the nearest straw, I checked the lobby directory, hoping that something might click.

Maybe my luck was changing. It was a small building. I stared at the directory. Maybe my luck wasn't changing.

"Let's see . . . two attorneys, a CPA, a palm reader — what's WOW?" I asked.

"I haven't the slightest idea. Look, are you OK?"

"Fine. I'll just jot all of these names down and check each one out. Did she seem like she was coming here intentionally?"

"Headed straight for the building. Are you sure you're all right?"

By this time I was out of the door, on my way back up the street. A connection. It had to be a connection. The voice on the tape, the woman in the Arcade and the Godzillette who attacked me were the same person. Calico Jack was being used by someone. There had to be something we were overlooking about the three male victims prior to Israel Chance. It may have been a wild goose chase, but it was the only goose I had to chase.

"Tom, I'm going over to *The Plain Dealer* and see if any of these folks ever made the papers. Want to come?"

"No. I have work to do." He was looking at me oddly.

"I really am all right, if that's what's bothering you. This is something really big. You and I could end up stars."

"Please be careful," he said as I got into my car.

"I never have so far. Why start now? Don't worry, silly.

111

With my luck, the worst thing that will happen to me will be a pie in the face. Highly amusing, but nothing to send sympathy cards for. Pratfalls are my life."

I blew most of the afternoon and about three-quarters of my eyesight in the microfiche department of *The Cleveland Plain Dealer*, our only remaining daily newspaper. There were scant references to both attorneys, who seemed to defend small time lowlife. No mention of the CPA. The palm reader had once run an ad around Halloween. Then we came to WOW.

Back in the sixties, a woman named Helen Gottschalk made a name for herself by making speeches about the use of violence as a means to an end. The organization she claimed to represent was Women of the World. WOW. She seemed to be supporting some fuzzy-edged ideology, terrorism in the name of women's rights. There were few takers and, when Ms. Gottschalk actually planted a bomb at City Hall, it turned out that she was apparently the only member of WOW. Worse than that, she wasn't much of a bomb manufacturer. The bomb was a dud, she was caught in the act, and her attorney opted for an insanity plea. She ended up in a home for the bewildered. She was reportedly furious with her attorney, Felix Goodman, because she would have preferred jail. She was, she insisted, not crazy. Felix Goodman? Why was that name so familiar? Felix Goodman. It fell into place. Felix Goodman had been the third murder victim, the well-dressed, middle-aged man.

They could have been pieces from different puzzles, but they sure as hell fit together. I decided to visit the WOW office, myself. They knew who I was, but I figured it would be their style to play it cool.

In the meantime, I had a date to get ready for — George Armitage, Ivy League Frog.

5.

He picked me up in a Rolls Royce. I didn't know what model or year — I really didn't care. Every once in a while, life gives you something. The ride wasn't nearly long enough. I wished the house were in Buffalo, New York instead of Bratenahl, Ohio, but the house was even more incredible than the car. I knew rich folks lived in this neighborhood — I

112

simply had not known how rich. The house was huge, set on the lakefront and furnished in the unambiguous good taste of old money.

The rooms all had fifteen foot ceilings. I had the impression that if it were humid enough, rain clouds just might be able to form somewhere up near the beams. I knew that if I had to go to the bathroom, I would have to leave a trail of breadcrumbs to find my way back. Are you getting the picture? This was a big house.

It was inhabited by George, when he was in town, a couple of noiseless cats and a blue parrot named Cookie, who chattered and chuckled meaninglessly, reminding me of some of my relatives.

The best thing was yet to come. The house was equipped with a no-kidding, real, live movie theater. Fifteen seats, a monstrous screen, a popcorn machine. "I'm moving in!" I shrieked. George laughed. He thought I was kidding. "I'll never look at a VCR again."

I can live without the cars, the housekeepers, the caviar, but this — I finally understood why it is that people want to be rich.

So we watched movies. We settled back while Mabel Normand, Fatty Arbuckle and the Keystone Kops cavorted for our personal amusement. Film, laughs, popcorn. For hours. I snuggled up to the frog, who was looking more princelike all the time. I could get used to this. Why did I want to chase some crummy psycho all over creation when this was available?

The last reel whirred to a finish. I became aware that there was no light in the room save that coming from the projector. George reached over and touched my cheek. Then, he leaned toward me and we kissed. I've been kissed in my life, more than once, I admit. But, never have I been kissed by an expert from the Ivy League. Oh Frog, thou art a prince! I probably lit up the room. I heard an orchestra start to play. So, OK, maybe it was just the string section, but there was music, I swear. More music than I'd ever heard before, even with the radio playing. I heard the parrot making noises in the distance. I realized that the kiss had ended. I looked up into George's smile. For a time we sat just that way . . . smiling in the darkness. Corny or not, it happens that way, sometimes even in real life.

"What's your story, babe?" he asked finally. "How did you

get to be a private eye? I'm not saying it's wrong, just kind of unusual for a woman to be on her own in the business of sleuthing."

"When I got out of high school, I decided that I would work for a while before going to college to give myself a chance to decide what I wanted an education for. I got a job at an insurance agency. It's one of the few industries where a female who cannot type or take shorthand can hold a position — if she doesn't mind having a tremendous amount of responsibility, not much of a salary, a lot of frustration, and no possibility of advancement."

"Sounds like a fine career for the feeble-minded."

"It is. I wasn't feeble-minded enough, however, to be successful at it. Oh, I tried. I dealt with customers. I dealt with the boss, whose name was on the door and who never tired of reminding us of the fact. Every day was like going to take an algebra test. When anything went wrong, no one tried to fix it. All they cared about was where they could lay the blame."

"I've heard that the White House runs that way, too."

"Indeed, it may. One day something went seriously wrong with a very large account. The boss, whose name was on the door, had neglected to pass a message along about the renewal of a big commercial policy. They had a large claim. They had no coverage. We lost the account, were sued by the former client and I drew the Wilmer."

"What's a Wilmer?"

"Well, you remember the gunsel in 'The Maltese Falcon'?"

"Sure. Elisha Cook."

"OK. Someone had to take the fall to get everyone else off the hook. Bogey suggested giving Wilmer, that was his name, to the police. Sidney Greenstreet, although he loved Wilmer like a son, agreed that he would make the best sacrifice. They gave out a lot of Wilmers during Watergate."

"I understand the concept. So they laid the blame on you."

"Yup. I won an all-expense-paid trip to the unemployment office. My parents offered me an easy-term loan. I took it. I went to college, law school, and passed the bar exam."

"But you don't practice law."

"No, I really didn't want to. Large law firms are stifling and sometimes unethical and private practice is a ticket to starvation."

"And you need tax shelters now?"

"No. I'm still starving. I'm just starving on my own terms."

114

"I like that in a woman." He took my hand in his.

"I do make a living, contrary to popular belief and rumors spread by my mother. I do enough business to get by. It has crossed my mind that I grew up on those great old black and white movies from the forties about hard-boiled private eyes. Possibly that's why all this appeals to me. I'm waiting for it to turn romantic and glamorous."

"We all have our dreams. I wanted to be a movie actor."

"You're kidding."

"No. From the time I understood what movies were, I wanted to be in them."

"But you're a graduate philosophy student."

"Useless. Completely and totally useless in the real world. It started out as a way to get back at my parents who insisted I could not do anything so crass as to work in 'entertainment.' So I picked the most useless degree I could think of to work toward. It got out of hand and now I'm getting a doctorate."

"But," I waved my hand at the screen, "all of this . . .?"

"I still love the industry. Someday if I can get enough money together, I want to produce. Thank God, I'm still in the will." He moved closer.

"Here's to dreams," I said.

We kissed some more. Serious kissing. Then it was late. He drove me home. I would have stayed the night, but he didn't ask me. I didn't press the matter. There was no rush. There would be lots of time.

As if to confirm my thoughts, as I was about to step from the Rolls, George moved toward me, taking my hand. In a passable Bogart imitation he said, "Louie, I got a feeling that this is the beginning of a beautiful friendship."

6.

I felt the satin of my dress. I knew that the deep green color set off my red hair. The coldness of the string of brilliant pearls at my throat was gradually warmed by the fire. People were always amazed when I changed from sea-faring garb, which I wore aboard my father's brigantine ship, into feminine cloth-ing. How, they marveled, could a creature who fought like a man, side by side with the men, become suddenly so much woman? I, for my part, reveled in their wonder. When young, I had learned to be first aboard a captured vessel, for that was

*the way to get the best of the spoils if you were quick and true
with your blade. My weapon shed blood as well as any of the
others. Better, even, for some were cowards and hung back
until the fighting was nearly finished. My thirst for gold was
surely as great as any man's. Now, after the day's victory, I
was the ultimate woman. The rum warmed me. I laughed
easily. Campfire, companionship, food, drink. Happiness was
mine. I was complete.*

And then I saw him.

*I could not see his face clearly. He wore a great broad-
brimmed hat which cast a shadow over his features, but the
way he strode into the noisy camp excited me. Muscular
sailor's thighs covered in calico put lust into my blood. He had
an air of authority that excited me even more than his strong
body. I heard his name spoken by someone I did not see. Jack
Rackham, called Calico Jack. I had heard the blood-thirsty
legend. He came closer, nodded to my father. He turned then
and spoke my name. "Anne Bonney," I heard him say. My
breathing grew difficult. He came closer. At last I saw . . . .*

What I saw was the cracked plaster of my own bedroom
ceiling. Whew, I thought, this thing is really beginning to take
its toll. I'm trying to solve this one after hours. The irritating
thing was that I hadn't gotten a good look at Calico Jack's face
in the dream. It was one more itch in a place I couldn't
scratch. Damn. I hate mysteries. Then I chuckled. That was a
strange thing for a detective to be thinking: if there were no
mysteries, there would be no detectives. Silly me.

I looked at the clock. It was almost time to get up. I had
determined to visit the WOW office to sniff around, but I
wanted to down a cup of coffee in my office first. I can rise in
the a.m., I just don't shine much.

The day was gray, the office was gray, and my thoughts
were turning gray. My hair was getting gray, too. I had noticed
it in the bathroom mirror. I looked at the phone, thinking
about the newest frog. Is there life after custard pie? George
was wildly attractive, painfully rich, fantastically interesting
and well — almost too perfect. I have made a career out of
looking gifts in the mouth. That is probably the single main
reason why I'm still unattached. I sighed. Calico Jack, come
out and play. Two cups of coffee later, I was ready to take on
WOW.

The building was right where we had left it the day before.

I soft-shoed to the elevator, stepped in and pressed the fourth-floor button.

"Catherine Nelson," I announced to the receptionist. "I'm with Case Western Reserve University. We were wondering if your little organization would like to take out some ads in the sports programs?" Now was the time to find out if they knew who I was. I was fairly certain that they wouldn't kill me outright. Not here, anyway.

She seemed to buy my act, talked briefly to someone on the phone and nodded in the direction of the inner office. A dignified-looking woman sat behind a desk surveying me as I entered. She stood up, reached across the desk and shook my hand. "I'm Helen Gottschalk."

Suddenly I become totally stupid. I hadn't expected this. "My mother's name is Helen," I announced brilliantly. I like to believe that I was playing for time, but the truth of the matter is that I was shocked into idiocy because I never expected to start at the top of the pyramid.

"Sit," she said.

"Freedom is not a cheap commodity to be easily gained by empty rhetoric." I took her measure as she talked. She was impressive. About forty, graying hair cut severely short. Brown eyes behind minimally corrective lenses that did not detract from the intelligence. And something else, something more elusive.

"The fight for freedom is long, hard, and sometimes brutal. Cruelty can be a tool. It can be used to pay debts and to gain attention. Ms. Lewis, we have known about you from the beginning. We have ways of gathering information. Do you understand what I am telling you?"

"Yes, ma'am." I would try brass. "Of course, you know who I am. Did you identify yourself to Felix Goodman before you had him killed? Did he know why he died? I don't think so. You keep secrets. Well, your secrets are about to become known." I rose and reached the door as she raised her voice just slightly.

"You're putting yourself in danger, Ms. Lewis. Don't continue with this." I glanced back. She was shuffling papers as if I were already gone. I decided to ruminate on the meaning of her last remark later, elsewhere, somewhere that felt a little safer.

As I passed the receptionist, she smiled cheerfully. "Have a nice day," she cooed. I never liked that line.

"I have other plans," I shot back. My first real murder case
. . . and I was scared witless.

7.

I crossed the street to a neighborhood greasy spoon. I
ordered coffee. It came saucerless. No Frills Cafe. There are
better places to drink coffee. There is better coffee. However,
there was no better place to watch the building that housed
Helen Gottschalk's office. After three swallows, yesterday's
Amazon showed up coming out of the building.

"How much for the coffee?" I called to the drill sergeant
dressed as a waitress.

She ambled over to me and looked pointedly down at the
cup. "You didn't like it?"

"It was ambrosia. How much?"

"You didn't drink much."

"I'll drink two cups next time. I've got to go now." My
quarry was getting away.

"Fifty cents," she said after thinking it over. I threw three
quarters on the counter and made like a bunny for the door.
If you don't tip, they remember you.

The woman was still in sight when I hit the street, getting
into some late model blue Ford. Luckily my car was parked
nearby, so I was right behind her in a matter of seconds.

I was so busy concentrating on not losing the blue car in
the dozens of other vehicles on the street (doesn't anybody
have a day job?), I didn't recognize the part of town she was
leading me to. She pulled into a driveway. I pulled off the road
just beyond the driveway. I turned around, took a look, and
suppressed a scream. I had gone up that very same driveway
the previous evening. Loose ends threatened to tie themselves
up in a most unpleasant knot. A lover's knot, to be exact. The
house belonged to George Armitage.

Maybe, I thought, there was some simple explanation. No.
Even as I shivered at the memory of the way he kissed me, I
knew he was a fox in frog's clothing, this George Armitage.
Tears blurred my vision momentarily. I watched the blue Ford
pull out of the driveway in my rearview mirror. I didn't have
the heart to follow. Not professional, I hear you say? True. Did
it make a difference that I knew I was behaving like a child?
Not one damned bit. And, just to be consistent, I was about to

118

do something even more unprofessional and childish. I was going to confront Mr. Ivy League Philosophy Student.

I stomped up the driveway and pushed the doorbell button. Some of Ma's blind dates turned out to be dogs, some had turned out to be stupid, but this was the worst ringer she'd come up with yet.

He opened the door. I looked at that gorgeous kisser. It was an old Bogart flick again. He was good. He was very good. I knew I'd have a few bad nights. I wanted to laugh and cry at the same time, it was so absurd.

I came right to the point. "The female who was just here. Who was she?"

"That was no female," he laughed. "That was my sister."

"Your —?"

"Sister. You know, sibling? Same mother and all that? My sister, Betty."

"She sure doesn't look at all like you." I felt he was lying. His smile was too smooth.

"What is this?" he asked, looking mildly annoyed. "If she were my girlfriend, I'd tell you. We've only had one date, you know. My mother was married twice. Betty is my half-sister. We have different last names, too. Hers is Noire."

"OK. I'll buy who she is. What concerns me, George, is who she's involved with."

"Look, come into the living room. No point standing in a draft." I followed him. If she was his sister, it didn't necessarily mean that he was involved in the same activities. Or that he even knew about them. Still it seemed an odd coincidence.

"Now," he said, sitting on the couch, motioning me to an overstuffed chair, "what's this all about?"

I sat, took a deep breath and went for it. "George, the young woman who just left here attacked me yesterday in the lobby of my building. She's made threatening phone calls and she was at the scene of Calico Jack's latest send-off. He is some nut who's running around carving people up because he thinks he's a guy who's been dead a couple of hundred years. After she attacked me, I followed her to a woman who I have good reason to believe is controlling this psycho. These people are terrorists, George. They believe in using violence to get attention. Now tell me what your sister, Betty, would be doing in this kind of company."

He said nothing, just stood, took my elbow, and pointed toward the door.

"I think you had better leave now. I think you have a vivid imagination. You have mistaken Betty for someone else." When we reached the foyer, he opened the door. "I'll call you," he said as he shoved me out the door. Like hell, you will, I thought. If I had had any doubts, they vanished as I looked into his eyes. I saw nothing. Easy come, easy go . . . back to the pond for another try, Livia.

The confrontation had, of course, been thoroughly stupid. I had now warned everyone. I had probably blown the whole case from hell to Sunday. Best thing I could do now was call the cops, tell them everything I knew, and gracefully retire from the fray. Who wanted to be Sam Spade, anyway?

The more I thought about the way he pushed me out of the house, the angrier I got. I sat in the car and thought. I hate being taken in. And I hate being taken advantage of. Most of all, I hate the humiliation of thinking that someone is sitting somewhere laughing at me. Since I'd probably blown it anyway, could it hurt to go back and tell the creep what I thought of him? Back up the driveway I marched.

He must not have latched the door, because it was standing open. Never one to stand on ceremony, I walked in. I heard voices coming from the living room. Finally, my P.I. instincts kicked in. I crept to the door to listen. George was talking to a woman. I didn't recognize her voice.

"Well, Goddamnit, Frieda, you guys promised me a lot of money to go through this charade. Nobody told me I was gonna have to do this kind of confrontation. I mean, I liked her well enough. We had a lot in common."

"Right," the female voice shot back. "You're a nice guy. You just need a little more money to produce a movie. Mr. Nice Guy."

"You didn't say anything about murder. Or kidnapping."

"Those turkeys deserved to die. Helen's attorney got her locked up in a nuthouse. The college kid was a witness to a rape and refused to testify. And Mr. Corporate Executive got Betty pregnant and wouldn't even pay for an abortion. They got what they deserved. The jeweler was an accident. Jack got a little carried away with his new weapon."

"Well when did kidnapping get to be part of this story?"

"Look, you didn't ask a lot of questions until now. The money was all you cared about. We've decided a hostage will make that money easier to get. She's the best hostage so far. She's too nosy for her own good."

"I don't like it."

"You like her, that's your problem."

"No, it's just —"

"Armitage, I'm leaving now. You're in this and you're going to play it out." I stepped back from the door and hid in the shadows, holding my breath. They walked right past me. Frieda was a uniformed policewoman. More things crashed into place. They had someone right in the police department.

I watched him let her out, praying he wouldn't turn around and look right at me. Fortunately, he turned and went up the stairs. I got myself out of there as quickly as I could without attracting attention.

Apparently I was going to be the target of a kidnapping. I didn't dare go home or back to the office. I checked into a small motel not too far from downtown. Nobody seemed to be following me. They didn't know that I knew. I tried to call Tom but got no answer. I had a couple of drinks, went to bed, and slept badly.

Early the next morning, I picked up a copy of *The Plain Dealer*. Scanning the front page, I saw that my kidnapping worries had been premature. The ladies of WOW had made their announcement during the night. More men would die. They were at war. Calico Jack was their field marshal. They had kidnapped a reporter and were holding him hostage.

Kidnapped a reporter? Could it be Tom? I felt as if I'd swallowed a stone. I flew to the pay phone in the motel lobby. There was an assistant editor at *The Plain Dealer* I knew. "The reporter who was kidnapped by the WOW people, who was it?"

"I don't know if I can tell you, Livia. The man's life is certainly in danger. The cops are real hairy about giving out information."

I had to know. "I'm involved, Ray. You've got to tell me."

"Livia, we don't want to put him in any worse —"

"Dammit, Ray, I have to know. It's Tom, isn't it? Tom Jennings?" Please let me be wrong.

"Take it easy, Livia . . . OK . . . it is Tom. They grabbed him late last night. They called us and we talked to him." He paused. "Uh, Livia?"

"Yes," I whispered.

"Don't do anything silly, huh?" He didn't know that I already had. "He'll be all right. The cops will handle it." They sure hadn't so far.

121

"Right. Thanks, Ray." This was great. While I had been looking in another direction, my best friend had been snatched by the bad guys. So far I had really messed this whole thing up. I went back to the office hoping something brilliant would occur to me. The next move turned out to be simple. The phone rang as I walked in. I understood how to answer a phone. Maybe I could become a receptionist.

"Lewis," I said into it.

"Livia?"

"Tom! Where are you? Are you all right?"

"Liv, dear, listen carefully." I heard another voice in the background. Female. "They tell me I've got to make this quick. Please, luv, forget your involvement in this affair. You'll be safer. These people are killers. All of them." Did I really hear someone laugh in the background? "Are you listening, Livia?"

"Yes, I . . . is there anything I can do? Anything, darling. Just say."

"There are two things. You can call me 'darling' again and, if you get to the palace, say hello to the queen." The line went dead. The palace? That was a bizarre remark. Maybe it meant something. It was too weird not to be some sort of clue. I lit a smoke and let my mind wander. What had he been trying to tell me?

I called Chief Beardsley, pouring out all of the information I had. I left out the palace thing. It was obviously meant for me. Bearsdley thanked me, even sounding sincere. "I hope you get them," I said. "They're giving feminism a real bad name."

"We will. And your friend will be OK. Don't worry." He wasn't all that bad for a police chief and a male chauvinist.

So I figured I had done what duty required. Now how was I going to find Tom? The business about the palace was making me crazy. Tom never made a lot out of the fact that he was British. It wasn't his style. Palace? What did I know about palaces? The big one, of course. If you're talking about the queen, it's Buckingham Palace. Buckingham? It clicked. A year or so ago, when we had been dating, Tom and I had done a lot of driving around Cleveland Heights. It was an activity we could afford. We had laughed about all of the British street names like Coventry and Surrey and the Victorian architecture was a treat that we never tired of. There had been a marvelous old apartment building on one of those streets called The Buckingham. We said it was probably where the queen stayed when she came to Cleveland.

Twenty minutes later, I was parked out in front of The Buckingham. I stepped into the entryway and hit the buzzer marked Custodian. "Yes?" the intercom crackled.

"I need to talk to someone about a tenant."

"We don't have a tent."

"No . . . no, a tenant," I pronounced carefully.

"Oh. You're a tenant. Lose your key?"

"Look, could I just talk to you for a minute?"

"You want to come in? Just use your key."

"I don't have a key."

"Lost it, did you?"

"No . . . I . . . just buzz me in, please."

"Wait a second, I'll just buzz you in."

After a while the buzzer sounded and I stepped through the door. He was standing in the doorway at the bottom of the stairs, adjusting what I was certain was a hearing aid. "Do you live here?" he asked, obviously bewildered to see a total stranger.

"No, I don't." He looked relieved. "I want to ask about someone who might. I notice there are no names on the mail slots, just numbers."

"Yup. Protects people's privacy."

"Does Helen Gottschalk or Betty Noire live in this building?" He answered so swiftly, he probably didn't notice the contradiction about privacy protection.

"Oh, sure, the Noire woman lives in apartment 5. She sure is a tall one . . . ." He was about to go on, but I turned to go up the steps, so he merely said, "A little strange, that one."

I was in front of apartment 5. I knocked on the door. No response. I tried the knob. Oddly, it was open. On entering I could see why. Someone had left in a hurry. Things were scattered everywhere. I had missed them.

OK, don't panic, I told myself. You're a detective, so detect where they went. On the coffee table I discovered a pile of literature about a group of islands on Lake Erie. They were a popular summer resort. It looked to me like a great place for a pirate camp. It was a hunch, but it was better than nothing. I went home, threw some things in a bag and was off.

8.

I drove until I reached Route 90, which I knew would take me in the direction of Port Clinton. There I could board an old Ford tri-motor plane called the Tin Goose and make the eight-minute trip to Put In Bay on South Bass Island.

I figured to cover the distance to Port Clinton, some seventy miles or so straight out on Route 90 in a couple of hours. Dodging big trucks and the usual contingent of crazy people who should never have been issued licenses kept me busy until I got to Sandusky.

I pulled off the highway in search of lunch. It was only another ten miles to Port Clinton and the Tin Goose flew every hour. The hostess at the Harbor Restaurant sat me down by a big bay window. The sun that had earlier warmed the day was gone. The sky was now a deep shade of gray. I ordered lunch which arrived fifteen minutes later, followed closely by George Armitage. I'll be dipped, I thought. This guy's got all kinds of nerve. He seated himself across from me. "George, what the heck are you doing here?"

"I'd like to say following you, but unfortunately it wouldn't be true. I have an aunt who lives near here. I was on my way to visit and thought I'd stop for lunch." Yeah. Coincidence again. "What brings you here?"

"My battered, but faithful MG, actually. With the help of good old Route 90, of course. The truth is I'm working."

"Oh?"

"Yes." For the first time I took a really good look at this guy with my faculties intact. Was he following me? Or worse, was I following him? Why were we headed in the same direction? "Yes, I've got a missing persons case that has been dragging out for quite a while. I'm really going over ground I've covered before in case I missed anything."

He bought it. I saw him relax. He thought I was stupid. I had, in fact, been stupid. I was better now. Stupid detective, one; frog, nothing.

"Can I see you for lunch tomorrow?" the Swamp Thing asked innocently. "We have to talk about what happened yesterday."

"Sure thing. Call me tonight."

I watched as he left the restaurant. It as a dead give-away. People who come to a restaurant to eat usually stay and eat. He hadn't been in the dining room when I arrived. Now he was leaving. This place didn't do carry out. I threw a few bills on the table, following him at a discreet distance. I hit the parking lot just in time to see him get into a 12-passenger van. I recognized two of the other occupants, a very tall woman and a kidnapped journalist. Looking closer, I noted one other person who stood out. His identity was immediately apparent. Hair, beard, the light glinting off of a gold earring. Calico Jack on vacation from some home or other.

As the van pulled onto the highway, I jumped into my faithful car, turned the key and got no response whatsoever. Now what? I opened the car's bonnet. I'm no expert, but I knew that all of those things should have been connected to something. Of course I should have expected that they'd try to slow me down in case I'd been chasing them.

By the time I hoofed it to the nearest gas station and brought back Mr. Goodwrench (who sneered at me, thinking God knows what, then reconnected the disconnected), it was getting late. Since everyone was so far ahead of me now, I thought of doing something I should have done earlier. I found a pay phone, told the operator to charge the call to my office number and dialed my parents' home.

"Hello"

"Hi, Pop."

"Livia, how nice." He meant this. He is a sincere, if housebroken, man.

"Can I talk to Ma for a minute?"

"Certainly." My father is not what you would call a communicative man. He lets Ma do all the talking. "Livia?"

"Yeah, Ma . . . uh . . ."

"Call the newspapers. My daughter actually picked up a phone and called her mother."

"Ma."

"This is a first, isn't it, Livia? Shouldn't we at least alert the press?"

"Ma, stop a minute. I gotta ask you a question."

"My permission to marry that nice young man from the other night? You've got it. When's the wedding?"

"Well, not exactly, but this is about George Armitage."

"You want to live together first? Well, I guess I would survive. As long as you marry before the babies come."

And she wonders why I never call. "Ma, this is a toll call, I can't afford to let you guess the question. George Armitage is not a nice person. He's mixed up in at least four murders and one kidnapping." That got me some silence. "How well do you know his parents?"

"I don't know."

"What do you mean you don't know?"

"Well, actually I don't remember them at all."

"Then how did the little dinner happen?"

"I was in the grocery store when George came up and asked me if I were Helen Lewis. I said I was and he said we had met in Connecticut where his parents live. You remember when we took that vacation? Well, I met an awful lot of people that time, so I figured I just didn't remember. And he seemed so nice, intelligent and polite —"

"How'd the dinner get arranged?"

"He said, hadn't I mentioned a daughter that I was very proud of. I said I had and one thing led to another and he was free that night so when I got home I called you and —"

"The rest is history. I gotta go."

I hung up before she could take a deep breath to start anew. Obviously Officer Frieda had swung immediately into action as soon as it looked like someone knowledgeable might be getting involved. I marveled at the speed with which they had assembled their little plan.

"OK," I muttered, getting in the car, "we're really on our way now."

9.

I finally arrived at Island Airlines and bought a ticket. "Are you sure Amelia Earhart started out this way?" I joked, boarding the small plane. No one laughed. They were a long eight minutes, but we landed safely on South Bass Island.

Where to start? What to look for? There wasn't much light left. I spotted the island lighthouse nearby. An excellent place for someone to have noticed anything out of the ordinary. I walked to the structure and pressed the doorbell. The door opened. Good heavens — first Lon Chaney at the museum, now Boris Karloff at the lighthouse.

I had the urge to scream, "It's alive," and run. I controlled it. I get these urges. If you watch a lot of movies, your hold on reality occasionally becomes just a teensy bit fuzzy.

"Yes?" His voice wasn't as scary as I had anticipated. I got my mouth in gear.

"I'm Susan B. Anthony from the North Coast Marketing Survey Group," I fibbed rapidly, "and I was wondering if you could spare a few moments to answer some questions." He thought it over.

"Well, I suppose. I mean I really don't have what you'd call a crowded schedule. Come in." He withdrew his bulk into the doorway. Apparently he had decided that I wasn't dangerous. He led me to a good-sized, seriously nautical, living room. From the ship's wheel over the mantel to the luxury liner spittoon in the corner, this room was about the sea. I took out my notebook and sat down in the captain's chair he motioned me to. I watched his large frame settle into a matching chair. His head really was somewhat square.

"Now," I took out my pen, "what's your name?"

"Douglas. Douglas Victor."

"Ah, two first names, eh? Probably caused a lot of confusion over the years." He stared at me. I tried again.

"So, Doug, tell me about yourself." The floodgate opened and Douglas Victor gave me a detailed picture of his life, starting with genesis. A veritable glut of information, all of it pretty boring.

After about twenty minutes I knew I was going to have to stem the tide or I would be there for weeks. "Gee, that's great, Doug, but I've got another appointment and I'm going to have to run. So, just tell me how long you've been playing this lighthouse gig?"

"About six years. And I can tell you . . . ." I bet he could.

"Whoa, Doug, listen, could you show me the actual light? I've never sen the inside of one of these things." I ignored the renewed stream of information as we climbed the stairs. This really had been what I was after. From the top of the lighthouse, you could see all over the islands. Something immediately caught my eye.

"What's that small woodsy island over there?"

"That's Bob."

"The island is named Bob?"

"Yeah. Nobody ever got around to naming it. I think it's got like a land parcel number. There's nothing much there. Nobody ever goes there. But it's there and I see it all the time, so I named it Bob."

"Uh huh." Does Mike Hammer run into stuff like this? Is the world filled with comedians? I tried to come up with the best way to ask the next question.

"Doug . . . you see that good-sized yacht moored right near Bob?" I felt silly calling a place by a persons' name.

"Oh, yes, ma'am. Lighthouse keeper's got to have good eyesight."

"Right. Well, do you have any idea who that boat might belong to? Have there been any strangers hanging around who seem, well, different?"

"Gosh, I really wouldn't know." He looked slightly embarrassed. "I don't get out much."

"OK, Doug. I'll be going now."

"By the way," he asked as we reached the front door, "What is it that your company does?"

"Demographics, Doug. We're researching the feasibility of someone opening a new kind of store on the island."

"What kind of store?"

I thought quickly. Nothing came to mind. I opened my mouth. "Fondue pots. They want to sell fondue pots, Doug." That's what came out.

"Fondue pots?"

"Yup. Fondues R Us." I left quickly.

10.

They were here, all right. Unless I missed my guess, it was their boat anchored off Bob. A check with the Chamber of Commerce told me that to get to Bob (yes, everybody called it that), I had to cross the island and rent a boat. In order to cross the island, I would have to rent a bicycle. I could also rent a bicycling outfit if I wanted. I had no choice. There were very few cars on the island and no public transportation of any kind. I rented the bike, practiced staying on the damned thing and I was off.

As I passed the lighthouse, I looked up. There was Douglas Victor, namer of islands, waving from his little balcony. It was a lonely wave. I didn't know if it was his lonely life that made him such a non-stop talker or if it was the other way around, but I waved back and silently wished him well.

Thanks to good directions, it took no time at all to locate the shop that rented outboard motor boats. "You rent boats, right?" I asked the old man who stood in the doorway.

"Yup."

"Can I rent one?"

"I reckon."

"How much?"

"For how long?"

"Couple days."

"Well . . . ." He scratched his chin.

I had had just about enough local color. "Sir, no offense, but could we wrap up this negotiation during my lifetime?"

"You ain't a tourist, then, Miss?"

"No. I'm a private investigator and I've got to get to this island over there pronto." Sometimes the truth works.

"Gee, I'm sorry. I thought . . .well, you know, tourists like a little eccentricity, so I sort of play this character. Boat's fifteen dollars a day. You better carry extra gas. No gas stations over there."

Arrangements concluded, I hopped into my rented conveyance and headed for the island everyone called Bob. We'd had a summer place on a small lake when I was a kid, and it didn't take me long to remember how to run the boat. I figured I could play Treasure Island with the best of them.

Fortunately, the equipment that came with the boat included a big flashlight. Before long, I pulled the boat ashore and crept toward the wooded area beyond the beach. I melted quietly through the trees toward a flickering light which I hoped was a campfire.

In a few minutes, I came to a large clearing containing several Quonset huts, and indeed there was a campfire. I heard a man laugh as I crept closer. Looking out through the foliage I saw a cheery scene. There was Helen Gottschalk, dressed in army camouflage fatigues. Next was Frieda, who had abandoned her police uniform for jeans and a sweatshirt. And, of course, my old friend, Betty Noire, in black leather pants and a jacket to match. Last of all, Calico Jack II. Dressed entirely in pirate garb, cutlass at his side, he seemed not to notice that he was an anachronism. I strained to hear what they were saying.

"Aye, I was a lost man until you lassies gave me purpose. My great, thirsty knife will not be quenched so long as ye have need. Tell me who have offended ye and they shall die."

I didn't see Tom anywhere. One of the huts was set farther away from the others, so while Jack had everyone's attention, I darted toward it. It wasn't empty. Much better than that. It had Tom in it. He was very efficiently tied up.

"Are you all right?" I whispered, leaning close to him.

"Yes. What are you doing here?"

"Rescuing you, you dope."

"How did you get here?"

"Why are you making small talk? Tell me about Jack." I fumbled with the knots, but it seemed useless. I needed a knife.

"His real name's Charles Perkins. They nabbed him from the place where Helen Gottschalk spent her time. I guess she got to know him there and charmed him. The doctors were convinced he was harmless. Helen thought otherwise. She was right. He really thinks he's Jack Rackham. He talks about Anne Bonney. He's waiting for her to come back."

There was a pile of women's clothing in the corner. It gave me an idea. "Listen," I said to Tom. "Sometimes we forget who our friends are. Armitage turned out to be in on this whole thing. They were originally going to let me play hostage."

"I know. They came looking for you at your office. I convinced them that I would be a suitable designated hostage."

"What were you doing in my office?"

"Waiting for you. I was worried about you."

"Oh, swell. Well, I think I can get us out of here and eliminate these crazies. You just stay put."

"Not much else I can do." He nodded in the direction of the rope which bound his hands and feet.

I quickly assembled the more colorful items of discarded clothing and put them on. The effect was gypsyish, but it would do. I stuck my pistol in the band of the skirt, gave Tom a quick kiss on the cheek, and was off to catch a pirate.

I concealed myself in the shadows. It was very dark now, a moonless night with only the last vestiges of the campfire giving any light at all. There was no activity in the clearing. I looked around and spotted Charles Perkins standing at the edge of the woods. He was alone. Perfect. I circled around until I was almost in front of him.

"Jack," I called softly. He looked directly at me and started to walk slowly in my direction. His face was a foot away from mine. Even in the almost total darkness I could see the glitter of madness in those eyes. I prayed my voice wouldn't crack.

"Don't you remember me, Jack? It's Anne. I was as good a sailor and as fine a fighter as ever served aboard a ship." His eyes peered at me curiously. I could feel his breath on my face. I continued.

"If you do not fight like men, you shall die like dogs. I told you that one time. Remember, Jack, when you discovered I was a woman in masquerade? The nights aboard my father's ship? Feasting in camp? We were a team, weren't we? Always in front, first at the spoils." I forced myself to laugh. I didn't want to shoot this poor demented creature. I gave it one last push.

"You loved me, Jack . . . ." That did it. The crazy slob broke. He fell to his knees, kissing my hand, sobbing.

"You've come back. They told me you would if I proved I was worthy."

Those were the only words I heard him speak as I brought my knee up under his chin with all of the force I could muster.

"Ugh," he said and was out cold.

"Ouch," I said, rubbing my knee. It never looked that painful in the movies.

It was at that point that my old friend, Betty Noire, made her appearance. She was probably searching for Perkins, but before she could take in what had happened, my gun was out.

"Hold it right there, Noire. And don't even think about yelling. You'd be dead and I'd be hidden in these woods before you could say 'Calico Jack.'"

To her credit, she understood. I made her drag Perkins into the nearest hut, and I gagged and bound her with some of the scarves I'd been wearing. I did the same with Jack after I'd relieved him of the beautiful dagger that he had been sporting. It looked like the one in the police photo. Israel Chance had duplicated his own original work exactly.

All that remained now was to get to Helen Gottschalk and Frieda. As I tried to decide how to deal with them, there was a powerful commotion in the woods. A loud voice, enhanced by a bullhorn, bellowed, "Throw down your weapons!" and a light blazed in the clearing.

By the time I got there, at least fifteen uniformed police officers were surrounding Helen and Frieda.

"Chief Beardsley," I said as I strolled out of the shadows."

"Where —?" he began.

"There are only two others. One of them's your killer. They're trussed up like Thanksgiving dinner in that hut over there. You followed me?"

"You left more than breadcrumbs, lady. You cut a swath. Wherever you go, they remember you."

"Chief, there's a guy on the mainland — George . . . ."

"We got him already. He was driving a van registered to Ms. Gottschalk. I never saw anyone so eager to confess . . . and to implicate everyone else."

"Well, then, if you'll excuse me, I have a rescue to complete." I gave him a mock salute with the dagger.

"That's evidence," he grumped.

"I'll take as much care of it as you would yourself, sir." I winked at him.

Tom was obviously relieved when I opened the door of the hut. It only took a few seconds to cut through the ropes with the dagger.

"Presto," I said. "You're free."

"Not altogether, I think," he replied. I tried not to understand what he meant.

"So, my friend, shall we get off this miserable island? I know a place where they serve really strong coffee and absolutely no seafood whatsoever."

"Sounds good to me," he said, smiling. "And thanks for the rescue."

"Anytime. After all, what are friends for? It's an even deal. I had my case and you have your story."

Faces of Fear

Carol Costa

The press called him the Midnight Strangler. He had already murdered five women. Now he was staring into the eyes of his next victim. She was perfect, exactly what he was looking for.

Both she and her companion stepped out of the elevator with him. The woman with the light brown curls and hazel eyes smiled and extended her hand to him. "Hi, I'm Dana Sloan. Didn't we meet at The Stewart Gallery last week?"

"Oh, yes, Miss Sloan." Gingerly, he took her slender hand in his. "How nice to see you again."

"So, how are you?" Dana asked.

"I'm sorry, but I'm in a terrible rush. I'm late for an appointment."

"Oh, sure. Nice to see you again," Dana said.

The tall, muscular young man walked off quickly, leaving Dana and her secretary, Marianne, staring after him.

"Thanks for introducing me," Marianne said sarcastically. "Who was he anyway?"

"I don't know." Dana laughed. "I'm sure I met him at the gallery, but I'll be darned if I can remember his name."

"Then why did you say anything to him?"

"Because I was embarrassed. Didn't you see the way he was staring at me?"

"Oh, I thought he was looking at me."

Dana laughed again. "You're probably right. Come on, we'll be late, and Clarice will write nasty things about us in her column."

The two women walked out of the huge office building that housed the newspaper that employed them. They hurried down the street to a nearby restaurant.

Clarice was already seated in a high-backed booth, sipping a glass of wine. She waved at them, producing a perfect smile that was dazzling against her flawless, ebony complexion.

133

"As usual, she looks like she stepped out of *Vogue*," Marianne whispered as they crossed over to the table. "I hate her."

Dana shook her head, amused by her secretary's remark. Marianne never seemed aware of her own striking good looks. A natural redhead with emerald green eyes, Marianne had a face that belonged in an Ivory Soap commercial.

"I'm so glad you could come," Clarice said, as Dana and Marianne slid into the booth.

"You sounded so secretive on the phone," Dana answered. "Is something wrong?"

Clarice put a finger to her red lips. "Let's order first, shall we?" Using the same finger, Clarice motioned for the waiter to approach their table. He sprang forward instantly as if he were waiting for her command.

With their lunch order in the kitchen, and their wine glasses filled, Clarice was now ready to explain her mysterious lunch invitation.

"I need your help, Dana. I asked you to bring Marianne along so she could take notes for you."

"Notes? I didn't bring my steno book, Clarice," Marianne said impatiently.

"What is the problem, Clarice?" Dana asked with a touch of annoyance. Leave it to Clarice to make this a big production, Dana thought. She probably wants me to verify one of her gossip column rumors.

Over the last five years, Dana Sloan had become one of the city's most respected investigators. With the power and resources of *The Globe* to back her up, Dana had earned a reputation for getting to the truth. One of the drawbacks of having such a reputation was that people burdened her with all sorts of requests for help, requests that were sometimes trivial and time consuming. Convinced that Clarice was about to take advantage of their friendship, Dana's mouth fell open in surprise when Clarice stated the reason for their meeting.

"My niece was the Midnight Strangler's last victim. I want you to investigate the murder. I'll pay anything you ask."

"Clarice, I'm so sorry. I didn't know," Dana said.

"Your niece was that beautiful black model who was found in the park?" Marianne asked sadly.

Clarice nodded then turned and looked directly at Dana. "I want you to find her killer. LaVonne was my sister's only child. Delia's still in shock. She hasn't uttered a word since

134

LaVonne's death." Her voice broke and her eyes filled with tears. Then as quickly as they appeared, Clarice blinked them away and continued in a low, angry tone. "Whoever did this must be stopped before he kills again. Five beautiful, young women have been murdered and he's still walking the streets. He's probably out looking for his next victim right now."

"Clarice, have you spoken to the police? Surely, they must have some clues. For all you know, they may be very close to solving the case."

"The police are nowhere on this case, Dana. That's why I came to you."

"I don't usually get involved in murder cases of this magnitude. The police have an entire team of detectives working on this."

"But you will try? Please?"

Back at the office, Dana and Marianne went over every detail *The Globe* had printed about the five murders.

The dead girls had been found in various locations around the city. In each case, the police were called at midnight by a man, who told them where the victim's body could be found.

"There has to be a common link," Dana said, thinking out loud. "Some small thread that will tie it all together. I'd like you to make up a chart on the victims. List their hair color, height, weight, occupations, whatever information you can find, so we can study and compare."

"I'll work it up right away," Marianne promised, as Dana stood up and slipped the strap of her handbag over her shoulder. "Where are you going?"

"To see Bruno."

"Is he assigned to the case?"

"I don't know, but it doesn't matter. Bruno knows everything that goes on in that squad room."

Dana left the building once more, unaware that the sandy-haired man from the elevator was watching her from across the street. He ran his tongue across his upper lip. He felt excited, anxious to get on with it. But he knew he must be careful, move slowly so as not to scare his victim.

Perhaps he could arrange an innocent meeting, like the one on the elevator this morning. Then again, maybe he could just walk into her office and ask Dana Sloan to investigate something for him.

The last girl had been so easy. A chance encounter at the

gallery as she admired one of his paintings. He remembered the way the smile on Lavonne's face had later dissolved into silent terror. He smiled, his blue eyes squinting in the sunlight as they followed Dana to her car and watched her drive away.

There's lots of time, he cautioned himself again. In a few days, he would have her, and she would be even more beautiful, more stimulating, than the others.

The downtown police station was in its usual state of uproar. An assortment of crooks and derelicts were being shoved through the booking process by uniformed policemen. In the crowded area outside Bruno's office victims waited to be interviewed. Their faces reflected bewilderment at the paperwork and red tape that caused the arm of the law to move so slowly.

Detective Al Bruno was at his desk, hunched over a thick stack of papers, sipping coffee from a styrofoam cup.

"Hi, big guy," Dana said with true affection in her voice. "Can I talk you into buying me a real cup of coffee?"

Bruno's massive shoulders straightened, bringing his head to an upright position. In an instant he was on his feet, wrapping his arms around Dana in an enthusiastic bear hug that trapped her against his broad chest and left her breathless with laughter.

"What are you doing here?" Bruno asked as her released her.

"I came to see you, what else?" she replied.

"Sure. I haven't seen you for six months, not even one lousy phone call, and all of a sudden, you just stopped for tea, right?"

Dana grinned up at him. "No, coffee."

"Okay, you got it." Bruno yelled to the guy at the next desk to take his calls and ushered Dana out of the station house to a small coffee shop across the street.

Bruno's dark eyes looked black as he studied Dana across the table. "I guess you've been too busy to call, huh?"

"Bruno, the phone lines work both ways. You haven't called me either."

"Yes, I have. I dialed your number a thousand times."

"That's funny. I never got any of those calls."

"Because I hung up before you answered." His ruggedly handsome face looked wistfully sad. Dana reached across the

136

table and patted his hand, as if she were comforting a small child.

"For such a big brute, you are such a chicken," she said.

"When it comes to you, I'm a mound of jello. Like I told you, when you're ready to pick up where we left off, you call me or, better yet, come by and invite me for coffee."

"Oh, Bruno." Dana felt frustrated. "Why can't we just be friends?"

"I get it. Today's not your lucky day, Bruno. Okay, honey, what did you stop by for?" He attempted a smile, but somehow it only made him look a little sadder.

"Do you remember Clarice Walker, the gossip columnist?"

"The attractive black woman with a smile that could melt a glacier?"

"Right. Well, she's asked me to investigate the murder of her niece, LaVonne Burton."

"Hey, hold on, sweets, that's one of the Strangler's victims."

"I know. Please, Bruno, I need some information." Their coffee arrived and Bruno concentrated on stirring sugar into his cup.

"Come on, Bruno," Dana pleaded. "Don't go into one of your moods on me."

"You know I'm not allowed to discuss a case with an outsider."

"I didn't think I was an outsider, at least not with you."

"You can't get involved in this one, Dana. It's too dangerous."

"Look, what if I promise you that whatever leads I come up with, I'll share with you."

"You won't make a move on your own? Promise me."

"I promise," Dana said solemnly.

Dana took notes as Bruno reluctantly told her what the police knew about the Midnight Strangler. When he finished, Dana looked at him with obvious disappointment. Two things were written on her pad. The man had light hair, and there had been traces of chalk dust found on one of the victims.

"What about the chalk dust? What kind was it?" Dana asked.

"As near as we can tell, it's the stuff artists sketch with, but none of the victims had any known contact with artists. Even the model, Clarice's niece, worked only with photographers."

"Marianne is making up a chart on the victims," Dana told him."

"Looking for the common link? Well, there isn't any. Two of the women were Caucasian, one blond, one brunette. The other victims were Asian, Hispanic, and black. It seems our killer likes variety. I wish there was more to tell you, Dana. Unfortunately, we have no other leads, which makes this case all the more frightening."

In the next few days, Dana began to follow the same route the police were taking. She and Cliff, one of the investigators who worked for her, made the rounds of all the shops that sold artist supplies, as well as the local art schools and galleries.

Their efforts were fruitless. No one remembered seeing any of the victims and without a description of the killer it was impossible to connect the Midnight Strangler with the art world.

A week passed and Dana reported to Clarice that she had no new leads on the man who murdered her niece.

"There must be something," Clarice insisted over another half-eaten lunch.

"The only piece of evidence that's turned up is that the murderer might have had artist's chalk on his hands. But then the police have questioned the families and friends of the girls and none of them have been able to connect the victims with an artist of any type."

A glimmer of hope flashed in Clarice's eyes. "Artists' chalk? The police never questioned me about that. They may have asked Delia, but she wouldn't have known. It was going to be a surprise . . . ."

Dana sat forward in her chair. "Clarice, this could be very important. Take your time, let the details surface in your mind, and tell me everything you can remember."

"I'd forgotten all about it." Clarice pressed her fingers against her forehead, willing her mind to accurately recall her niece's words. "Delia's birthday is next month, and LaVonne wanted to surprise her mother with a portrait. She said she was going to visit some of the galleries to inspect the work of local artists."

"Did she mention any particular gallery?"

"No, I'm sure she didn't, but wait, she did say something else. It was a joke. She made a joke about finding a realistic

138

artist with a good supply of black paint."

Dana left Clarice and went directly to The Stewart Gallery. A bizarre theory was forming in her head, and she needed Noel Stewart's help to work it out.

"Dana darling, back again so soon?" Noel greeted her in his phony effeminate voice. Dana knew for a fact that Noel was not gay, but for some reason it was the image he liked to project.

"Your gallery only represents realistic artists, am I right?" Dana asked as she returned Noel's token caress.

"Absolutely. None of that abstract junk will ever hang here."

"I know a lot of your artists discuss their paintings with you. In the past few months, has anyone talked about doing a painting on death?"

Noel's face turned a little pale. "You're still on that thing about the Strangler being an artist, aren't you? Well, my dear, I assure you that no one associated with this gallery is a murderer."

"I'm just trying to work out a theory. Humor me, please."

Noel shuddered uncomfortably and thought about Dana's question for a few minutes before answering. "The only one I can think of is Juergen Jamison. He's been dropping hints about a painting he's working on for some European exhibit. He calls it Faces of Fear."

"Tell me about it."

"I don't know very much. He said something about capturing the emotion of fear on the faces of the victims. . . ." Noel stopped in midsentence.

"Victims?"

"That was his word, not mine."

"Did he say anything about using models for his piece?"

"No . . . well, he did say . . . ." Noel was starting to sweat although the air-conditioned gallery was very cool.

"Noel, just tell me whatever it is, even if it docsn't make sense to you."

"That's just it, darling. It does make sense. Juergen said he was painting uniquely different faces, all wearing a mask of fear." Noel's voice had reverted to its natural low register.

"Have you told any of this to the police?"

Noel recovered his composure enough to sound indignant. "Of course not. The idea that there could be a connection between Juergen and the Midnight Strangler is preposterous. He's been exhibiting his work here for years. And despite his considerable talent, he is a quiet, modest individual."

"What does he look like?" Dana asked.

"He's tall, blond, rather muscular. You met him at the opening. I introduced you myself."

"Yes, I do remember him. He's the same guy who was staring at my secretary and me in the elevator. Please, Noel, I've got to get a look at that painting. Do you have an address for Jamison?"

While Noel looked up the address, Dana put a call through to Bruno. He wasn't at his desk, so she called her office. Cliff answered the phone on the fifth ring."

"Where's Marianne?" Dana asked impatiently.

"At lunch, I guess. Is something wrong?"

"I'm checking out a lead on the Midnight Strangler and I want you to keep calling Bruno for me. When you get through to him, tell him to meet me at this address." Dana glanced down at the paper Noel handed her, then read the information to Cliff.

Dana left the gallery and drove to the address Noel had provided, only to find that it was an empty lot.

As she paced in front of the vacant property, trying to determine her next move, Bruno arrived in an unmarked police car.

"So much for promises," Bruno yelled as he approached her.

"I'm sorry," Dana explained. "I wasn't going to do anything until you got here." She quickly told Bruno about the conversation she'd had with Noel Stewart.

"You could be on to something," Bruno agreed. "It's worth checking out. Let's go back to Stewart. If he's sold any paintings for Jamison, he may have a social security number and we can trace him through that."

Back at the gallery, Noel searched his records once more and came up with Jamison's social security number. Bruno called the information into the station.

While they waited to be called back, Dana phoned her office again. Once again, it was Cliff who answered the phone.

"Did Marianne go home already?" Dana asked.

"She never came back from lunch," Cliff replied.

The news alarmed Dana. It wasn't like Marianne to take

off without telling anyone. Dana tried calling Marianne's apartment, but there was no answer.

Dana took a deep breath, as her mind replayed the scene in the elevator with Juergen Jamison. Dana assumed he was staring at her, and it had made her uncomfortable. But Marianne thought he was looking at her, and maybe Marianne had been right.

"Hey what's wrong with you?" Bruno asked jolting her back to the present. "You look scared to death."

"I think the Strangler's got Marianne." The words came out in a hoarse whisper.

"What?" Bruno yelled at her. "How do you know?"

"She left the office for lunch and never came back, and she's not at her apartment. Call it a hysterical reaction, but the other day Marianne and I met Jamison in the elevator. He was staring at us, as if he were hypnotized or something. When I spoke to him, he ran off like a scared rabbit."

"What does that prove? We don't even know for sure if this Jamison character is our man."

"Think about it, Bruno," Dana insisted with panic in her voice. "The common link could be that all his victims have looked totally different. He's already chosen a colorful array of women, a blond, a brunette, a black, everything but a redhead. Marianne is a . . . ."

Bruno didn't wait for Dana to complete the sentence. He was already on the telephone calling the station, demanding the information on Jamison.

Ten minutes later, Dana sat beside Bruno as the dark blue sedan zig-zagged through traffic with its siren blaring. They squealed to a stop in front of the address the police computer had provided for them. The house was set back from the street, partially obscured by trees and overgrown shrubs.

Inside the house, the artist was at work. He spoke quietly to the young woman he had tied to a straight-backed chair. "That's it, Marianne, go ahead and try to get free. Ooh...yes, that's good." Jamison raised his brush and made a few more strokes on the likeness he was transferring to his huge canvas. There were five other faces captured there, faces of beautiful women. All of them appeared to be terrified. One was obviously screaming.

Marianne wasn't screaming. She was saving her strength for the ropes that bound her, knowing that if she was unable to free herself she would surely be dead by midnight.

Juergen Jamison was in his own special trance, hypnotized by the picture he was painting. Every now and then he walked over and stroked Marianne's creamy skin, telling her how beautiful she would look in death. "I will wrap my hands around your throat, and in a few minutes, it will be over."

His words had always caused his victims to become more frightened, and Marianne was no exception. Her eyes were wide with terror, and she struggled harder to free herself.

Jamison returned to the canvas to capture her expression, but as he raised his brush once more, there was a crash of glass and the sound of splintering wood. A dark head and massive shoulders burst through the doorway. Juergen reached for the gun next to his easel, but Bruno was already firing. Juergen gasped as the policeman's bullet hit his lower arm, sending his gun flying across the room.

Marianne cried with relief as Dana untied her. "I was going to lunch. He was in the lobby. He was down there waiting for me."

Bruno handcuffed Juergen, ignoring the blood that ran from the killer's wounded arm, and then called the station for assistance.

Dana stared at the bizarre work of art Juergen had murdered five women to create. "This painting is quite realistic," she said coldly. "I'm sure it will be all that's needed to convict him."

Requiem for Billy Daniels

Edie Ramer

Some said Billy Daniels was a rutting pig. Some said Billy Daniels was better than Christmas. Some just minded their own business. Those last were few, mighty few.

When Joe, my husband of four months and the town deputy, heard about Billy's murder, he said the Tuccawanee Reservoir was going to rise a foot once all the tears began to flow. When my father, the sheriff, came to pick up Joe, he said it would take them days to question all the women Joe had fooled with. Daddy and Joe should've stayed with me.

Carol Muller was the first to come, dust flying beneath the tires of her red Toyota. A bandana tied back her fuzzy orange hair, and the purple cotton skirt and top she had on made me wonder if she was color blind.

"Who did it? Who did it, Bonnie?" she called through the screen door, pounding on the aluminum frame and altogether making more racket than a cell full of singing drunks on a Saturday night.

"Hush up, Carol. You trying to raise the dead?"

Carol scrunched up her eyes and opened her mouth and gave a Lucy Ricardo wail. My cat ran screeching out of the house.

I steered Carol to the kitchen table, handed her a glass of iced tea, and plunked a box of tissues in front of her. She wiped her eyes, then blew her nose hard enough to pop *my* ears.

"Who killed Billy Daniels?" she asked.

"How should I know?"

"Who does your daddy suspect?"

"Why I believe he's on the way to your house this very minute." I smiled nicely.

"Me!" She reared back in the chair. "It's been eight months since Billy and I went out. I wouldn't've waited till now if I was going to kill him. I'd've done it in the heat of the moment."

143

Carol painted modern pictures that no one bought, and she prided herself on her passionate temperament. During the two months she went out with Billy, she acted as if they were Frankie and Johnny.

Through the open window, we heard tires crunching gravel. I excused myself and let in Sue Ann Wendt. Sue Ann was big and built like a linebacker, while Carol was small and looked as if she was anorexic, but they fell on each other's necks as if they were identical twins reunited after being separated since birth. Unless town gossip had let me down, it was the first time they'd spoken to each other since Billy broke up with Carol to go out with Sue Ann.

"I can't believe it," Sue Ann cried.

"Neither can I." Carol sobbed louder so as not to be outdone by Sue Ann.

"It's been six months since Billy and I broke up, but I always thought he'd be back."

"Me too."

I shook my head and went to the door to let in Helen Rodale. It'd been over two months since Helen and Billy stopped going around together, but some of the first grade mothers were sill grumbling that Helen wasn't fit to teach their unsullied children. Helen had been heard to say that the loudest complainers were the ones Billy had never looked at twice. A lot of heads nodded agreement when that went around.

"Does your father have any suspects?" Helen followed me into the kitchen.

"Lord, I don't know. Join the crowd."

I was mixing up a pitcher of lemonade when I saw a bottle-green station wagon driving up the road. I put the pitcher on the table and went to the front door. Maggie Crenshaw pulled up behind Helen's blue Chevette. If any more townfolk came, we'd have enough people to vote on the new road.

Maggie and her daughter, Cindy, slammed out of the car and ran up to me. I'd been expecting Cindy. She'd just graduated from high school and, like Maggie had been, was the prettiest girl in school. I'd heard that Ben Crenshaw, the president and owner of the Tuccawanee Bank, had been mighty perturbed when Billy took Cindy to Big Al's Movie House the Saturday before last.

"Daddy didn't do it," she said to me. Her face was pink from crying, but she still looked cuter than a new-born kitten.

"Of course he didn't." Maggie hunched her shoulders at me from behind Cindy.

I hunched my shoulders back and invited them inside.

In the kitchen, Cindy plopped into the last chair without asking her mother if she wanted to sit. When I came in from the extra bedroom carrying two folding chairs, Cindy, Helen, Sue Ann, and Carol were all making use of my box of tissues.

"Billy was so artistic," Carol was saying. She waved her bony fingers in the air as if she were holding a paintbrush.

Helen and Sue Ann made room for me, their chairs clattering. Maggie squeezed in between her daughter and Carol.

"Billy was intelligent," Helen said. "He asked me for our first date at the library—in the biography aisle."

Sue Ann leaned forward and her arm muscles flexed. "Billy was strong. He helped me and Pa dig post holes one day, and when we were done he was as frisky as a stallion in the morning."

Cindy sighed. Maggie glowered.

"He was a hunk," Cindy said, closing her eyes. At just eighteen, you got down to essentials.

Another group sigh heaved through my kitchen.

"His muscles . . . ." Sue Ann grabbed a tissue.

"So big and hard." Helen wiped her nose.

"I wanted to paint him nude, but he wouldn't stand still long enough." Carol hiccupped a giggle. "Not that I objected too much at the time."

"Stop this!" Maggie pounded the table. "Next you'll be describing the shape of his noodle and the dimples on his buttocks."

"But, Mama —"

"No! Your father was right, and all this talk proves it. You're too young to go out with men like Billy Daniels." She stood, her chair legs scraping across my linoleum. "We're leaving."

"No, we're not." Cindy jerked away from Maggie's arm. "I want to hear what Bonnie knows about Billy's murder."

"Cindy."

"Mama."

After they glared at each other for thirty seconds, Maggie sat down. Everyone turned to me.

"C'mon, Bonnie," Carol said. "Tell us."

"I shouldn't tell you . . . ." But I was going to, and they knew it. I waited to be persuaded.

"We loved him," Helen said.

"All right. Agatha told my dad that she heard Billy come home last night about midnight." Old Agatha Freeling rented the top of her home to Billy. Agatha was half blind, but not too much was wrong with her hearing. "I suppose he was with you, Cindy," I added.

Cindy nodded. "Mama waited up for me."

"She went to bed right after she came home," Maggie said.

"Agatha went to bed too. Loud voices woke her up a little after one. She heard a woman yelling, then a bang. Before she could get to the window—" I paused to heighten the suspense. They nodded. They all knew about Agatha's arthritis. "—she heard a car squealing out of her driveway. She went upstairs and, well , you know what she found."

Four hands reached for the tissue box.

"Who would've hurt Billy?" Helen asked between sniffles.

"Most likely it was Billy's girlfriend between you and Cindy." They all dropped their jaws and stared at me. I went on, "I was never a genius at school like you, Helen, but I can add. Carol, you and Billy went out for two months. You had two months, Sue Ann. And you had two months, Helen. Between Helen and Cindy, there's two months unaccounted for."

"There was another woman, but he never told me her name," Helen said.

"Who?" Cindy asked me.

"How should she know if Helen didn't know?" Maggie snapped.

"Oh, I know. It was someone who couldn't go out with Billy openly. Someone who was married." I stared at Maggie. "Someone who was mad enough to kill when Billy dropped her for her daughter."

"Mama!"

"Shut up, you little tramp. Billy Daniels didn't deserve to live." With that, Maggie ran out of my house. Cindy grabbed the box of tissues.

Later, when Joe asked how I guessed that Maggie Crenshaw had been having an affair with Billy, I shrugged and smiled. How could I have told him it was because Maggie knew about the dimples on Billy's buttocks?"

I knew because I'd had the two months between Sue Ann and Helen.

And in my opinion, Billy Daniels *was* better than Christmas.

Death in the Borsky Ballet

Naomi Strichartz

Plié

Marya Cherkova, former ballerina with the Borsky Ballet, smiled at herself in the mirror. Trained at the famous Kirov ballet school in Leningrad, she sometimes amused herself in her new role, as a professional psychic. Marya sat in her most comfortable chair, sipping hot coffee and eating sweet buns with a crumbly sugar and cinnamon topping. They were good. It was such a pleasure to have as many as she wished after the years of dieting. She was certainly not slim any more, she thought, admiring her handsome, round face. Why did dancers have to be so skinny? A shame. Just so not-so-strong male dancers could lift them high in the air without apparent effort. Why can't the men lift weights and get stronger, she thought, still annoyed about it. Good. Still fifteen minutes before her next client. Time for another cup of coffee and a bun or two. After leaving Russia, Marya had toured the United States with the Borsky Ballet for thirty years, back and forth through big and small towns on an uncomfortable bus. After so many years of dancing, her body finally said enough, and ten years earlier, at the age of fifty, she packed up her theater case and said good-bye. Well, she thought, this is over, I wonder what will come next.

The obvious profession for a retired ballerina was teaching, passing on experience and knowledge to the young so that the art could continue. But no one really, if they are honest, wants to teach after a career on the stage, so Marya, who still enjoyed being center stage, chose her new role as a psychic.

Once she decided, she knew it was right; it felt like a piece of a puzzle triumphantly falling into place. Marya had been quite psychic as a child and her grandmother had taught her how to read tarot cards. Now she had a steady flow of satisfied customers, some more interesting than others, but all willing to pay handsomely to hear about themselves, what was apparent and what was not. Marya kept her readings light and upbeat, trying not to frighten anyone but occasionally venturing a warning if she felt a client was in danger.

Of course, there were times she still missed dancing, the sheer physical joy of it, but she wouldn't let herself get stuck in the past. So many ballerinas did, she knew, and it struck her as sad. Nothing stands still, she told her friends, not the sun, moon or the earth, so why should I? As her reputation as a psychic grew, the police began consulting her. This was fun since it allowed her to combine her psychic talent with her clear analytical mind. It was like the crossword puzzles she enjoyed doing in several languages. She finished her last bun and took a final sip of coffee. It was time to get ready for her next reading. She tied a blue scarf around her head and adjusted her robe. Her costume was as much for comfort as for effect, since Marya disliked clothes that were tight across her ample middle. Her robe was a lovely rusty silk, the color of an autumn sunset. Like herself, she thought, an autumn sunset in all its variety and color, but not winter — not yet. She took her tarot cards out of a sweet-smelling cedar box and picked up her small crystal ball, the rock with all its beautiful imperfections that she had found in an antique shop on Broadway and knew she must have. Then she went into her study where a client was nervously waiting.

Marya introduced herself to the girl. Sylvia Walters spoke with a slight accent, Eastern European, Latvian perhaps, and was so clearly a dancer, Marya had to smile. This would be easy, she thought. Her muscular legs, long slender neck and neat bun were enough of a give away, but her huge tote bag clinched the impression. Marya instructed the girl to give her a personal object to hold and to state her problem.

Sylvia handed her a toe shoe, obviously very worn, which would serve perfectly. "I've received a threatening note and I'm frightened," she said shyly. "Maybe you can tell me what to do."

Marya looked uneasily at the girl. She was very nervous but didn't look like a hysterical type. Holding Sylvia's toe shoe, a thousand memories exploded simultaneously. The Borsky Ballet, she thought wistfully and then pushed nostalgia aside. This, after all, was her business now.

"May I ready your cards?" Marya always asked before she began.

"Yes, please," Sylvia said.

Some people, Marya knew, were unreasonably afraid of the tarot. They took the cards, with their dramatic images, literally, and out of context, getting all worked up for nothing. It was the entire layout that told a story, for those who could see. It told what might happen if all other things stayed the same, which of course they generally didn't. To understand this movement of the universe and the life in it was to understand everything, Marya felt. Everything in the universe was born, matured, and died only to be born again and again in different forms, she believed, as the moon waned and waxed each month. But everything, like the moon, had a dark side, better faced than ignored and, if possible, dealt with.

Sylvia's cards did have a dark side with the tower of destruction looming dangerously over everything and death lurking sneakily in the background. This card almost never meant the literal death of the client, she pointed out.

Sylvia sat tensely, twisting and untwisting her hands in her lap. Marya thought for a few minutes. She felt herself slipping into another dimension. Her sense of the present fell away.

Then she spoke slowly and carefully. "You were born in Eastern Europe, in Latvia perhaps, and have lived here for about ten years. You dance, of course," she said, holding up the toe shoe and smiling. "You have been recommended to me by someone who knew I was a dancer years ago, so you know or work with someone from the Borsky Ballet. I think you dance there at the school or, from what I see, you are dancer already, a young member of the company. You are right to be worried. I think someone in the company is trying to harm you or your career. But you will have help. It is dangerous but not hopeless; you must be very careful."

"Madame Niderlova told me you were wonderful," Sylvia said.

Marya's face lit up at the mention of her old friend. "And how is Irina? I must call her. When you get older, people slip away like pearls on a broken strand. I don't want to lose touch with her. Let me know if I can be of further service to you and good luck."

Marya returned half the money Sylvia handed her.

"A professional discount to a budding ballerina," she said, aware of the small check Sylvia would take home each Friday. And what about the long summer layoffs with no pay at all? Marya sighed. So unfair; ballet is the hardest work in the world and just about the worst paid. She said good-bye to Sylvia and glanced at her clock. Good, just enough time for a cup of coffee before her next client arrived.

But the phone rang, and it was Inspector Cohen. Last year she helped him solve a case and he developed, she knew, a bit of a crush on her. Inspector Cohen had been amazed at the way Marya used her intuition to solve the mystery of a clever jewel thief who had plagued Greenwich Village. The thief was foolish enough to break into Marya's apartment and steal some rings that had belonged to her mother. Marya discovered his identity without even leaving her apartment.

Inspector Cohen had asked her out to dinner after that first case was successfully finished. Marya went in order to celebrate with him but had no wish for romance in her life right then. She was busy working and reading the books she had had no time for when she was dancing.

But this was not a social call. "Madame," he began formally, "there has been a death, a murder, in the Borsky Ballet studio. A young girl, about eighteen, from the company. She was discovered early this morning by the cleaning woman. We know she was already dead for many hours before the body was discovered —the cleaning woman isn't a suspect. But just about everyone else in the company is. I've convinced the precinct to hire you since you know so many of the dancers and teachers in the company. Will you help?"

Marya was stunned. She thought of the agitated girl who had just left her apartment. "Yes, a good time for a new case," she said. "I do it." As always, when she was excited, Marya lapsed into imperfect English.

"Can you come up to the precinct right away?" the inspector asked.

"In an hour," Marya said. She never canceled a client, the way she had never canceled a performance, except for that terrible time when she fell and broke her foot. The show must go on.

It was this discipline, developed when she was very young, that helped her to concentrate on her next client, a regular, who couldn't decide whether or not to get married. Not a terribly interesting case. And she couldn't come right out and tell him that the cards confirmed her impression of him as a foolish and shallow young man.

Finally he left and Marya took the Madison Avenue bus uptown to the police station. "Madame," the inspector said, looking at her admiringly, "you are lovelier than ever."

"You don't need lovely, you need perceptive, clever maybe — lovely won't help," Marya said, eyeing him squarely, "or is this just a pretext for a date?"

"Oh, no," he assured her, "we need your help. The girl was probably poisoned. We'll have the lab report tomorrow. We think she was killed between nine and eleven last night."

"Is there a motive?" Marya asked.

"Too many, I'm afraid. It seems everyone in the company hated Caroline Parks. I've already spoken with Irina Niderlova who knows everything that goes on at the school and the company. She said Caroline had a lot of enemies. She danced tolerably well but wasn't special. She thinks Caroline wouldn't have gotten into the company at all if her daddy hadn't been in oil. Made a huge donation to the company. Lately Caroline had been getting large roles and the whole company was incensed."

"What do you want me to do?" Marya asked.

"Why find her killer, of course."

"Yes, of course," Marya said, smiling graciously.

"Madame Niderlova expects you. We believe this is an inside job. Remember, Marya, everyone who was in the building last night is a suspect. *Everyone.* So be careful."

Tendues

Marya climbed up the three flights to the Borsky Ballet studio on West 57th Street and opened the door to a familiar scene. Dancers in colorful practice clothes were warming up, drinking coffee, and relaxing with their feet propped up against the walls. Some dancers stood in little groups whispering anxiously. They could have been discussing anything.

But in this familiar tableu, there was a police officer standing near the door, looking ill at ease. And she could feel the tension in the room. Most of the students seemed aware of yesterday's death. But dancers are among the most disciplined people in the world. They would take class today as though it were an ordinary day, the work banishing all else from their minds.

The School director, Irina Niderlova, stood up to greet her old friend. "Marya, how good to see you, how good you could come," she said as they exchanged kisses on both cheeks, Russian style.

"I will watch Boris' class," Marya told her. "Can you tell me who is who?"

"Of course. Here comes Boris now."

A large uncoordinated man lumbered towards them. Looking at him no one would imagine he had once been a dancer. But even now he danced smoothly, although he couldn't cross a room without crashing into the furniture. Boris wore a baggy shirt and pants and a beanie to keep his bald spot warm. Boris was pathologically afraid of catching a cold. Marya remembered this kind, neurotic man with great fondness. And he had been a wonderful partner, often supporting her in *Gaieté Parisienne*.

"Marya, darling, how good to see you. You know about Caroline? Terrible. And a terrible girl. But to kill her?" Boris held on to his beanie as if afraid it, or his head, would fall off. With Boris you never knew which.

"I hope to be of some service," Marya said, squeezing her old friend's hand, and returning two more sloppy kisses, one on each cheek.

Marya sat down on a wide bench next to Irina and watched the dancers milling about. Some were stretching on the floor, others, legs propped up on the barre, were still talking. Towels reserved favorite places at the barre. They were very beautiful, Marya thought, men and women in the prime of life, lean and fit, with the taut expression of those with a calling in life. Marya allowed herself one moment of envy and then, impatiently, returned to the business at hand.

Zoya Akimova, the pianist, entered the studio with her tote bag of music. Marya got up to kiss her, another old friend she had neglected to see. When Marya stopped dancing she decided it would be easier not to see her old friends from the dance world for a while, but now she realized how much she missed them. Zoya looked terrible, Marya thought sadly. Her skin was clammy and pale and her hands were shaking. She seemed to be taking Caroline's death very badly. Zoya went and sat down at the piano and Boris clapped his hands for attention. Suddenly all the confusion ended. The dancers rose quickly to their feet and took their places at the barre. Moving like a single organism, they were almost frightening in their discipline and purpose.

"One, two and," Boris said, and the barre began. It was another world, Marya thought, a world the audience doesn't see when they watch the apparent effortlessness of a performance. Boris demanded a lot of his students, and they strived to do better and better, their faces transformed with sacrifice and joy. It was quite easy to pick out the company members from the other dancers. They were all good, naturally, but there was that something more, a fluidity and ease, a regal carriage of the head, the extra reach of the arms, and legs like liquid steel. It was called the Borsky Ballet style.

"Sylvia, what are you doing?" Boris suddenly shouted and strode over to the girl who had spoken to Marya in such distress a few hours ago. "Higher, hold your back," and he slapped her thigh hard. "I don't care what happened," he said. "You must work."

Sylvia seemed relieved to be distracted from her thoughts. She was obviously distraught. But her arabesque lengthened and got higher and her attention focused on the exercise. Boris patted her back fondly. He couldn't walk away from an upset dancer, even if he was the one who upset her. Although Boris could be a holy terror in class, the dancers sensed his genuine love and didn't resent the discipline. He sometimes made the class repeat all the long hard barre exercises again if they looked sloppy. Everyone obeyed, even the most famous dancers. No one even thought of rebelling. And in this perverse world of ballet, it was his favorites who got picked on most and were most grateful for it.

"Sylvia is a lovely dancer," Irina whispered, "and a lovely girl. Everyone was so upset when Caroline was given solo billing instead of her and then when Caroline was given the Queen of the Willis to dance, it was just too much. My God, I almost forgot, Caroline is dead." She shook her head, disbelievingly. "That is Andrew, over there," she said, pointing to a tall, handsome boy standing in the corner. "He was Caroline's boyfriend, but they had broken up."

"He doesn't look particularly upset," Marya noted as she appraised the boy with disfavor.

"He is a brash country boy. I think he was really in love with Caroline, or thought he was, but she treated him so badly. Treated everyone badly. You know, the company is like a family, a lot of squabbling and a lot of love. We never had anyone like Caroline before. I warned Anatol not to take her on. If only he had listened to me. But her father donated money that was needed for the tour, and Anatol said there would be no tour at all without it. Still, the dancers were all very resentful."

Marya immediately recognized her old rival, Helena Rubova. Helena was now prima ballerina of the Borsky Ballet but before, it had been Marya who was ballerina and Helena was just a minor soloist. Helena was very beautiful with her dark chestnut hair, widely spaced eyes, and a full mouth. She became radiant when she smiled. She could be quite imperious and, next to Anatol, was now the most powerful person in the company. Marya knew that Helena had fought her way to the top, refusing to let anything get in her way. She stood now at the center barre, carefully regarding herself in the mirror. Sitting against the wall, as close as she could get to Helena without getting in the way, was Nora, Helena's secretary and maid. She sat sewing Helena's pointe shoes, looking up frequently to cast a loving eye on her idol.

"Do you remember Nora?" Irina asked.

"How could I forget," Marya said, smiling. "She spent seven years trying to convince me to retire so Helena would get my position. 'You must be tired, I suppose, of dancing after all these years,' she would tell me. But I went on and on until my body refused to dance."

How did Helena feel about Caroline?" she asked Irina.

"She hated her," Irina said. "Helena was used to Anatol obeying her every wish, but somehow she couldn't stop Caroline."

"She has been stopped rather effectively, hasn't she?" Marya said thoughtfully.

Barre over, the class moved into the center floor. Helena and her partner, Erik Serkin, went to the front of the room and the other dancers fell into place, pretty much according to rank. The students who were not company members waited for the second group so they might find a place in front of the mirror. A sad looking girl in the second line caught Marya's eye.

"That's Ellen Trager," Irina said. "She's been in the company a long time, ten years, I believe. She is very well liked by the other dancers. She is competent at what she does and very helpful to the new ones coming in."

155

Competent, like the word capable, meant not particularly talented, Marya knew.

"She remembers everything," Irina went on, "everyone's roles and their birthdays, too. I think she has given up hope of ever being promoted; she loves to dance and I guess that is enough for her."

"How did she feel about Caroline?" Marya asked.

"I think, well, I don't really know how she felt about her, but she was friendly. She is friendly to everyone."

"Does she have any special friends in the company?"

"I don't really know; she's just naturally friendly, but, I think, not close."

Marya nodded.

The class was now doing grand allegro, a long, joyful combination consisting of turns and large jumps. The dancers leaped broadly, like gazelles, and Zoya, having regained her composure, played her Mendelssohn piece magnificently.

But there was beneath the music incredible tension in the room. Right after class the police would question all those who had been in the Borsky Ballet Studio last night. And Marya would be there too, listening and watching. It was unthinkable, really, that any of these beautiful people had cold-bloodedly committed murder. We are capable of everything, all of us, Marya reminded herself, it is just a question of circumstance.

Eventually, the class came to an end, and the students applauded their teacher, in the time-honored tradition.

Marya went with Irina and Boris into the company office. She accepted a cup of coffee and sat down to wait for Inspector Cohen. She looked over the list of names that he had given her earlier, at the police station.

Anatol Borsky, company director

Andrew Gaines, company member

Ellen Trager, company member

Sylvia Walters, company member

Erik Serkin, leading dancer

Helena Rubova, ballerina

Zoya Akimova, pianist

Irina Niderlova and Boris Popoff, company and school teachers.

"Are you and Boris really suspects?" Marya asked, amused.

"I don't think so. Boris and I went to the Russian Tea Room and then to the ballet. We were seen by people we knew in both places," Irina said, obviously not worried.

Suddenly, Inspector Cohen burst into the room. "One of the suspects has disappeared," he said.

"Who?" Marya asked.

"Zoya Akimova, the pianist. She's gone."

Degagés

"We will proceed as planned," Inspector Cohen said, "and question the suspects one by one."

"One by one?" Marya asked. "No, I don't like that, is too uncomplicated."

"What would you suggest?" he asked sarcastically. "That is the way we always do it."

"I want to see them all together, to see how one relates to the other. No one stands alone. Like time, bending in on itself, it doesn't begin or end. Is mistake to think like that. First we see them all together and then later we simplify."

He remembered that Marya's methods were unorthodox, but they worked, although Inspector Cohen could not understand why.

"We'll do it your way," he sighed. "Send them all in," he said, turning to the policeman who waited at the door.

"All together?" the man asked, startled.

"That's what I said," the Inspector barked.

Chairs were hurriedly arranged in a circle. Marya sat like a cat, relaxed, but wary. They entered. The young man, Andrew, came first. Shallow, was Marya's first impression. Shallow and perhaps a bit stupid as well, and the trait she most disliked in a male, cocky. She found herself wishing he had done it. Unfair, she scolded herself, unfair and prejudiced and, a last scalding rebuke to herself, unprofessional. Helena stalked in and flounced into a chair as though attacking it.

"Do you realize, Inspector," she began, without acknowledging Marya, "that I have a television appearance tomorrow with Erik, and this is my rehearsal time?"

"And do you realize, Madame," Inspector Cohen said, "that a young woman has been murdered and that you are a suspect?"

Helena looked shocked but still imperious. "Marya, darling," she shifted her attention, "how nice to see you. You have put on a lot of weight, but it becomes you."

Marya smiled at this piece of malice. "It is a relief to be able to indulge myself, after years of deprivation, and yes, I agree, the weight does become me, but I think we had best concentrate on the poor murdered girl."

Sylvia sat looking pale and shaky. She was chewing her lips. "Don't worry, dear," Marya said, smiling at her, "try and relax."

Anatol Borsky was outraged to be sitting there with his subjects, his harem as it were. He was a man used to being deferred to. Anatol was portly, graying, and slightly breathless. He must be over seventy by now, Marya thought; oh well, it happens to all of us, if we're lucky. Anatol enjoyed dangling roles in front of his dancers and watching them respond like hungry dogs. Not a fool, but too self-important. Anatol Borsky was not her favorite person.

Ellen held a tissue in one hand and rested her cheek in the other. She was crying quietly and steadily. She looked honestly distraught as she gazed at them with wide watery eyes.

Erik was not there. He felt a sore throat threatening and they had let him go home because of his performance the next day. But they would talk to him in the morning.

"So Marya, do you want to ask the questions?" Inspector Cohen asked her.

"No, you go ahead, I'll listen," Marya said.

How they react is as important as what they say, she thought. One can always lie, but it is harder to hide the truth that expresses itself in body language.

"Very well," Inspector Cohen began. "We'll go around the circle. Please tell me what you were doing between nine and eleven p.m. last night."

"I was rehearsing *Swan Lake* pas de trois with Sylvia and Ellen. Caroline was there for a little while and then left," Andrew began.

"Do you always rehearse at that hour?"

"No, but it's hard to get studio space during the day. We felt under rehearsed. It wasn't unusual for us to do that," he added carefully.

Not stupid, just shallow; Marya adjusted her opinion.

"I was rehearsing also," Helena said, "what I should be doing now. I'm going to dance the *Black Swan* with Erik for NBC. It's being taped tomorrow so I must be in top form. Last night we worked on the pas de deux but I haven't practiced my solo enough." She still sounded imperious and annoyed.

"So you and Erik were here at the Borsky Ballet studios last night between the hours I stated?"

"Yes, and Zoya too, she played for us."

"I was in Studio Two with Andrew and Ellen. Caroline was there for a while and then left for her appointment with Mr. Borsky," Sylvia said.

"Were you all cast in the *pas de trois* this season?" Marya asked.

"I was, I hoped, and Andrew had danced it before; Ellen was standing in for — Caroline," Sylvia said, quietly.

"It's all your fault, you idiot," Helena shouted at Anatol Borsky. "Pushing that ninny of a dancer, with no thought for who you were hurting, no thought for anyone."

"Caroline was a lovely dancer, Inspector," Anatol said smoothly. "The better the dancer, the greater the jealousy and bad feelings, if you know what I mean," he said, smirking at Helena.

"You mean Helena was jealous of Caroline?" Marya asked him softly with a note of incredulousness.

"In a way, yes," Anatol said.

Helena glared at him but said nothing.

"Mr. Borsky, were you at the school between nine and eleven last night, then?"

"I was here for a while. Caroline did have an appointment with me, but when she didn't arrive — I don't wait for dancers, Mr. Cohen — so I left. It was about nine forty-five."

"And where did you go?"

"Home, Mr. Cohen, my wife can attest to it."

"We don't generally take alibis from wives, Mr. Borsky," Inspector Cohen said with a smile.

Helena gave a nasty laugh.

There is definitely trouble between those two, Marya decided. She was paying more attention to Ellen, however. The girl was crying continually, but pulled herself together when it was her turn to speak.

"And where were you last night, Miss Trager? The others have said you were with them rehearsing, is that true?"

"Yes. Andrew asked me to stand in because Caroline had an appointment with Mr. Borsky. I love that dance, but I'm not cast for it. I was just doing it until Caroline came back."

"But she didn't, did she?" Marya asked, watching her closely.

"No," Ellen said, beginning to cry again. "We went on dancing, lost track of time, until almost ten o'clock, I think."

"Did any of you leave the studio during that time?"

"Sylvia did," Ellen said. "She left twice, I think, but I don't know why."

Inspector Cohen looked inquiringly at Sylvia.

"I did leave. I tried to call my mother to tell her I'd be late. But the line was busy. I called again later and got through to her."

"Irina and I were at the ballet," Boris said.

The visiting Bolshoi were creating a sensation, Marya knew. She made a mental note to herself to try and get a ticket.

"First we had supper at the Russian Tea Room," he continued. "Alexis waited on us."

Marya was still musing about the Bolshoi. She hated paying fifteen dollars for a ticket only to find she was sitting behind a pole. The Met was nicer to perform in than to attend, but still, the Bolshoi is the Bolshoi.

"So, we will check out your alibi and, if it holds, you and Irina Niderlova are not suspects in this case. Perhaps you can help us with your observations," Inspector Cohen added.

They both nodded.

"How did you feel about the deceased, about Caroline Parks?" he asked no one in particular.

Marya immediately drew herself up attentively.

"She was my girlfriend," Andrew began, "until recently. We broke up last week."

"Why?"

"I realized I didn't love her, I didn't like her attitude and . . . and I found out she was seeing someone else."

Marya saw his eyes rest briefly on Anatol.

"Anyway," the boy continued, "she didn't really love me, she only loved herself. She enjoyed having a male escort, but frankly, on my salary, I couldn't afford to date her; Caroline had very expensive taste. I began to — hate her — but I didn't kill her," he added softly.

"Caroline was not a nice girl," Helena said. "Her daddy was in oil, and that's how she happened to join the company. He made a big donation. I warned Anatol not to take her on. She wasn't as good as our weakest dancer."

"She was damn good," Anatol shouted.

"So she was trying to climb to the top, with Anatol's help," Marya said, looking suggestively at Helena.

Helena ignored her. The woman had nerves of steel, had to have, Marya knew, to have become the ballerina she was today.

"She was an arrogant young girl," Helena continued. "You know, Marya dear, they think they can dance, just because they can do steps. It's artistry that makes the dancer, the star," she said, drawing herself up.

"So how did you feel about her, Madame?" Inspector Cohen repeated.

"I hated her, of course," Helena admitted, crossing herself as she remembered Caroline was dead. "She got roles she didn't deserve and gloated about it, too. It was unfair to the rest of the company."

"Any idea, other than her daddy's money, how Caroline might have gotten all this?" Marya asked.

"Why don't you ask Anatol, darling?" Helena said with a leer.

Anatol Borsky sat sullen but uncharacteristically quiet.

"I hated her, too," Sylvia said, wincing. "She had everything, but she wasn't such a good dancer." She looked nervously at Anatol Borsky, who continued not to respond. "Lots of better dancers didn't even get into the company and she was being made a soloist," Sylvia said, clenching her hands nervously.

"In a way, you were the one with the most to lose, weren't you?" Inspector Cohen asked Sylvia.

"Yes. I was to have been made a soloist this season. Helena told me. *Queen of the Willis* would have been my first major role. But Caroline got it instead."

"I was fond — of Caroline," Anatol Borsky said finally. "Despite what you've heard, she was a lovely dancer. Beautiful, talented, and young. Helena hated that. They all did. Caroline was coming to see me so we could discuss her new contract as a solo dancer. You know, Inspector, Caroline looked a little like Helena. A dark beauty. She had better legs and feet. Helena was sick with jealousy. But it is my job to nurture young talent."

"Nurture, yes, let's put it that way," Helena said, looking at him sideways.

"So your interest in Caroline was purely professional," Marya asked, looking at him squarely.

"Of course," he said, too loudly.

"I can't believe anyone did this," Ellen said. "I mean, how could anyone kill her? I liked Caroline. We used to have coffee together. I think I was her only friend."

"What about her friendship with Andrew?" Marya asked.

"They broke up," she said, blushing and looking at Andrew.

"Were you jealous that Caroline was being made a soloist?" Marya asked.

"Jealous?" Ellen seemed to be entertaining the thought for the first time.

Oh come on, Marya thought to herself, she is too good to be true.

"I feel very fortunate," Ellen continued. "Here I am, a member of the most famous ballet company in the country. I dance in all the classics, get free toe shoes when we're performing, and free classes at the company school. Dancing is my life; it makes me very happy."

"How long have you been with the company?" Marya asked.

"Eight years," she said, "and I would like to stay forever."

"But you can't dance forever, can you?" Marya asked gently.

The younger woman didn't answer, but dried her eyes on her tissues.

"It's very important to me, to be a good person," Ellen said after a few moments.

"It's all that fool Anatol's fault. He is an idiot," Boris shouted angrily. "Falling in love with a young girl, there is nothing worse than an old fool. Terrible dancer, arrogant, wealthy bitch. Anatol can't see the nose in front of his face. An idiot!"

But of course this was very interesting, Marya thought, although she had come to this conclusion herself long ago.

Boris added, "I think that Caroline was not liked by most of the dancers in the company or by the teachers. But murder is against nature. I can't imagine who could have actually done it."

"One person did, and we will find out who," Inspector Cohen said with finality. "Before you all leave I would like a word with you in private, one at a time," he added, glaring at

Marya. "Please leave one by one and we will talk to each of you in the hallway."

"Any idea who might have done it?" the Inspector asked Andrew in the hall. He always learned more from this question than from any other. The best way to know someone fast, he felt, was to see whom they would accuse in order to exonerate themselves.

"No one really liked Caroline, it's hard to say," Andrew began. "I don't think any of us would actually kill her either."

"But someone did, didn't they?"

Andrew nodded.

"Have you ever seen this before?" Inspector Cohen asked.

"Sure, it's a pointe shoe, all the girls wear them. This one is from England, called Freeds," he said, looking at the peach color. "Some of the girls wear them even though the company buys them Capezios, which are American-made shoes," he explained. "But they like Freeds better because they don't make as much noise on stage."

Marya looked at the Inspector's befuddled expression with superiority. She was beginning to like Andrew despite herself, although she wasn't sure why.

"Who are the dancers who wear these Freeds?" Inspector Cohen asked.

"Sylvia and a few of the new girls. Why?"

"This shoe was found next to Caroline's body," he said, frowning.

Andrew grew pale and showed nervousness for the first time. "Why would anyone leave a clue like that?" he wondered.

"We want to know even more than you do," Inspector Cohen said as he motioned Andrew to leave.

When they took Helena aside she laughed nastily.

"If I were Sylvia, I would have killed her," she said. "She had everything to lose. She was to become the soloist this year and bang, the position was given to Caroline. I was coaching her in the part of the Queen of the Willis for this season, but that was taken away, too. Sylvia is a good dancer for a young girl, not enough style yet, but flexible and strong, good line."

"Have you seen this before, Madame?" Inspector Cohen asked, holding up the pointe shoe.

"Have I seen a toe shoe before, Inspector?" she asked, smirking. "Yes, I have seen them."

"Have you seen this particular shoe before?"

She looked. "Five and a half X, yes, it is Sylvia's. I tried it on, we are the same size, three and a half D in Capezios and five and a half X in Freeds. The English size them differently."

Marya nodded and Inspector Cohen looked confused as Helena left and Anatol joined them.

Marya felt uneasy. Inspector Cohen had the habit of jumping to conclusions, the wrong ones. What if he decided to arrest Sylvia?

"It is deeply distressing to me, Inspector, that you think a member of my company, the Borsky Ballet, has committed a murder," Anatol Borsky began, pompously. "Are you sure it couldn't have been an outsider?"

"Relatively sure, Mr. Borsky, but nothing has been ruled out yet."

"Listen, Inspector, this girl, Caroline, she was my favorite. Surely you can't imagine that I could have killed her."

"Well, just suppose someone here did do it, who might it be?"

"She was not popular, Inspector. As I said before, the better they are, the more jealousy and bad feelings."

"Was Helena jealous?" Marya asked.

"Insanely."

Anatol Borsky wouldn't say any more, so they dismissed him.

Ellen Trager had been crying, Marya noted, as the young woman approached, still clutching a damp tissue. "I can't believe anyone in the company did this," Ellen said. "I mean, I know she's dead, someone killed her. But I just can't believe it."

"Do you have any idea who might have wanted Caroline out of the way?" Inspector Cohen asked.

"I know everyone is saying Sylvia ought to have done it. But the Borsky Ballet is like a family. Sure there are squabbles and problems, but murder?"

"Families are excellent material for murder, Miss Trager," the Inspector said.

"Were you aware that Caroline was very rich?" Marya asked her.

"Yes, of course, we all knew that. It was the way it was."

"Did you feel any jealousy?"

"Me?" she asked, with the same air of astonishment as before. "No, I felt myself — feel myself — to be very fortunate.

I love dancing in the company and if it doesn't make me rich, it does make me happy."

"You dance in the corps de ballet, don't you?" Inspector Cohen asked. "Any hope of promotion?"

"Everyone hopes, but no, the company doesn't think I'm good enough."

"And Caroline, she was good enough?" Marya asked.

"I'm a better dancer than she was," Ellen admitted.

"What were you and Andrew doing when Sylvia left rehearsal to make her phone calls?" Marya wondered.

"Andrew and I just talked," she said. "I like him a lot."

Amazing that she blushes like a fourteen year old, Marya thought. And amazing, too, she is so unaware of herself and out of touch with her feelings. And all this crying for others, perhaps it is for herself that she weeps, Marya thought.

"So," Marya said, "Caroline had money, solo billing she didn't deserve, and the boy you like and still, most amazingly, you felt no jealousy?"

"I liked Caroline. It wasn't her fault she had all those things. Besides, she and Andrew broke up," she said, with a hint of a smile. She was dismissed and left looking uncertain about the impression she had made.

Boris asked to talk to them, although he and Irina were no longer suspects. His evening with Irina had been confirmed by a policeman who made a quick visit to the Russian Tea Room. After dinner, they had met other friends at the ballet who were eager to confirm their alibi; Irina and Boris were well known in the ballet world.

"Anatol is responsible for this. I don't mean he killed her. I doubt that, unless she refused him, and then anything would be possible."

"What do you think of Ellen?" Marya asked, disturbed by the girl's total lack of self-insight.

"Ellen? A friendly girl. So-so dancer. She seems grateful for the opportunity to dance in the company, as she should be. She got in a long time ago before the standards got tougher."

"Any chance she might get promoted?" Marya asked.

"No, none, unless that fool, Anatol, develops a crush on her."

"Do you think Helena might have killed Caroline?" Inspector Cohen asked.

Boris thought for a moment. "Helena is a tough cookie.

She got to the top somehow, anyhow, and she wants to stay there. But there's a limit to what Anatol could give to Caroline. She couldn't dance, and there was the reputation of the company to consider. Caroline wasn't a direct threat to Helena, I don't think."

"But if threatened, you think it is possible," Marya said.

"If threatened, if her position were threatened, Helena would stop at nothing."

"And what do you think of Sylvia?" Marya asked, sensing the answer, but wanting it spoken for the Inspector's sake.

"A lovely dancer and a lovely girl. A budding ballerina, as you can see, Marya darling."

"Do you think she might have done it because of all the provocation?" Inspector Cohen asked.

"Not a chance, Inspector, and now I must go. My dog is expecting his walk. And Marya, let's not be strangers," he said, squeezing her hand.

Marya thought it was ominous that the Inspector wanted to talk to Sylvia last.

"No one in the company could have done it," Sylvia said. "Although Mr. Borsky seemed very upset lately. I think it had to do with Caroline and Helena, but I'm not sure."

"What did you really do when you left the rehearsal last night?"

Sylvia looked upset. "I wasn't phoning my mother. I followed Caroline to the bathroom. I knew she would be prettying up for her appointment with Mr. Borsky. I showed her the threatening note I told you about," she said, appealing to Marya. "I said she'd better stop writing those or I would tell the management about it. She called me a lying bitch and I slapped her. She pulled my hair and I scratched her face. There was blood on her cheek. Then I went into the phone booth until I calmed down. The second time I left, I did call my mother," she said.

"Do you have this note with you?" Inspector Cohen asked.

"No, it's at home, but I will bring it to you," she said. "Caroline was alive when I left her, you must believe me," she said, a note of hysteria in her voice.

"You do realize you may be the last person to admit to seeing Caroline alive?" Inspector Cohen asked. Sylvia gasped and held onto the wall for support. "About what time did all this occur, do you recall?"

"About nine thirty, I think."

"Is this your shoe?"

"Yes," she said, her lips trembling.

"It was found with the body," he informed her, watching closely. "Don't leave town, Miss Walters. We will be needing you again."

"Don't worry, my dear, I will help you," Marya said reassuringly, although at the moment she couldn't imagine how.

Fondues

Marya stepped gratefully into the bathtub. The hot water relaxed her and eased the twinges of arthritis she had been feeling lately. After her bath she put up a pot of coffee and took out her bag of little buns. Two or three wouldn't be too many after a day like this. She sat at her round pine table and looked around the room with satisfaction. Home felt good to her after all the years of touring. Home was where she rested and worked now, saw clients, got ideas and was —herself. She sat eating and sipping the hot coffee. How lovely are these little creature pleasures, especially as one grows older, she mused. After eating, she went into her study and carefully laid her tarot cards out into the formation known as the Celtic Cross. She asked the powers of the earth to give her the insight to understand. She chose the fool, an unnumbered card, to represent herself, the questioner. And she was him, the fool just beginning a journey towards enlightenment. But she would find out in time, it would all be there for those who could see. She meditated on the cards, not to predict the future, or even to unlock the past, but to activate her own intuition and the power that resides within. She thought about the known facts in this case. Circumstance pointed to Sylvia as the murderer but Marya was certain she was innocent. Zoya had run away. Did that mean she was guilty? Afraid? And where was she? No one liked Caroline, but who possessed the obsessive hatred that could lead to murder? Helena? What if she was insanely jealous because Anatol had taken Caroline as his mistress? Marya thought about the aging man with his pendulous stomach and shook her head. Anatol claimed to be genuinely fond of Caroline and Helena confirmed this. What, then, could be his reasons for killing her? Andrew had broken up with Caroline, so why would he kill her? Why would Caroline send Sylvia a threatening note? It was all so confusing, and Marya felt something important was missing. She studied the cards. The magician was the final card in her layout, symbolizing, to her, sleight of hand, and things not being what they seem. Carefully she put her cards away, first wrapping them in a piece of blue silk, then returning them to their cedar box and placing them in a special drawer in her bureau. Marya smiled at herself. She reserved a small corner of her mind for amused skepticism and doubt. This she had inherited from her father, who had been a physicist. The combination of glimpses into the non-material world and hard analytical thinking gave her the insight for solving mysteries. She knew the answer would come in time, but meanwhile there was still a lot of work to do.

Too early the next morning, the phone rang. It was Inspector Cohen.

"I just got the lab report. Caroline Parks was poisoned. The medical examiner found two poisons in her system — cyanide and aconite. Enough to kill ten dancers. And that must have been quite a fight Sylvia had with the deceased. Caroline had an ugly scratch on her face and some strands of brown hair were clenched in her hand. We have to run some more tests, but I'll bet you that the hair turns out to be Sylvia's. If nothing more turns up I'll have to arrest her."

Marya swallowed her anger, a feat not natural to her. She knew quiet reasoning was more effective than temper when dealing with the police. "You hired me to work on this case. I am telling you, the murderer is not Sylvia. No, I don't know yet who. The case is just a day old. I need time."

"It's eight o'clock. I can give you until this time tomorrow — no later. If nothing new turns up, I'm arresting Sylvia Walters." And he hung up.

"Damn." Marya couldn't understand the police. They rushed with everything. The truth could not be rushed, but unfolded in its own time. The earth itself unfolded the seasons with infinite calm and patience. "Damn," she said again. Rush she must, for Sylvia's sake at least. First she needed to talk to the girl right away. Then she would question Erik Serkin, as planned. And then it looked like she had better find Zoya. Too much for one day, she thought, sighing. She put on a favorite green cotton skirt and a T-shirt that had once been black, but was now so faded it looked gray and pearly, like the inside of a sea shell.

Marya looked up Sylvia's home number from the list of suspects Inspector Cohen had provided her. A woman with a heavy, weary voice answered on the third ring.

"Sylvia is still in bed. She was up most of the night. Can you talk to me instead?" she asked worriedly.

"No. You must get her up. Tell her it is an emergency. She should meet me in one hour at Brownies Coffee Shop on 55th Street. Tell her to bring the note. She will understand. Oh yes, you must tell her it is Marya Cherkova calling." I am getting all muddled, I must be nervous, Marya thought, hanging up the phone.

By 9:15, Marya and Sylvia were seated in a private booth at Brownies. "Exactly what happened between you and Caroline in the bathroom?" Marya asked, after they were served cups of strong, steaming coffee. She tried not to sound too urgent; the poor girl was obviously frightened enough already.

"We had a fight, as I said. Caroline sent me this note saying I was to refuse all new roles. It didn't make any sense, because Caroline had so many new roles of her own, but I was furious. First she got my billing, and then the Queen of the Willis. How dare she threaten me after all that? I confronted her."

"Then what happened?"

"She was in the bathroom preening for her meeting with Mr. Borsky, just as I knew she would be. I shoved the note in her face, said she was crazy to have written it and I would complain to the management if it ever happened again. She called me a lying bitch and I slapped her face. I couldn't believe it, I had the evidence right there. She lunged at me and pulled my hair. I think I scratched her face when she grabbed me by the neck and I pulled away. I felt panicky. I have never had a fight like that in my life. I pretended to make a phone call but I just sat in the booth until I felt calmer. Then I went back to rehearsal."

"Inspector Cohen said you were the last one to admit to seeing Caroline alive," Marya said, as gently as she could. "Will you show me the note please?"

Sylvia pulled the note out of her large tote bag:

REFUSE ALL NEW ROLES OR ELSE

— C

169

"Are they thinking of arresting me?" Sylvia asked, trembling.

"I am trying to prevent them from having that thought," Marya said grimly. "And now I must go and meet the Inspector at the studio," she said, leaving the money on the table to pay for their coffee.

Marya rushed through the hot mid-town streets. She still loved the heat-baked sidewalk, feeling its warmth in her. It made her feel like dancing again.

When she arrived at the Borsky Ballet, Inspector Cohen and his expressionless assistant were already there. A few minutes later, Erik Serkin walked in, looking stunning. His black hair was beginning to gray at the edges and his body was lean and strong. He was wearing gray slacks and a white T-shirt that showed off his year-round tan. He carried a large brown leather bag over one shoulder. It looked expensive. He looked, Marya thought, just a bit too jaunty for the occasion. There was something pathetic about his effort to look youthful. He appeared completely recovered from yesterday's illness. He probably hadn't wanted to be questioned with the ordinary mortals, Marya thought, amused.

"Where were you between nine and eleven on Tuesday night, Mr. Serkin?" Inspector Cohen asked.

"Rehearsing at the Studio with Helena. The Black Swan pas de deux, as you must already know, Inspector. Zoya can tell you, she was accompanying us."

"Zoya is not around, as *you* must already know," the Inspector snapped back. "Any idea where she might have gone?"

Erik looked around as though trying to conjure her out of the walls and shook his head.

"How did you feel about Caroline Parks?" Marya asked.

"Caroline was a little bitch and a miserable conniver. I tried to convince Anatol to fire her. He refused. At first I thought it was because of her father's donation, but now I think differently."

"What do you think now?" Inspector Cohen asked impatiently.

"I think she was blackmailing him," Erik said. "Anatol hinted as much, said he couldn't fire her, said he would if he could."

"Why was she blackmailing him? She certainly didn't need the money."

"That's for you to find out, isn't it, Inspector? Now I have a rehearsal, if you will excuse me."

A shadow crossed Erik's face and Marya saw it —there was more. He hated Caroline for some other reason, something deeper. Perhaps Caroline had wounded his ego, insulted him in some way. She would find out. He stood up, wincing slightly. His knees are starting to go, Marya thought, remembering how hers had started hurting when she was forty.

Marya and Inspector Cohen sat quietly for a few minutes.

"I think we will wait and talk to the great Anatol Borsky, what say?" Inspector Cohen said with a meaningful look.

"Close the door, Gabe," Marya said urgently. "Anatol's secretary is out for coffee, his office is right through that door; you stay here, don't let anyone in."

Marya went into the large office. The walls were as she remembered them, lined with bottles of cognac, vodka and blackberry brandy. Anatol's desk was disordered, also as she remembered. She began going through his drawers. The bottom drawer contained dancers' contracts. "Voila," Marya whispered. Clipped to Caroline's contract was a note:

NOT ENOUGH. WANT 200 MORE. WILL NOT DANCE
WITH ERIK. HE IS TOO OLD. AND HE HATES ME.
SAYS HE WILL DROP ME ON STAGE. WHY DON'T
YOU FIRE HIM?

— C

She stuffed the contract and the note into her tote bag, and went back to join Inspector Cohen.

"Look at this," she said, holding up the note triumphantly.

"You can't do that without a subpoena, it's against the law."

"Anatol doesn't know that, he's Russian," she said, smiling.

"So Caroline was blackmailing Anatol, and he killed her," Inspector Cohen said.

"So Caroline was blackmailing Anatol and someone killed her," Marya corrected him. "But yes, we need to talk to Anatol. He never comes in until noon, so let's go have a bite to eat."

"Is it a date?" Inspector Cohen asked, hopefully.

"Not at all, just a bite," Marya said, amused.

When they returned to the Borsky Ballet Studios, Anatol greeted them politely in his usual pompous fashion. Wasting no time, Marya showed him the note. As she expected, he didn't question the legality of her methods. He sat down and sighed, expelling air like a deflating balloon.

"I was afraid to tell you," he said. "It felt like admitting I killed her. And I didn't do it. But —I'm glad someone did," he said.

"I thought she was your latest, Anatol," Marya said, with some pleasure.

"No, I hated her; she was threatening to tell my wife everything."

"So, she *was* your latest?" Marya remarked.

"You lied to us yesterday," Inspector Cohen said mildly.

"Lied? Let us say I misled you. Caroline was blackmailing me. She had been for some time. Helena is right, she wasn't good enough for her roles, not even good enough to be in the Borsky Ballet. I decided to take her because of the donation — we needed it badly. I thought she would dance in the corps for a few years and then give up. But I was wrong. She was a very ambitious young woman."

"Anatol, do you know if she might have been blackmailing someone else?" Marya asked.

"I doubt it. She wanted roles, she wanted power over me. What could the others do for her?"

Inspector Cohen signalled Marya that they should leave. "Mr. Borsky, don't leave town," he said.

Marya's head hurt. She walked into the main studio where Erik and Helena were going through their final practice before their TV appearance. Black Swan. The familiar music soothed her. There was Odile, the wicked magician's daughter, pretending to be Odette, the Queen of the Swans. Helena was stunning in this role, majestic, pretending to be what she was not. She lost herself in the beautiful pas de deux. Yes, Helena was good. Much of the criticism against her was jealousy. She is right, Marya thought, all of them can do the steps, but to dance is something more. Marya looked around the room. Helena's bag was bulging with practice clothes, enough for a whole day of hard work. Her toe shoes were laid out on the floor, at least six pairs of them, Marya counted. One pair caught her eye. It was peachy instead of pink, Freeds. No need to go closer, Helena already said she wore the same size as Sylvia. Perhaps Helena did have more to lose than Sylvia, she mused.

Rond de Jambes

That evening, Marya sat in her comfortable chair, thinking. Something important was eluding her, something was not as it seemed. She was sipping a glass of cold white wine. Marya believed in being good to herself, as long as she didn't harm anyone else. She had the autopsy report in front of her and it was confusing. The cause of Caroline's death was poison, as suspected, but Caroline did not die from one poison, but from two. In addition to these, aconite and cyanide, both deadly poisons, all the poor girl had in her stomach was Coca Cola and coffee. The fact that Caroline had not eaten all day did not surprise Marya at all. It wasn't rare for dancers to starve all day, maybe have a small breakfast and then nothing but soda and coffee until ten or eleven at night. Terrible, but true. Dancers were much skinnier now, too skinny; they lacked the strength to jump well and the beautiful roundness of the female body was lost. Marya blamed George Balanchine, the influential director of the New York City Ballet, for this. He told his dancers to eat nothing at all. Monster, Marya thought angrily. The irony was that Balanchine was a wonderful chef and loved to eat. Marya had enjoyed several sumptuous dinners that George created for friends around the Russian holidays. It was as if he begrudged the dancers both joys at the same time. It was enough for them to dance, they didn't also need to eat. Marya's train of thought was interrupted by the insistent ringing of the telephone.

"Inspector Cohen here," the voice began with no preamble. "We have some information on our boy, Andrew. He has a record."

"What has he done?" Marya asked, interested.

"You name it. Truancy, vandalism, and an assault charge from his school days. Oh, yes, and drugs, drugs, drugs. We have a good case against Sylvia, but I think this is worth an investigation."

"That's very broad-minded of you," Marya said, smiling.

"So, how would you like to take a trip to Ithaca, New York? Talk to the police, and his family and friends."

173

"You mean Utica, New York?" Marya said, stalling for time.

"No, Ithaca, upstate New York, you know, where Cornell is."

"I never heard of it," Marya said, trying to recall all the small towns she had danced in when she was in the Borsky Ballet.

"That's because the Borsky Ballet probably didn't go there," he said accurately. "I can book you a flight first thing in the morning."

"Thank you, but in this wonderful world of electronics I don't need to travel there," she said. "I will use the telephone instead. You can add whatever you save on the plane ticket and hotel to my final bill," she added practically. "But first I will talk to Sylvia again. The poor girl is so upset."

"Marya, we don't have much time. I will drop off the police report first thing in the morning, and you should begin immediately. An unsolved murder looks terrible for the department."

"Why don't *you* do it if you are in such a hurry?" Marya asked.

"Please, Marya, you are so much better at talking to people — I get only half the information. I need you."

"Maybe you don't have much time, Gabe, but me, I'm only sixty, and I need time to think. But I will investigate Andrew tomorrow. I promise you."

Later that night there was a tiny scratching sound at Marya's door. Half asleep, she got up and found a brown envelope stuffed in her mail slot. That man simply has no patience, Marya thought, putting the envelope on the table and going back to bed. But she lay awake, thinking. Ithaca — it did sound familiar after all, and then she remembered why. Didn't Judith Sanders move there to open a ballet studio when she retired from the Borsky Ballet? Yes, and her husband taught at some university, perhaps Cornell. I wonder if Andrew studied with Judy? He certainly must have trained somewhere. He didn't spring up fully formed like a mushroom from nothing.

Marya remembered Judith had been a promising young dancer in the Borsky Ballet. She retired at a very young age so she could get married and have children. No one, not even Marya, could understand it. It was Marya herself who got Judith into the company, having had a bit of trouble convincing that idiot, Anatol, to take her on. He preferred a more Nordic kind of beauty, blond and blue-eyed with a tiny nose— like Caroline, Marya thought sadly. She always told him it was the dancing, the talent that counted, but once a fool . . . Marya thought, before she drifted off to sleep.

After breakfast, Marya dialed information and found the listing for a dance studio in Ithaca. A few seconds later she was talking with Judith Sanders on the telephone. It didn't surprise Marya a bit to learn that Judy had been Andrew's teacher. "Did he tell you that?" Judy asked.

"No, he didn't mention it," Marya admitted.

"They never do," Judy said with an audible sigh. "Before we talk about Andrew, there is someone else who wants to talk to you."

Luckily, Marya was used to surprises and she was blessed with a strong heart because the next voice she heard belonged to Zoya herself. "I think you may be looking for me," Zoya said. "I ran away because I was terrified. I didn't know where else to go, and I've been up here before to play the piano for Judy's classes. I know they must think I am the murderer to run. Do you think that?"

"I don't know what to think yet. Are you?"

"No, but I got a warning note. It said: If you talk, death! It was signed with the letter 'C'. But Marya, I received the note after Caroline was already dead!"

"The note may have been written by the murderer," Marya said. "What do you know that someone is afraid you might divulge?" she asked.

"Sylvia wasn't the murderer."

"How do you know?"

"Sylvia was in rehearsal, wearing practice clothes and woman's pointe shoes, pink shoes. I take break out in the hall. Someone carrying body, Caroline. Was dark in hall, I can't see who is, but shoes, some light on shoes and they are dark, black I think, man's shoes. I don't see who is, maybe he see me. You see now? I can't go back, even if they think I am murderer." Like many Russians, Zoya got less grammatical when she was excited.

"Zoya, come back," Marya implored. "Come, and I will protect you. You can stay here with me and no one will know you have been found."

"Aren't you afraid of me?" Zoya asked.

175

"I will take my chances," Marya said. "Now, please, I must talk to Judy.

"So, Zoya has told you about the murder," Marya began, after Judy came back on the line. "Andrew was the victim's boyfriend and he is, of course, a suspect. What can you tell me about him?"

"He was a difficult teenager, or so his parents told me. They didn't know what to do. I know he was suspended from school a few times, but I never had any trouble with him. He took to ballet right away. He had a good natural jump and he seemed to like the discipline of ballet. He danced with our small company. After just three years he was quite usable, a natural. Never pointed his feet enough — he started ballet too late for that. But when I sent him to New York City he got a scholarship at the Borsky Ballet right away. The rest you know," Judy said.

"Do you think he was capable of murder?" Marya asked bluntly.

"No, I do not. Would you like his parents' phone number? I know they are very worried."

"This I already have," Marya said. "Please promise me two things. One, you will put Zoya on the next bus to New York City. I will meet her at the Port Authority Station. Two, you will come and visit me, it has been a long time."

"Of course, to both," Judy said. "How fast the years have gone."

Marya had no sooner hung up when the phone rang. "Well," the irritable voice said, "what have you found out?"

"I just spoke to Andrew's ballet teacher. She thinks Andrew is nice boy," Marya said.

"Ballet teacher! What about the police?" Inspector Cohen asked.

"Next I speak to his parents," Marya said, hanging up quickly.

After an interesting conversation with Sarah Gaines, Andrew's mother, Marya was satisfied that Andrew was innocent. Mrs. Gaines told Marya that Andrew had been hyperactive and difficult as a young boy. He had trouble concentrating and so school was torture for him. At home, he knocked down shelves of books, tore up mail, and splattered his food. Finally, she and her husband transferred him to a private school. Mrs. Gaines made no attempt to whitewash her son. Drugs were a continual worry to her and her husband, but fortunately that was just a stage and Andrew no longer used them as far as they knew.

"And the assault charge?" Marya asked. She listened to the explanation and snorted. Wait until Inspector Cohen hears this, she thought, smiling with anticipation.

Later that day Marya made some borscht and a cucumber salad. She had a loaf of fresh pumpernickel and cold white wine. It would make a lovely supper. Zoya would not go hungry at her house, Marya thought happily.

She left her apartment and hailed a cab to the Port Authority bus terminal on West 40th Street, not her favorite neighborhood at any time of day. The waiting room was filled with street people huddled amid their belongings. One man sat imperiously in a corner glaring balefully at anyone who got too close. He is King of the Rags, Marya thought, shaking her head sadly. He, along with countless others, lived here in the bowels of the dirty bus station. Marya felt thankful for her lovely home, so private and so precious, where she lived in comfort with all her treasures surrounding her. She hurried downstairs to gate 68 and barely had time to look around when Zoya was embracing her.

Once safely in Marya's apartment, Zoya couldn't stop talking. "I was tired of playing and needed a break from rehearsal," Zoya said. "The hall was dark but light shone through the crack under the studio door. I see a shadow, a person is carrying someone. I see the murderer," she said, her voice rising. "I see shoes, black men's shoes, and I think, maybe I can't see his face but he has seen me. The shadows move into the women's room. I go back to rehearsal, worried, but don't know what has happened. Next day we hear. After I see you at studio, someone put note in my purse. It says:

IF YOU TALK, DEATH

— C

'My God,' I say to myself, "Caroline can't write me a note, Caroline is dead!' Something is very wrong and I am frightened. I call old friend Judy, she let me come stay with her."

"Let's eat and talk more later," Marya suggested. "Later, Inspector Cohen will come and we have a little surprise for him."

177

"He knows I am here?" Zoya asked.

"Not yet," Marya said, smiling in anticipation.

Marya lit candles and they ate her excellent borscht with sour cream and spread fresh sweet butter on the bread. The salad was crisp and refreshing. Zoya felt much better after her meal and several glasses of wine.

At eight o'clock, promptly, the doorbell rang and Inspector Cohen stood in Marya's living room, blinking in amazement. "You found Zoya! Marya, you are really something, I don't know how you do it, but you do. That's what I told the boys at the station, 'We need Marya, she knows things, she sees things, I don't know how, but she does. We need her.'"

Marya poured three glasses of wine, and told her story.

". . . and so Andrew beat up this boy in school who had been teasing him and wouldn't stop. The school decided to call the police although Andrew was only 13 at the time. And so Andrew is not Caroline's killer," she concluded.

"How can you be so sure?" Inspector Cohen asked.

"Mother tells me Andrew acts on impulse. He can punch someone if he is angry, but he can't plan anything, not even his own meals. He is incapable of premeditated murder, which this is."

"Mother said!" Inspector Cohen looked doubtful.

"Yes, parents know their children very, very well, regardless of what the experts think. And now, we must have protection for Zoya. The murderer may believe she recognized him."

"I can't spare a man, you know that, Marya."

"Then I must hide," Zoya said, "and I cannot play for rehearsals."

"The rehearsals will have to get along without you," Marya said.

"You realize you are still a suspect," Inspector Cohen told Zoya.

"No, she is not either," Marya said. "The murderer was wearing men's shoes."

"That is what Zoya says," Inspector Cohen said skeptically. "And if she is telling the truth, a woman can also wear men's shoes. But if someone was being carried, it probably was a man," he agreed. "So perhaps Andrew did it after all. I don't take character references from mothers."

"Maybe was Anatol and maybe Erik, but not Andrew,"

Marya insisted, "and certainly not Zoya," she said, gently leading him to the door.

"You are thinking maybe I am the murderer after all?" Zoya asked perceptively, before they went to bed.

"I don't know what I think yet," Marya admitted, "but no, I am sure it was not you."

Frappés

Marya believed in the power of human passions. A girl had been murdered, quite possibly by a fellow dancer. The answer would be found, she was certain, at the Borsky Ballet Studios. She must go there.

"Be careful," Zoya warned her as she left the apartment. "Someone capable of killing once can kill again."

Marya climbed slowly to the third floor of the ballet school and discovered that Boris was not teaching his class.

"He felt a cold coming on," Irina told her, "and went to bed with a hot water bottle and a cup of tea."

Boris was a hypochondriac, Marya remembered with a smile. He was afraid of draughts and constantly closed windows, even in July. Helena was teaching the class in his absence.

The dancers were working hard, especially those who wanted very much to join the company. It was well known that Helena controlled who got into the Borsky Ballet these days, except in the case of Caroline. Too bad. If Helena had had her way, the girl would be alive now.

Helena was a beautiful woman. She was dressed in pink tights, a black leotard and a long, transparent black skirt. She wore her old pointe shoes instead of ballet slippers and had a turquoise silk scarf tied around her head. Gold hoop earrings completed the picture. Helena was stunning.

She was picking on a pretty girl who looked about sixteen. "How do you expect to become a professional dancer? Look at you — your leg's all turned in! Impossible. Do it again."

The girl repeated the steps.

"Bad! Bad turn out. Bad control. You must work much harder." And Helena turned away.

The girl seemed elated. Probably this meant she would be joining the company soon. Strange perversity, Marya thought.

When did it start, the idea that cruelty was proof of caring and interest?

The company looked uninspired. You could see they preferred Boris' class. But Helena's class was very difficult, a test of endurance, speed, and control. Marya looked around the studio. Ellen was leaning on the barre and staring hopelessly at herself in the mirror. As usual, she was teary-eyed. She looked tired and nervous as well. It is as though she studies herself and forever finds herself lacking, Marya thought. Ellen's face, when she watched the young, talented dancers, wore a tense smile, but her eyes looked terrified, in the realization that these dancers will replace her one day soon.

Helena seemed genuinely interested in Sylvia, but then, why did everything Helena say seem to implicate Sylvia?

Erik stood in front center and admired himself frankly in the mirror. He looked like a slightly worn Greek god, no, like Narcissus, Marya thought with a chuckle. Erik liked to be treated like a star and Helena indulged him in this. Good partners are hard to find. Erik fiddled with his white T-shirt, alternately tucking it in and pulling it out of his tights as he studied his body sideways as well as straight-on, searching for the best effect. He settled for the shirt tucked in, accentuating the curve of his lower back melting into his tight, muscular buttocks. Marya knew Helena really adored him, but had to be satisfied with their mock romances on stage. She wondered what their children would have looked like.

Sylvia looked nervous and guilty, Marya thought, proving again that appearances are deceiving. She worked hard and her long lines were beautiful. She could be a lovely Queen of the Willis and Marya hoped she would get the chance. Helena ended her class with pirouettes, and the class applauded. Helena came over to where Marya sat, against the wall. "Not my best class. The pianist is no good. How I wish Zoya were here." Zoya would really be missed when the company started intensive rehearsals on Monday, Marya thought.

"Why don't we have lunch," Marya said. "Then we have some time to talk.'"

"I was supposed to eat with Anatol, but he is in such a state, I think he will be relieved. Wait here and I'll let him know."

"You know, he isn't himself at all, I am worried about

him," Helena confided over shrimp salad and a glass of white wine. "He is an old man and I'm afraid — no Anatol, no Borsky Ballet. Oh, excuse me a minute, I must put something in my eye."

"Contact lenses?" Marya asked.

"No, a little infection. The doctor gave me eye drops for it," and she squinted into her little hand mirror. "There, done," she said. Marya picked up the bottle and noted with a shock that it contained aconite.

"So! Oh yes," Helena said. "There's something I forget to tell the Inspector. There was another person in the studio the night Caroline was killed. I forgot to mention that Nora was there."

"Nora?"

"You remember Nora, my maid? She was there that night, of course. She is always there. I don't even notice her any more. No one does."

"I do remember her, of course," Marya said. "She just appeared backstage one night and said she had to see you."

"Yes," Helena said, "I thought she wanted me to sign her program, but she just stood there looking uncertain. Finally she told me she had followed the company all year in order to see me dance." Helena could not disguise her pleasure. "And that was when you were prima and I was still just a soloist. She offered to take care of me, to be my maid. I wasn't sure Anatol would allow her on the bus, but the idea appealed to him, the snob!" she said scornfully. "I moved her into a small apartment and paid the rent. In return she did my laundry, cleaning, and cooking. I still remember her that first night," Helena said, "standing there with her arms slightly open, as though making an offering of herself."

Marya thought back through all those years. How well she remembered Nora, who couldn't forgive her for having a higher rank than Helena. She would ask Marya if she was getting tired of dancing, tell her how peaked she looked, and suggest that she take some time off. Nora knew then that Helena would become the next prima but she was impatient to see her idol gain that position. Marya looked closely at Helena. Very soon, she knew, it would be Helena's time to retire. After forty, each performance is so much more precious because it could be your last. "Why did you wait so long to mention Nora?" Marya asked.

"She is always with me but as I said, I don't notice her any more. She is for me like the traffic beneath my window. I am used to her. She is like a piece of furniture that's stuck quietly in a corner."

"Well, I will have to pay Nora a little visit," Marya said, nodding to the waiter for the check. "How is she doing now? Still the same?"

"She is really wonderful, I should be much better to her, I guess. I come home each night to a clean apartment. Dinner is waiting in the oven and there are fresh flowers on the table. She sews my shoes and alters my dresses. She wants to do all this and doesn't resent it all. It's strange, isn't it?" Helena said.

"Hard to understand, yes," Marya agreed.

"She has no life of her own," Helena said, wonderingly.

As Marya walked towards Nora's apartment, she thought about the woman she was about to see for the first time in many years. She remembered how Nora studied Russian so she could speak to her loved one in her native language, although Helena, who had lived in America so many years, spoke perfect English. Marya recalled how Nora, ever vigilant, sat listening to company gossip while she sewed Helena's toe shoes. When someone kindly inquired how she was, Nora would respond, "Not too well. She has a bit of a cold. It must be the change in weather." Helena was fond of her but didn't respect her. How could she, when Nora threw her life away without even looking back?

She was treated like a dog, Marya thought. Tolerated and loved, in a way, but not given the full value of a human being. After a performance, if someone was there to take her out to dinner, Helena would leave without a glance towards Nora. If there was no one, Helena ate with her, reluctantly, in some out-of-the-way restaurant where she wouldn't be recognized. She was too much of a snob to be seen with such a homely companion. Nora believed her devotion was returned. She told endless stories about Helena that made her sound like a capricious child. How she missed her bus because she had to have on more chocolate ice cream. Or how she held up the curtain in Santa Fe because she was shopping late. Nora found all this enchanting, but Marya knew Helena was tough and appallingly selfish, for all her charm. So, of course, if Helena was there the night of the murder, then so was Nora.

182

Did Nora think the ever-climbing Caroline was a threat to Helena? Did Helena fail to mention Nora's presence deliberately, or was it, as Helena said, that she simply no longer noticed Nora's presence at all. It might be too easy to overlook someone who did all your chores, wore your favorite colors, and then retreated meekly into the background, asking for nothing in return.

Armed with these memories Marya arrived at Nora's apartment on East 70th Street, just around the corner from Helena's place. When Nora opened the door, Marya tried to hide her surprise: though Helena after fifteen years looked more beautiful than ever, Nora had aged for both of them. Her face was a network of lines, and she was bent with arthritis. Marya wondered how she herself looked to Nora. Her own thick brown hair was now streaked with gray which she left strictly alone. "I don't want to live with deception," she told her friends. Although she had gained weight, she still moved beautifully and her legs bore the definition of her early training. Nora looked at her uneasily. The last time they had met, Marya was a well-known ballerina and Nora was, after all, just Helena's maid. Marya hugged her warmly and smiled.

"It's been a long time," she said.

"Come in, I'll make some tea," Nora said.

Marya looked around the dining room which also served as the living room. It was small and nothing extraordinary, except for the walls, which were plastered with pictures of Helena in every imaginable situation. Helena posing, Helena taking a curtain call, Helena on the beach, on the street, in class. Helena posing with Nora and looking bored. The roses on the dining room table were red.

"Helena's favorite," Nora said.

"So, how are you doing these days?" Marya asked, settling into a chair that looked almost comfortable.

"Not so good this week. Her foot is bothering her. Tendonitis, I think. She really should go to the doctor, but you know how she is about doctors," she said in a conspiratorial tone.

"I don't wonder so much how Helena is since I just saw her, but Nora, how are you?"

Nora looked at her with surprise. Is it possible, Marya wondered, to so lose your own ego in another? And, if so, what would that make you capable of?

"I'm fine, really," Nora said finally. She went into the tiny kitchen and brought out a dish of cheese danish. Then she poured the tea. The danish were flabby and uninteresting. Marya longed for one of her delicious little honey buns, sticky, and smelling sweetly of cinnamon and spices.

Nora beamed at her. "We're having dinner together to-night," she said, blushing like a bride. "I prepared it already. She called and said Anatol isn't coming over after all and there is more than enough for two, so she said I might as well have some. Isn't that just like her?" she asked, smiling.

"Yes it is," Marya said, trying not to laugh. "What did you think of Caroline?" Marya asked as they sat drinking their tea.

"What a terrible girl!" Nora began.

Was it Marya's imagination, or had Nora developed the slight Russian inflection of her idol?

"Helena was right. Anatol should never have hired her. A troublemaker."

"How did she make trouble?" Marya asked.

"She sent Helena a letter," Nora said, lowering her voice. "It said: WE ALL KNOW HOW YOU GOT TO BE BALLERINA, and it was signed 'C.' It's disgusting. You know, Helena is a wonderful dancer. It's not her fault Anatol fell in love with her. But what they don't realize is that Helena is religious. She never had an affair with him. And Anatol is — a moral man — he admires her from afar."

"I see," Marya said, not venturing an opinion. "But still, I don't really know how you are."

"I don't have time to wonder about it, we're so busy. I would like to share Helena's apartment, to live with her and take care of her better. I'm afraid she is in danger. But Helena said I should be careful not to become a nuisance — she needs her privacy. Of course, I understand."

"Who do you think might have killed Caroline?" Marya asked. "You are always there, at class, at rehearsal, you see everything, hear everything."

"Helena would never hurt anyone," Nora said quickly. "She didn't like Caroline, but no one did. She spoiled the atmosphere of the company. But still, we are like a family here. I don't think anyone would actually kill her."

"Have you noticed Ellen's crying lately?" Marya asked.

"Oh yes. She is a crier, of course. Helena has decided to ignore her. She isn't improving but she's been in the company too long to fire. Helena protects her in a way. I think Anatol might let her go and hire someone younger and prettier but

Helena has integrity, feels responsible for the dancers. I think Ellen and Caroline were friends. Ellen is so good-hearted, she felt bad that no one liked Caroline. I think they sometimes ate together. I tried to comfort Ellen, but she is quite distraught, poor girl. I really love Ellen. Did you know when I had bronchitis so badly last winter she actually came here to make me tea. She gave me some herbs she grew herself. She brought me this, also," Nora said, pointing to a plant with delicate blue flowers. "And I've been to her apartment several times. We sit around and talk, about Helena I suppose, if I have anything to do with it," she said, laughing with a sudden bit of self awareness and humor.

"But, like Helena, you did not like Caroline," Marya repeated.

"No, like Helena, I did not."

Stretching

The company was rehearsing in a large cavernous Russian Orthodox church on 130th Street. Irina, a member of the congregation, had arranged for the intensive rehearsal period to be held there, since there were not enough studios at the company school. Warm-up class was at nine a.m., given by Helena, and promptly at ten, rehearsals began. They continued until five or six, Monday through Friday, for four weeks. Not enough time for the dancers to learn the repertory, but it was all the time the company could afford. Soon the company would hit the road; the case had better be solved by then, Marya thought.

The rehearsal space was huge, the size of four normal studios. There were tables and chairs along the sides where dancers could rest, eat, and sew their shoes until they were needed. The new dancers were easy to spot. They looked nervous and carried notebooks to write down the steps. The older dancers knew the choreography the way they knew how to breathe. The ballets changed little from season to season. The new dancers had ten or so ballets to learn in a very short time. Marya smiled with recognition at the young girl she'd seen in class the day before, getting hell from Helena. As expected, she had just joined the company. She stood clutching her notebook, looking terrified. First day in the company, she had good reason to worry. It wouldn't be easy, Marya thought. Five new girls and four new boys, a typical year.

They were rehearsing Swan Lake, Act Two, women only, and so the men sat chatting quietly. Some sipped lukewarm coffee and others warmed up, stretching and bending and adjusting their practice clothes. There were four acts in Swan Lake but the Borsky Ballet did only acts two, three and four. Ellen stopped often to wipe her face, or was it her eyes? She seemed always to be on the verge of tears. Were they tears of sorrow, or guilt, or shame, Marya wondered. The girl looked a mess, not strong enough to get through the tour. Helena ignored her. She shouted out sharp corrections to the new girls. "You are in the Borsky Ballet now! This was a good company before you joined. You must not spoil it."

Erik kept adjusting his clothing. He was, of course, exempt from any criticism. He was watching the two new boys. Erik was having more trouble now, beginning to look worn out. He had lines etched deeply into his forehead and around his mouth. Still, he had grace and elegance, that special something, Marya thought. Although he still looked stunning from the stage, the young men seemed to prefer each other. There would always be someone for him, though, who thought he would help their career. But he never did. Erik tended to think only about himself.

Marya knew one of Erik's carefully guarded secrets. He suffered horribly from stage fright, which began when he partnered her in Raymonda so many years ago. Erik took a preparation for a simple leap, his legs slid from under him, and he fell flat on his face. The audience laughed when he slipped again, trying to get up. Since then he was terrified of slipping, terrified of becoming a laughingstock. He never forgot his humiliation. And now he was aging, Marya thought, and like many older dancers he tried to cover his pain by seeking young dancers and their admiration.

Marya looked at them, beautiful gypsies. Did she ever really do this? Work so hard for so little, tour eight months of the year, mainly one night stands, and take class each day? She had, and she had loved it, too. She settled back to enjoy herself. Although she looked totally absorbed in the dancing, her mind was elsewhere. Motivations. Emotions. Who was capable of murder and who had the opportunity?

Erik sat down to wait until he was needed to do the pas de deux with Helena. He was with a group of male dancers, trying to act young. It made Marya sad.

Tchaikovsky's lilting score was being murdered by the new pianist. Zoya refused to emerge without police protection, which Inspector Cohen claimed he couldn't offer her.

"No, no!" Helena yelled. "Sarah, you are the worst swan I've ever seen. Ai ai, you new girls are spoiling everything."

Again it was the pretty one, Sarah. She looked as if she would soon be crying. But Ellen was doing it for her. The swans clattered noisily on the slippery wooden floor. It was not designed for dance and actually looked dangerous for the dancers. No one cares about the dancers, not really, Marya thought. The girls were perspiring, although the room was cool, concentrating on the steps, the lines, and staying absolutely together. It's easier to be a soloist than this thinking of everything at once. The new girls not only had to contend with Helena screaming, but they got endless corrections from the older dancers. "Get in line," "Where do you think you're going?" hissed in stage whispers. Somehow, most of them survive, but I don't know how, Marya thought.

Anatol walked in to survey the scene. He looked like a prosperous land owner watching his serfs.

"Sarah, come here," he commanded. "You must pay attention to Miss Rubova, do you understand?"

"Yes, Mr. Borsky," she said timidly.

Anatol looked around. Caroline had been his most recent mistress. Helena no longer had anything to do with him. He was looking for a successor. And he is capable of anything, Marya thought.

At noon the corps finally got a rest. Marya sat down next to Ellen. She took out some cheese, a crusty roll, and a bunch of grapes. She offered to share with Ellen but the girl refused. Her lunch was plain Dannon yogurt.

"How boring," Marya said, "is that your usual lunch?"

"Yes, I need to stay thin," Ellen said.

"You don't treat yourself very kindly, do you?" Marya asked.

As expected, Ellen began to sob.

"I'm just so upset by Caroline's death I don't know what I'm eating anyway," she said. "We used to stand together at the barre. And the way Helena treats the new girls, I just hate it! When she picks on them it feels like it's me. I identify with people too much, I guess."

"But in a way that is right, we are all the same, fashioned from the same stuff. But you must be giving yourself a treat, a rest, a special gift. To be stingy with one's self is bad."

"I don't deserve better," Ellen said.

Interesting, Marya thought. She is so deprived, allows herself no pleasures. So different from Helena who reminded her of a contented cat and who indulged herself without guilt. Ellen is pinched and looks older than her age. Helena was already forty but looked so much better. She looked still in her prime because she took such good care of herself, going to health spas during vacations and treating herself to expensive clothing. How does Ellen really feel about those who are more fortunate? Marya wondered. Could she be exempt from jealousy?

At twelve-thirty Helena clapped for attention. "We will do Act Two again, but first Erik and I will dance the pas de deux for our honored guest." She smiled at Marya and motioned to a chair in the front of the rehearsal area. Now Marya gave her full attention to this lovely dance. Helena's arms were especially good and Erik played his role well, the prince who falls in love with a swan. Marya clapped and bravoed when they finished, and they bowed to her. Then rehearsal began in earnest again. Sylvia and another girl named Janet Kent, were the big swans, a lovely duet. Marya admired Sylvia's fluidity, her effortless arabesque and classical proportions, definitely a budding ballerina. The other girl was good also, though a little more self-conscious. Marya liked it when each time a step was done it was as thought it had never been done before. Spontaneous. She herself had danced like that.

It was almost five o'clock when Marya realized she was hungry. She retrieved her bag from under the table and waved good-bye to Helena who, seemingly tireless, was still screaming at the new girls.

Marya arrived home exhausted, as though she had been dancing herself. She sat down and opened her bag to take out the remains of her lunch. She stifled a scream as a tarot card fell down onto her lap. The image of Death leered up at her. There was no note. Her initial shock over, Marya was amused. So someone didn't want her coming to rehearsals!

She poured a drink of cognac for herself and one for Zoya, who looked pale. "You know," Marya explained, "the death card rarely refers to an actual death. That is just a mistake made by those who can't see. Death card is a look at the bare bones, like an X-ray, a look at the essential. It sometimes means to drop the unnecessary and only carry the essential with us. Problem is to be able to recognize what is essential. The card encourages us not to hold on, not to force, because we die a little each day, like it or not."

"I doubt that the murderer had all that in mind," Zoya said with accuracy.

"No. I'm sure you're right," Marya agreed. "Murderer wants to scare me off and me, I won't scare. You know, my cards keep telling me, things are not what they seem. Death is not what it seems. Murderer is not what it seems. What is essential here and what not?"

She sat regarding the death card. She made friends with it and let it take her on a journey into her own mind. It was an especially pretty card. The skeleton, clothed in a hood, carried the traditional scythe. In the other hand it carried a rose.

Death, death of a young dancer by poison. Two poisons. Why? Aconite, so deadly that even a tiny amount can kill. Then why the cyanide, also? Why try to kill Caroline twice? Things are not what they seem, Marya mused.

Petit Battments

Marya began to prepare supper for Zoya and herself. A short time later the doorbell rang and Inspector Cohen burst in. He was not in a good mood, Marya was sorry to note.

"Death threats! It has been a whole week and *what* have you found out?" he blurted irritably.

"Here, we have a glass of wine. Sit down," she said, smiling ingratiatingly. "I will tell you what I find out. Amazing, the human beings, what they do! But always a murderer leaves a trail, somehow wants to be caught.

"What we know," she said, "Caroline is dead." Inspector Cohen sighed. "No, this is important, she is dead and can't tell us whether or not she wrote the letters."

"Of course she wrote them. And someone continued them after killing her," Inspector Cohen said.

"Good. Then Anatol did it! Arrest him!"

"Are you sure?"

"No," Marya said.

"How about Andrew?" he asked

"No, I don't think so."

"Why don't you think so?"

"Because it is out of character. Mother said he can be

189

violent but is always ineffective."

"MOTHER SAID!" Cohen roared.

"Yes. Someone put death threat into Zoya's bag, after Caroline is dead, and signed it with a C. They know is not possible we believe it is Caroline, so someone is trying to incriminate someone else. Zoya got a death threat. She saw murderer, or part of murderer, and he or she doesn't know how much was seen. Better scare her so she doesn't talk. What did Zoya see? Black shoes carrying Caroline's body into the bathroom."

"Then it's either Anatol, Andrew or Erik," Inspector Cohen said, with conviction. "I'll remind you I wanted to arrest Anatol," he said.

"Yes, you did. But just because Zoya sees man's shoes, doesn't mean the murderer is a man."

"No?"

"No. Everything is not what it seems. See?"

"No."

"Well, woman could wear man's shoes, right? You said this yourself."

"Right," Inspector Cohen said, sighing.

"And then Helena forgets to mention that her loyal servant, Nora, is also a suspect. This is woman completely lost in the life of another. What would she do if she thought Helena was threatened? Then there is Ellen. She is too hard on herself. She nibbles on plain yogurt, not even allowing herself a drop of flavoring. She wears unattractive second-hand clothing and is continually weeping for the sadness of others. What does she have to look forward to when she is forced to stop dancing? And she looks terrified of something." Marya glanced at her watch. "It's not too late for me to pay her a visit." In a moment she was out the door, leaving a startled Zoya and Inspector Cohen behind her.

Ellen lived on 74th Street and Broadway, on the fourth floor of a walk-up. Although the halls were painted dreary brown and the banisters shook, good smells wafted from under doors and the hallways were spotlessly clean. There was a small, delicately colored wreath made of dried flowers hanging on Ellen's apartment door. As the door opened, Marya was surprised by the lush foliage which seemed to cover every surface of Ellen's living room. There were dozens of plants all over the window sills, tables, and shelves, and many pots of herbs hung from the ceiling. A huge, ancient looking vine crept its sinuous course and covered an entire window. Here was Ellen's one gift to herself, Marya thought. Plants of every description for her to love and care for. Marya had imagined her apartment quite bare with nothing frivolous or extravagant. Ellen herself looked tense and drawn.

"Well, so Ellen, it is beautiful, plants, curtains, a special place to rest."

"Yes, please sit down. I'll bring some tea — is herbal all right? I have peppermint, camomile and skullcap."

"Oh, how nice! Skullcap and peppermint is so soothing. So you are, I see an amateur herbalist?"

"Yes. I love herbs. They are my children," she said, reaching over and fondly touching a purple sage leaf. "The only ones I'm likely to have," she added with a self-deprecating laugh.

"You would like to someday have children?" Marya asked curiously.

"If I were married, I would," she said, "but I'm not likely to meet anyone at the Borsky Ballet. Anyway, dancing is my life and I wouldn't change anything."

Marya looked around. Aside from the plants, which made the apartment look like a tropical island, Ellen's furniture was plain and the apartment seemed to be decorated in Salvation Army style. No taste, Marya thought sadly, but she noticed that everything was meticulously clean.

"I wonder if it's possible to earn a living with plants," Ellen said. "When I have to stop dancing I worry how I'll manage." She spoke quietly, but with a desperation that caught Marya's attention.

"Why not?" Marya said. "Unlikely is sometimes likeliest. Look at me — once Ballerina and now psychic. Who would have imagined it!"

Marya noticed a typewriter and a pile of papers on the table. "What's this?" she asked.

"That's my part-time job. I need a little extra money to help out my mother and sometimes I send money to Cecily and Ann."

"Cecily and Ann?"

"They are my sisters."

"I see, so you work two jobs so they don't have to work at all?"

"Cecily is retarded. She is able to live on her own and gets disability insurance. But it's not much so I like to send her a little extra. Ann works in a department store so I don't send her much, just presents and sometimes I help her pay for a trip. I wish I could do better for them. I'm really not too good at making money. I think of mother, living all alone since my dad died. It's so sad." She began to cry.

"Seems to me you expect too much of yourself. You give to mother, give to sisters, have two jobs. What about Ellen?"

"I feel like the fortunate one, really. I guess I feel guilty because I'm so much better off than the rest of my family. I'm doing what I love!"

"Well, it sounds like they are lucky to have you," Marya said.

"There's a lot of room for improvement," Ellen said, brushing non-existent crumbs from the immaculate table.

The apartment was so clean, you could eat off the floor, Marya thought. Everything about it was meticulous, so unlike the chaos of her own home. Marya watched Ellen carefully. She looked as though she was in turn watching herself and finding herself lacking, Marya thought.

"I wonder if you notice anyone in the company acting strangely," Marya asked. "Sooner or later the murderer will give self away."

"We are all acting strangely," Ellen said, "it is the strain."

"True," Marya agreed. "I know you were close to Caroline. Did she ever tell you where her mother was?"

Ellen appeared to be puzzled by the questions, but she answered promptly. "Yes, her mother ran off with a younger man, years before Caroline's father died. She never visited Caroline and I'm not sure Caroline even had her address."

"That is sad."

"And if her mother married again, she might have changed her name. How could anyone reach her?" Ellen asked.

"So, Caroline was really an orphan, with no one to go to for help. The Borsky Ballet was her only family and no one there liked her."

"That's right. I know she acted badly sometimes, but she was always decent to me. I guess she needed someone. I told her it was best to stay away from Mr. Borsky. I must tell you, Madame Cherkova, that I had the feeling Caroline might be blackmailing him. I told her that could be very dangerous."

"I see. Do you have any idea who might be writing letters now?"

"No. It's too awful." Ellen was crying. Her eyes were always ready, Marya thought, always filled and ready to spill over with some unnamed sorrow and, Marya realized, terror.

"Have you always been so depressed, so sad?" Marya asked, gently.

"I'm not depressed. I'm fine. It's just a very hard time, for the whole company."

"Yes, is true," Marya said, finishing her tea and wishing there were something to go with it. "I want to admire your plants before I go," she continued. "I am a bit of an herbalist myself. But I don't have, how do you call it — your green thumb. Who takes care of all your plants when you are on tour?" Marya wondered.

"My sister Ann. But I worry myself sick," she admitted. "Ann waters them but she doesn't really care and they know it. After a long tour they are mostly all alive but they look — neglected," she said, her eyes beginning to water once again.

"Ah, larkspur," Marya said appreciatively, hoping to distract Ellen from another siege of crying.

"No, that's monkshood, though it does look like larkspur," Ellen said.

The two women stood admiring the delicate blue flowers.

"You must spend a lot of time caring for your plants, they look so well," Marya said.

"A lot of time, it's true, but they are worth it — my babies," she added, with an apologetic smile.

"Please, you must invite me over sometime soon, this has been lovely," Marya said, exaggerating a bit and giving Ellen a hug. She left her standing at the door, looking like an abandoned puppy.

Grands Battments

That night, Marya tossed fitfully in her sleep. Her dream was almost a nightmare. Her beloved old teacher, Tamara Androvna, lay dying and wanted to see Marya once more before she left for the other world, but Marya was away dancing in another country. And so Madame Androvna died before Marya could reach her bedside. But then Marya arrived and her old teacher died again, in exactly the same way, so that this time Marya could be there. The death had to be the same in every detail, just like a movie that plays on and on.

When Marya woke up, a sadness enveloped her like a mourning cloth. She longed for her teacher and missed her again, as though she had died only yesterday. As the mist of her dream world began to evaporate, Marya sat up in bed. How mysterious the workings of the sleeping mind, she thought. Now she understood.

And so, it was time to talk again to the director of the Borsky Ballet, Anatol Borsky himself.

"Marya, what a pleasant surprise." Anatol rose nervously to greet her. "Have you discovered who did this terrible thing?"

"Not yet, but I am getting closer. Should you drink so much, Anatol, with all your heart medication? Is it not as they say — contra-indicated?"

Anatol glanced at the bottle of cognac on his desk. "It isn't, I don't think so. How did you know I took medication? Oh, of course, you're psychic, aren't you? Marya, I tell you, I didn't do it," Anatol said, rubbing his hands together.

"I must tell you, you are in trouble," Marya said. "Caroline was blackmailing you and you seem to have a strong motive. You wanted to fire her but couldn't, and your old mistress, whom you still adore, is furious with you. And then Zoya, yes I found her, saw a man's black shoe, your shoe she thinks, moving Caroline's body into the bathroom. You were the one Caroline had an appointment with the night she was murdered. I wouldn't be surprised, Anatol, if Inspector Cohen arrests you soon."

Anatol slumped in his chair. He looked ill.

"I didn't do it," he said, "but I *was* the one who brought her into the bathroom. She collapsed in my office. I tried to revive her, but she was unconscious. I tried splashing her with cold water, but then I realized she was dead. I panicked and left her there. Yes, I should have called the police right away but I was afraid."

"You have been less than honest, Anatol. You have caused a lot of trouble," Marya said, as she made her exit from his office. There was a lot to do and she was in a hurry, she had no time to waste on Anatol. On her way out of the building Marya stopped to use the ladies room. She had always hated the fact that there were no windows, but only an exhaust fan

194

that didn't work too well. She groped in the darkness for the light switch and realized that she was not alone. She was suddenly afraid. The death card, with its intimation of doom, was still in her purse. Had she been foolish to confront Anatol so openly? She felt the air move behind her and reeled quickly around, but it was too late. Marya crumbled in a heap to the floor, without even seeing her assailant.

At first there was only pain and then she began to hear voices. In a few moments Marya realized she was home, in her own beautiful bed.

"Someone doesn't want you around," Inspector Cohen said, "and that someone can't be Sylvia since I've had her in custody since early this morning."

"Oh, let her go," Marya groaned, touching her throbbing temple. "I told you she didn't do it."

"This is a little note for you, by the way," Inspector Cohen said, handing over a small scrap of paper.

GIVE IT UP OR DEATH!

— C

"Oh, how stupid of me!"

"What, that you got hit?"

"No, not realizing before," Marya said.

"Here is some more ice for your head," Zoya offered.

"How long have I been unconscious?" Marya asked.

"Only a few hours," Inspector Cohen replied. "The doctor says you have a slight concussion. I don't think you need to be in the hospital, but you do have to rest."

"I wonder, was my assailant not trying to kill me or just not very strong?"

"You're the psychic, you tell me," Inspector Cohen said. "By the way, I've assigned an officer to look after you."

"That is very kind of you," Marya said with some irony. "Ouch! Oh, my head. I'm going to rest now, but I want you to bring all the suspects here to my apartment tomorrow morning. Then you will learn who the murderer is."

Marya closed her eyes and ignored Zoya and Inspector Cohen until they finally left her room. When she was alone, she found she could think quite clearly, in spite of the throbbing in her head.

Tracking a killer was dangerous, as she was discovering. They thought they didn't want to get caught, although their guilt often made them careless, forcing them to call attention to themselves, to try too hard to seem innocent. Murder spoiled the karmic balance of the world, disturbing not only the deceased and the killer but everyone around them as well. It was the ultimate arrogance of man, and of woman too, she admitted reluctantly, to dare and disturb this balance.

Marya let her thoughts focus once again on the dream she had had just before waking in the morning. Sometimes dreams were ordinary and dull, filled with trivia and irritation from the day before. But this dream was significant, a glimpse into the other world which gave her important clues about Caroline's death. How free the mind is, she thought, looking ruefully at her stiffening legs. Lately her dreams were filled with warnings, delicate, like spider webs that evaporate in daylight. As she went over every detail of her dream she knew, more surely than ever, what it had been trying to tell her.

Finale

The next morning Marya's head felt heavy and sore. She dressed slowly while Zoya prepared strong Russian tea. Zoya was terrified that she would soon be confronted by the murderer and Marya tried to reassure her.

"Soon they come and we must be ready," Marya said, between bites of sticky bun and sips of good hot tea.

At ten o'clock the suspects, followed by two uniformed policemen, filed into Marya's sitting room. Inspector Cohen glared at the cushions that had been laid out on the floor.

"Sorry, but I do not have enough chairs," Marya said, "so we will all sit here together in a circle on the floor." The policemen looked at Inspector Cohen questioningly and then dragged their cushions toward the doorway and sat down. Marya looked around at the suspects; Anatol looked less majestic than usual, and Ellen was weeping, as usual. Helena refused to sit on the floor, feeling it to be beneath her dignity, so Inspector Cohen brought her a chair from the dining room. Erik sat on the floor without protest, trying to look as young as possible, Marya thought. Andrew arranged himself comfortably and looked apprehensive. Sylvia appeared to be upset and nervous, and Nora sat protectively at Helena's feet, much to the latter's evident annoyance. Inspector Cohen chose the last available cushion.

"So, welcome to you all, including the murderer," Marya began. "Please, I ask you to be patient with me," she said, smiling at the inspector, "because first I must tell you about my dream."

"Marya, please, this is not a game. Be serious," Inspector Cohen shouted.

"I am completely serious, Inspector Cohen," Marya said, offended. "You see, my dream has helped me to know the truth."

"Go ahead, then. You will anyway," Inspector Cohen said, trying to ignore the smirks of the two policemen.

"Yes, in any case I did not ask you for permission. *You* asked me to solve a murder, if I recall correctly."

"For God's sake, Marya, get on with it," exploded the Inspector.

"All right. Two nights ago I had a dream. At first, I didn't understand it, but now I know that it was Caroline's way of telling me something. In my dream, she let me see that she died, but it was all wrong, and so she had to die again, the way it was meant to be. Well, I was at first quite confused, but then, I remembered the two poisons and it was all so clear. Probably, you all see it too," she said, looking around. The sea of questioning stares made her realize this was not so.

"Then we have to proceed in a more usual way. That will please the Inspector," she said.

"It would probably help," he agreed.

"So, here we have sitting, seven people who all hated Caroline. Some with stronger reasons than others, but all with hate."

"No, I cared very truly about Caroline, I honestly did," Ellen said, wailing.

"Please don't interrupt me dear," Marya told her. "So, to me, in a way, you are all guilty by, as you say, intention. But the law cares only about who actually succeeded in killing her. And so I am happy to say that Sylvia is innocent of any crime and should be released from custody. Yes, there is proof," she said to Inspector Cohen.

The other six began to shift nervously on their cushions.

"Anatol had the most reason to kill Caroline. He was being blackmailed by her, something most serious, often leading to murder. Is that not so, Inspector?"

197

Inspector Cohen sighed.

"And then, Zoya recognized Anatol's shoes in the hallway the night of the murder; he was carrying Caroline's body to the bathroom." The others gasped. "And since Caroline had an appointment with Anatol that night, he may well have been the last one to see her alive!"

"Shall I arrest the man?" Inspector Cohen asked.

"Look at him," Marya said. "Does he look like a man about to be arrested? No he does not, and that is because, although I almost wish otherwise, Anatol is not guilty."

"What the hell was he doing with a dead body then?" Inspector Cohen asked.

"Caroline collapsed in my office, Inspector. I carried her to the bathroom hoping to revive her, but she was dead. I panicked, and told no one, until Marya found out for herself."

"So then I think, could it be Helena?" Marya continued.

"No, it could not," screamed Nora. She clutched Helena's knee.

"Let go of me, you idiot," Helena snarled. "Let Madame Marya Cherkova tell everyone how I did it."

"From the beginning I was puzzled about the two poisons. Why two, I think to myself? Could there be two murderers? Why not, if she has so many enemies?" Marya said.

Ellen began sobbing as though her heart would break.

"When I ate lunch with Helena she had to use eyedrops for an infection. Eyedrops sometimes contain a bit of aconite, one of the deadly poisons that killed Caroline. So I ask to see the bottle and, yes, it does contain aconite, but it is almost full. Still, couldn't there be a second bottle somewhere? And aconite is so deadly it would take very little, anyway. Helena had a lot to lose because of Caroline. And, I believe Helena would do anything to protect her position, even kill."

Helena sat with a sneer on her face. The two policemen got up to arrest Helena, who began to laugh hysterically.

"No! You can't arrest her," Marya said, alarmed.

"Why not!" Inspector Cohen yelled.

"Because she is innocent," Marya said, smiling.

"Marya, I must insist that you stop playing games," Inspector Cohen said. "Seriously."

"If you want to discover the true murderer then I will do things my way and not yours," Marya said.

"So we come to Erik." As Marya looked towards him Erik

rushed for the door, only to be stopped by the police.

"Erik?" Helena gasped. "It's not possible."

"Erik hated Caroline because she refused to dance with him," Marya explained. "He tried to get Anatol to fire her but instead she got promoted and was given even larger roles. If I am not mistaken Caroline tried to use her influence to have Erik fired. With ego wounded, Erik is capable of anything," Marya said.

"You bastard," Andrew shouted, making a sudden lunge for Erik.

"You may not be violent while in my sacred home," Marya said sternly.

"Not quite anything, Madame," Erik sneered. "Yes, I hated Caroline for refusing to dance with me. Who did she think she was? She was just a little nothing and I am a leading dancer. I should have refused to be seen on stage with *her*. I would have dropped her gladly, even injured her, but I couldn't kill her, or anyone. I couldn't go that far."

"Couldn't you?" Inspector Cohen snarled.

"No, I could not."

"He is telling the truth," Marya said.

The tension in the room was getting unbearable.

"So we come now to Ellen," Marya continued, looking compassionately at the weeping girl. "Ellen has had a hard life, she supports her family and has very little money left for herself. How she hated those more fortunate than herself and then condemned herself for hating. Caroline had everything that Ellen did not: beauty, youth, money, roles and, most important, Andrew. It started like a game, didn't it, the notes?"

Ellen continued sobbing and hardly reacted to Marya at all.

"No, I can't believe this of Ellen. Ellen is a nice girl," Helena protested.

"First she got Caroline in trouble with Sylvia by writing a threatening note and signing it "C". Caroline didn't understand why Sylvia was so upset. The strain has been showing on Ellen, she is anxious, cries constantly and is not nice to herself."

"It's true, I deserve to die," Ellen sobbed. "My life is meaningless anyway. I've never been loved and don't deserve to be."

"So Ellen may be somewhat responsible for Caroline's

death. But she is not the actual murderer. At first I think it is her, but then I think, Ellen is disturbed but she really wants to be good person, so I look further. My magician card and then my dream has solved this, finally."

"So it's Andrew after all," Inspector Cohen said.

'No, his mother was right, Andrew is not a violent person," Marya said, looking at the Inspector pityingly. "It will be hard to arrest the murderer because she is dead. Caroline wanted to kill Andrew. She was furious that he had abandoned her. That is the way she looked at it, like a baby. You see, her mother abandoned her when she was still very young and then her father died not long ago. When Andrew broke off their relationship it was the last straw for her. She was a spoiled and willful young woman, used to having her own way. So she put cyanide in Andrew's coffee cup. They were rehearsing. Ellen drank herb tea, never coffee. Sylvia takes her coffee with cream. It was only Andrew who drank his black. But Caroline was very nervous that night and she became confused. She drank the poisoned coffee by mistake. So the murderer was Caroline and Caroline is dead. You can't arrest her," she said smugly, looking at the bewildered Inspector.

"Amazing," Inspector Cohen said. "You are a genius," he told Marya admiringly.

"I thought so too," Marya said immodestly, "until my dream. You see, I had forgotten about the aconite found in Caroline's blood. My dream told me, Caroline died twice. She was her own murderer, but there was another one, too. When Ellen told me that plant I thought was larkspur was actually monkshood, I went home and looked it up in one of my herbal books. It is," she said, looking slowly around the room, "aconite. You knew the aconite plant you gave to Nora was poison. You know a lot about plants, don't you, Ellen?"

"I knew it was poison and I taught Nora how to make it into a salve. I knew she would try to kill Caroline with it, she wanted to do it before Helena did."

"You showed Nora how to make a deadly salve and mix it with Nupercainol. Nupercainol is what all dancers use to numb the pain of blisters they get from their pointe shoes. I used it all the time myself. Aconite placed on an open wound might very well be deadly, enough to kill, I don't know. So Nora, you gave this to Caroline and she must have used it on a bleeding toe. And so, as in my dream, Caroline was killed not once, but twice."

"I should have hit you much harder," Nora screamed. "I'm glad she's dead, she was hurting my baby," she wailed hollowly. "At least now you'll be safe," Nora said, looking up at Helena with adoration.

"You poor idiot, I never intended to kill her, I just wanted to fire her," Helena said, glaring at Anatol.

"I do not know if there was enough aconite in the salve to kill Caroline and I don't know how we will ever find out. Perhaps we leave that one for the medical experts and I will leave the decision of who to arrest to my good friend, the Inspector," Marya said with a bow that was reminiscent of her curtain calls of the past.

Contributors

Helen and Lorri Carpenter, a mother/daughter writing team, live and work in central Florida. Their stories have been published in a variety of magazines and an Emma Twiggs mystery, "The Disappearing Diamond," appeared in *The WomanSleuth Anthology: Contemporary Mystery Stories by Women*.

Carol Costa is an award-winning, off-Broadway playwright. Her story, "The Best Bid," appeared in *The WomanSleuth Anthology: Contemporary Mystery Stories by Women*. She has completed a mystery novel featuring Dana Sloan, and is currently writing television scripts.

Rose Million Healey has had short stories published in *Cosmopolitan*, *McCall's*, and *Redbook*. Her detective, Thelma Ade, was first introduced in *Alfred Hitchcock's Mystery Magazine* and then appeared in *The WomanSleuth Anthology: Contemporary Mystery Stories* by Women. She lives in Manhattan, where she is completing a play.

Dolores Komo is the author of *Clio Browne, Private Investigator*, which was published as part of the WomanSleuth Mystery Series (Crossing Press) in 1988. She is currently working on her second Clio Browne novel, *Affairs of Death*.

Judi Lind is a life-long mystery buff who lives in San Diego, California. She has published short stories and articles in numerous magazines, and is a member of Mystery Writers of America and Sisters In Crime.

Bonnie Morris has recently completed a six-year stint as a graduate student in Women's History and is about to launch a career as a college professor. She has had stories, poems and essays published in a variety of feminist and academic publications. One of her stories was recently published in *Finding Courage: Writings by Women*.

Elizabeth Pincus is an ex-San Francisco private eye. She currently lives in Boston where she writes for *Gay Community News* and the *Boston Phoenix*, and is working on her first Nell Fury novel, *The Two-Bit Tango*.

Edie Ramer lives near Milwaukee, Wisconsin. "Requiem for Billy Daniels" is her first short story to be published in an anthology. She is currently at work on a mystery novel.

Naomi Richardson Strichartz was born in Brooklyn. She was a member of Ballet Russe de Monte Carlo and is currently directing the Dance Circle Studio in Ithaca, N.Y. She has written two children's books, *The Wisewoman* and *The Wisewoman's Sacred Wheel of the Year* (available directly from Cranehill Press, 708 Comfort Road, Spencer, N.Y. 14883). "Death in the Borsky Ballet" is her first published mystery.

L.A. Taylor has published seven mystery novels, a science fiction novel and a collection of poetry. Her most recent mystery, *A Murder Waiting to Happen*, was published in 1989.

Linda Wagner was born in New Jersey but has lived most of her life around Cleveland, Ohio. "No Man is an Island" is her first published mystery story. She is currently working on a novel featuring Livia Day Lewis.

Irene Zahava (editor) is the owner of a feminist bookstore in upstate New York. She has edited several short story anthologies, including: *The WomanSleuth Anthology: Contemporary Mystery Stories by Women; Finding Courage: Writings by Women;* and *Through Other Eyes: Animal Stories by Women.*